Praise for the Giulia Driscoll Mystery Series

NUN TOO SOON (#1)

"Exciting and suspenseful."

...rs Weekly

"For those who have not yet read these incredible mysteries written by an actual ex-nun, you're missing out...Brilliant, funny, a great whodunit; this is one writer who readers should definitely make a 'habit' of."

– *Suspense Magazine*

"With tight procedural plotting, more flavoured coffee than you could shake a pastry at, and an ensemble cast who'll steal your heart away, *Nun Too Soon* is a winner. I'm delighted that Giulia– and Alice!–left the convent for a life of crime."

– *Catriona McPherson,*
Agatha, Macavity, and Lefty Award-Winning
Author of the Dandy Gilver Mystery Series

"You'll love Giulia Falcone-Driscoll! She's one of a kind—quirky, unpredictable and appealing. With an entertaining cast of characters, a clever premise and Loweecey's unique perspective— this compelling not-quite-cozy is a winner."

– *Hank Phillippi Ryan,*
Anthony, Agatha and Mary Higgins Clark
Award-Winning Author of *Truth Be Told*

"Grab your rosary beads and hang on for a fun ride with charming characters, amusing banter, and a heat-packing former nun."

– *Barb Goffman,*
Macavity Award-Winning Author

"We're hooked! Entertaining characters and a twisty plot make *Nun Too Soon* a winner."

– Sparkle Abbey,
Author of the Pampered Pet Mystery Series

"Colorful characters and a unique, lovable heroine make for another enjoyable read from Alice Loweecey. *Nun Too Soon* is a funny, snappy, well-paced mystery with a whodunnit that kept me guessing till the end."

– Jennifer Hillier, Bestselling Author of *Creep, Freak, and The Butcher*

"I love Giulia (I've always been a sucker for kick-ass nuns), and Loweecey really knows how to turn a phrase. The sense of detail is deft; the timing is exquisite, the characters are real."

– James D. Macdonald, Author of *The Apocalypse Door*

Nun Too Soon

The Giulia Driscoll Mystery Series
by Alice Loweecey

<u>Novels</u>

NUN TOO SOON (#1)
SECOND TO NUN (#2)
(Fall 2015)

<u>Short Stories</u>

CHANGING HABITS
(prequel to NUN TOO SOON)

Nun Too Soon

A GIULIA DRISCOLL MYSTERY

Alice Loweecey

HENERY PRESS

NUN TOO SOON
A Giulia Driscoll Mystery
Part of the Henery Press Mystery Collection

First Edition
Trade paperback edition | January 2015

Henery Press
www.henerypress.com

ISBN-13: 978-1-940976-65-5

Printed in the United States of America

To my fans.

ACKNOWLEDGMENTS

It's been a long and interesting road here to the Hen House. Never give up, folks, and never surrender.

Huge thanks to my awesome agent, Kent D. Wolf. And thank you, Henery Press. Giulia loves her new home. Thanks as well to all my writing friends who encouraged me with virtual hugs and chocolate. The trenches are better with good people to share them.

One

Giulia Falcone-Driscoll—formerly Sister Mary Regina Coelis—slammed open the door to her private office.

"Sidney, I'm going to kill my husband."

Driscoll Investigations' pregnant assistant jumped a whole inch out of her chair. "Don't startle a woman in her thirty-seventh week, please."

"Sorry, mini-Sidney," Giulia said to the almost-ready baby. "I didn't mean to scare your mama. Make sure you spit up on Frank the first time he holds you."

Sidney—named for a rich uncle who had the gall not to leave all his money to Sidney's parents—giggled. "If you kill him, cover your tracks, okay? I don't want to get dragged into a murder investigation while I'm nursing."

Giulia slumped against the doorframe. "No jury in the world will convict me when they hear his latest gem, assuming the lawyers select twelve married women for the trial." Her curly brown hair bounced over her shoulders. It was distracting, but still preferable to trapping it beneath a black veil.

Across the sunny room, Giulia's admin stared at her from beneath white-blond bangs. Sidney glanced at Giulia, then drew Giulia's gaze toward the admin.

"Zane," Giulia said, "please stop shrinking into your chair like a cornered rabbit."

"Sorry, Ms. Driscoll."

He began typing at an alarming rate. Recently hired away from a gigantic accounting, loan, and paycheck processing company, Zane still tended to react like an escaped prisoner.

Giulia huffed. "Zane, stop. You are allowed to take part in our conversations. You're not in Cube Hell anymore. I'm not micromanaging you. You're here because you have incredible analytic skills and because you fit in with our group dynamic."

"Sidney said it's because I sound like Humphrey Bogart when I answer the phone."

"Sidney has a big mouth and she will need to go to confession this Saturday."

The phone rang. Zane turned away from both of them before picking up the receiver.

"Good morning, Driscoll Investigations."

"Schweethaht," Giulia finished in a whisper. Sidney spluttered into her hands. Giulia bit the inside of her cheek so she wouldn't do the same.

"Why are you planning Frank's funeral service this time?" Sidney asked in her stage whisper.

"He called to say he invited his oldest brother and his wife and their three kids for dinner. Tonight." Giulia kept her voice low so Zane wouldn't be distracted.

"It's almost noon," Sidney said.

"I pointed that out to him. He said he knows I can do it and whatever I make will be fine. I wonder if broiled Leg of Frank Driscoll will taste good with a garlic and red wine sauce."

Sidney put her hand on her phone. "I'll call *The Scoop* and tell them to be at your house at...seven-thirty?"

Giulia made a gagging noise. "That pack of TMZ-wannabes gives pond scum a bad name. If they stick their camera in my face I might forget my Franciscan ideals of peace and reconciliation."

Sidney adjusted her position in her chair. Pregnancy hadn't altered her college athlete physique much. And nothing could change her perky disposition—not even a baby kicking her ribcage.

Zane put the call on hold. "Ms. Driscoll, Colby Petit of Creighton, Williams, Ferenc, and Steele is on line one."

Giulia's eyebrows disappeared into her too-long curls. "Solid law firm. I don't know that particular lawyer's name...wait..."

Zane's fingers worked magic on his keyboard. "He successfully litigated the 'bus stop pickpocket' trial last November."

"Right." Giulia came around behind Zane's desk. "Got the guy's sentence reduced to probation and restitution," she read from the news report on his screen, "and got himself a commendation from the judge. So he's a do-gooder with a smooth tongue. I'll take it on my phone. Thanks."

Giulia closed herself into her half of Driscoll Investigations' office space. When her husband had run the business, the room's only personalization had been a basketball hoop attached to the off-white wall above the wastepaper basket. Seven months earlier he returned to the police force as a detective and Giulia became the owner of Driscoll Investigations.

Now the walls were painted a soft lemon yellow, linen-like curtains covered the blinds on the window, and every piece of visible wood glowed from hand-polishing and buffing. "You can take the gal out of the convent," Giulia used to say, "but the convent still tries to cling to the gal." That clinging included ten years of manual labor skills learned at the altars of stovetop cooked starch, Lime-Away, and Wood Preen.

She sat in her ergonomic secretary chair—secretaries did all the real work so their chairs gave the best support—and pressed the button for line one on the phone.

"This is Giulia Falcone-Driscoll."

"Ms. Driscoll, this is Colby Petit." His voice blended a nasal quality with the melodious tones of a trained elocutionist. "I'm representing Roger Lambelin Fitch. Does the name mean anything to you?"

"Uh...it's a fancy frilled rose that won first prize at last year's home and garden show."

"Jesus Chri—sorry. Sorry." He inhaled and coughed. "Those

leeches from *The Scoop* tried to catch me with that reference at six this morning. Hadn't even had coffee. I nearly said something that would not have looked good on the news. Anyway. Mr. Fitch is accused of murdering his girlfriend, Loriela Gil, last April. The Silk Tie Murder?"

Giulia typed the phrase into Google. "Of course. Roger the pianist. We've worked in the same community theater orchestra a few times." She picked out highlights of the news summary. "Roger was released shortly after the murder. What's changed since then?"

"I don't want to go into details over the phone. Can you meet me for lunch? I have a proposition for Driscoll Investigations."

Giulia chewed her bottom lip. She shouldn't. They were in the middle of that discreet embezzlement investigation for AtlanticEdge in which Roger Fitch's name was prominent. Plus the Diocese of Pittsburgh's background checks. Plus two interviews this afternoon for a temp to cover Sidney's maternity leave.

"Ms. Driscoll." The attorney's practiced voice became brisk. "I'm only asking an hour of your time. Did I mention lunch reservations at Airi?"

Visions of homemade wasabi plus ginger ice cream danced in Giulia's head. Well, she needed lunch. And she could pay for it herself. She wouldn't bring up the conflict of interest. Client privilege, plus she trusted no attorney. If she said the words "conflict of interest" to this one, he'd be all over it like a rash.

"All right, Mr. Petit. Half an hour, then? I'll meet you there."

She regretted her decision half a second after she hung up the phone. "Falcone, you're not as devious as you pretend."

She opened the door between the offices. "Guys, I'm meeting that lawyer for lunch."

Sidney nodded, deep in a transfer of handwritten notes to her computer.

Zane said, "I sent the background documents for the new Seminarian candidates to your iPad."

"Excellent. Thank you. One of the best things to come out of my years at the convent was the Diocese trusting an ex-nun with their private business. I should be back by two at the latest. Go ahead and stagger lunch."

"I can eat at my desk, Ms. Driscoll. We all had to inhale our food at PayWright."

Giulia glared at Zane. "Get out of here and breathe different air. Walk. Enjoy a warm early March day because we're bound to get snow by the end of the week. The brain works better with different stimulation." She wrinkled her nose at herself. "Why do you make me feel like I'm your Scout Leader?"

Zane smiled, wiped it from his face, then raised his right hand. "On my honor, I will do my best to do my duty." When Giulia groaned, he said, "I got to the rank of Star before I rebelled."

"If next winter is as bad as the one a few years back, we know whose house to descend on for heat and shelter." She grabbed her houndstooth blazer from the coat rack by the door. "Sidney, no labor pains 'til I hire a temp, please."

Two

Giulia parked her eight-year-old copper Saturn Ion—secretly dubbed the Nunmobile—in the last open space in Airi's parking lot. The deceptively beautiful March day appeared to have lured out every office worker in Cottonwood, Pennsylvania.

The decibel level of the combined conversations in the small Japanese restaurant stopped Giulia cold in the doorway. There wasn't a free booth or table in the place. She inhaled garlic and tuna and ginger and barbecued beef.

A hostess appeared before her just as she saw a close-shaved black man in a sober gray suit waving from a booth near the front windows.

"I think I'm with him," Giulia said, pointing.

"Right this way, miss." The hostess weaved through the tables and Giulia followed, apologizing twice to diners for bumping the backs of two chairs.

The lawyer stood and held out his hand. "Ms. Driscoll. I'm Colby Petit. Pleased to meet you."

They shook hands and Giulia slid into the other side of the two-person booth. A waitress set glasses of water and menus in front of Giulia and the lawyer. They studied the Guaranteed Ready in Five Minutes lunch specials without conversation until the waitress returned.

"Tempura vegetables with miso soup, please," Giulia said.

"Spicy beef with seaweed salad, thanks," Petit said.

The moment the waitress turned away, Petit smiled at Giulia and she understood how he charmed judges and juries.

"Thank you for agreeing to meet with me on such short notice. I don't know if you're aware of the history of the case?"

Giulia debated on taking out her iPad to make notes. Too deceptive. Instead, she put on her polite face. "Not any longer, no."

He nodded. "That might be good. You'll have a fresh perspective. In brief, last April first my client and his girlfriend went to sleep together and when he woke up she was out on their balcony, strangled with one of my client's neckties."

Their food arrived. The ambient noise remained at a level above one of Frank's rec league basketball games. Good thing Giulia's ears had two years of navigating that kind of racket.

She started her soup. Petit talked through his salad.

"He was arrested immediately and called me that same morning. Forty-eight hours later, the police released him because all the evidence was circumstantial."

Giulia resisted the temptation to tilt her soup bowl up against her lips to catch every drop. Instead she dipped a battered slice of bell pepper into the restaurant's signature wasabi and closed her eyes against the moment of flame in her sinuses. Wonderful.

"You eat their wasabi? You're a brave woman." Petit blinked at his first mouthful of spicy beef. "This is as hot as I can take. It's delicious, but I'll be eating plain rice and Maalox for dinner." He swallowed. "Every bite is worth it. To continue. For the past eleven months, the police have been, shall we say, less assiduous than I would like in trying to discover the actual killer."

"Did you think they were convinced your client was in fact the murderer?" More wasabi. Giulia breathed through her mouth for a few heartbeats.

"Damn skippy. For my part, I'm convinced my client is innocent." He chased a particularly saucy rib with several gulps of water. "After the usual tests and evidence gathering," he panted slightly from the spices, "my client was indicted for first-degree murder twelve weeks ago."

Giulia finished the last piece of tempura with regret. On any other day, this quirky, charming man might convince her to add another case to DI's two-ton workload. This despite his disparagement of the local police, since she assumed good intentions on his part. He must have done his research and known that Frank's knee rehab and return to the police force as a detective—and transfer of DI to Giulia's control—happened last June first. A smart lawyer like Petit would surely have those facts and would not include Giulia's husband in his blanket condemnation.

Petit must have picked up on her body language, because he shifted tactics. Giulia reminded herself never to underestimate any lawyer ever.

"Here's the thing, Ms. Driscoll. The prosecution's piled up a tower of evidence, and it's pretty convincing. Locked-room mysteries play well on stage and in cozy novels, but in real life twelve random adults are going to make only one equation out of it."

"I can hazard a guess," Giulia said. "One man plus one body in one room minus anyone else around equals the man in the room committed the murder." She finished her water. Restoring her taste buds from wasabi numbness took precedence over this sob-story. Her conscience poked her with vigor. She had eaten at this man's expense without any intention of agreeing to his request.

On second thought, she hadn't. Her wallet had enough cash to cover her own lunch. Her conscience has no grounds for reproach.

"That's exactly the solution they'll come up with." He signaled the waitress. "It's what I want to prevent, but even I see how absurd any other conclusion sounds."

Giulia said as though she hadn't already figured it out, "I don't quite see what you brought me here to ask."

"Coffee and plum wine for me," Petit said to the waitress. "Ms. Driscoll, let me recommend the ginger ice cream. I understand it's won local awards."

Giulia saw no reason to mention she'd eaten their ice cream

many times. "Thank you. Green tea also, please," she said to the waitress.

Petit continued, "My client insists he's the only one who can prove his innocence. He knows he's trapped in a clichéd mystery and he has to try everything possible to extricate himself. He says everything includes hiring you."

Giulia frowned. "Hiring DI to do what?"

"To go over everything from before, during, and after the murder to find the real killer. He says that despite the DNA evidence, despite the circumstantial evidence, despite what the police and *The Scoop* and her relatives and his relatives say, you can pluck justice from the morass he's trapped in."

"Mr. Petit, I can see why juries love you."

His earnest expression didn't crack. "Juries can sense when I believe in the clients I represent. It's that simple, Ms. Driscoll. I believe in Roger Fitch's innocence."

They leaned away from the table to let the busboy clear their dishes and the waitress set out their desserts.

Before Giulia had a chance to reply to Petit's proclamation, he said, "Mr. Fitch has set aside funds to hire you. His assets are frozen but the judge has authorized this particular expenditure." He drank half the small glass of plum wine in a gulp. "I've researched Driscoll Investigations. You have a reputation for championing the underdog."

"Perhaps, but that doesn't mean I'm a pushover." She dipped her spoon in the ice cream. "We're up to our necks in work right now. I'd need a lot of convincing before I commit myself and my staff to more work." Giulia knew she was lying. Petit was already working his way under her skin.

"Convincing?" Petit smiled. "You just said my favorite word. It's—" he pulled out his cell phone and checked the screen— "quarter after one. My office is ten minutes from here if we avoid the construction on East Main. May I take up another hour of your time?"

Giulia did a quick calculation.

"I have a report to fine tune and two appointments starting at two forty-five."

"Challenge accepted. I'll finish what I have to say in less than an hour."

"Deal." She scooped more ice cream, free to enjoy it now. The extra hour would allow the lawyer to give her the full performance and feel that she hadn't dismissed him out of hand.

She took out her phone and typed in an alarm for ten a.m. Confession on Saturday. Nothing short of world destruction would make her skip this week. The number of half-truths she'd spoken in the last hour alone...

Three

The offices of Creighton, Williams, Ferenc, and Steele commanded half the fifth floor of the newest glass building designed by the town's architects *du jour*. Giulia once drove by them on a sunny summer day and the afterimages from the tinted glass nearly caused her to rear-end a Hummer. The Nunmobile would've lost that encounter for sure. Today she and Petit went around the back way to avoid any potential glare problems from the angle of the early spring sun.

The lawyer held the building's glass door for her. "Damn architects are going to get sued when someone blames a T-bone accident on their five-story mirror."

Giulia followed him to the elevators. "It's still better than another giant box o' cinderblocks."

The left-hand elevator *pinged* and they entered.

"Agreed." Petit pushed the button for the fifth floor.

Unlike most elevators Giulia had experienced, this one shot up so fast her stomach took several long seconds to catch up. She regretted lunch for those seconds.

Petit led the way to another glass entrance. Tasteful gold scrollwork outlined the double doors, the scroll pattern repeating in the pattern of the maroon carpets. The receptionist's desk looked like real wood. The receptionist's suit looked like it cost three times as much as any outfit in Giulia's closet.

She needed to get a grip. She now ran her own successful

business. Success outweighed fancy clothes any day. She also needed to disregard the little fact that the receptionist was younger and prettier than her, too. She was her own woman.

Giulia ignored the fact that every word of her lecture was much too familiar. Self-image issues much?

Petit led her down a slate-blue hall accented with watercolor landscapes. The office they entered differed only in its pearl-gray walls and watercolor winter scenes. And the man with surfer dude hair sitting at the Roycroft-style table waiting for them.

"Morning, first flute." He stood and held out his hand. "Haven't seen you since we shared an orchestra pit for *Working* last September. Remember those three actors who kept asking for their cues to be accented harder? Black Joe, White Joe, and Gay Joe." His laugh was half an octave higher than his voice.

Giulia remembered why she hadn't regretted his absence at the community theater. She smiled and returned the pianist's "I spend six days a week at the gym" grip. Professionals didn't let their personal opinions interfere with work. "That was an enjoyable show, Mr. Fitch. The Joes' various solo lines certainly added to the overall production value."

Professionals also knew the art of the subtle dig.

Petit pulled out a seat for Giulia before sitting at the table himself. "Roger, Ms. Driscoll has several other commitments this afternoon, so we're on the clock to win her to our cause."

Fitch grinned. When Giulia didn't respond, he wiped it off and went for the serious look.

Giulia mentally smacked herself for ascribing ulterior motives to everything he did based on eight weeks of rehearsal and performance for four musicals over the past few years.

If she factored in possible ulterior motives from that other interfering issue, however...Roger Fitch might not be a killer, but he could very well be a thief.

Petit slid a file folder over to Giulia. "I've prepared some photographs to encapsulate the problem." He gestured for her to open it. "Please."

When she did, the face of a smiling woman greeted her.

"That's Loriela Gil, the woman Roger's accused of murdering. She and Roger had been out to celebrate Roger's birthday last April first. They returned late and, frankly, shouldn't have operated a motor vehicle."

"Come on, Colby," Roger said. "Dodging a DWI is chump change. They're gonna pump me full of poison and my neighbors'll celebrate my execution with popcorn and beer if we can't prove I'm innocent." His voice lost its cocksure quality halfway through the last sentence.

Petit nodded. "Of course. That night, Roger and Loriela decided to end their celebration in bed."

"Sex. It's what's for dessert." Fitch winked at Giulia.

Petit's body jerked slightly in Fitch's direction. Fitch jerked a second later. Based on Giulia's observation of similar jerky motions at Frank's extended family dinners, the lawyer had kicked his client under the table. Petit cleared his throat. "Roger has deposed that both of them were so drunk they fell asleep right afterwards, and Roger slept through their alarm. He didn't wake up until a co-worker called to see if he was coming to the office that day."

Giulia studied the photographs as she glanced at the pianist from under her lashes. Perhaps the eleven months between the murder and now was an excuse for his callous attitude. It didn't make her any more sympathetic to him.

A smidge more persuasion crept into the lawyer's voice. Giulia had to be giving off neon-bright disapproval signals.

"You'll see the photos beneath that one are evidence of Roger and Loriela's enduring relationship."

Giulia dealt them onto the table like cards. The couple kissing on New Year's Eve. Dancing at someone's wedding. Cutting birthday cake. The photos could've been a montage from any one of the last dozen romance movies Giulia and her friends had seen on a girls' night out.

Giulia added "Ramp down the cynicism" to her internal to-do list.

"All right, Mr. Petit. What next?"

"The next set of pictures shows several angles of the apartment she and Roger shared, taken the morning after the murder. If you'll take a closer look at the fourth one, the one that shows the balcony from the outside, you can see the footprints in the landscaping mulch below the balcony." He waited for Giulia to deal those photos on top of the first set. "One of the prosecution's contentions is that Mr. Fitch deliberately planted those footprints to mislead the police."

Giulia picked that one up again. This type of evidence wasn't her area. Frank's eyes on these pictures would give him buckets full of information.

Her hands set down that print and picked up another one, giving it the same apparent scrutiny. What really captured her attention was her brain trying to pull off an internal shift from "DI has no time for another case" to "What is the truth at the heart of this?"

"Roger," the lawyer said.

The pianist switched attitudes as though the lawyer had snapped his fingers.

"Ms. Driscoll, when I talked Colby into contacting you, it wasn't just Driscoll Investigations I wanted to see. It was you."

Giulia set down all the photos.

"Bet you didn't know the orchestra pit started a pool when you took over the agency. The Second Violin ran it like one of those baby pools at work. We bet on the month and day you'd screw the pooch and declare bankruptcy."

Giulia's smile stiffened.

"Don't get mad or anything." Fitch's return smile all but sparkled. "All in good fun. Besides, the money's still in the safe in the conductor's house because you didn't fold." He leaned across the table. "The conductor said you'd succeed because you're the opposite of those old-movie detectives. You have what modern people want. Women in charge, but who aren't pushy or bitchy or too masculine. That's what I need: The right kind of woman."

Giulia put as much distance between them as she could while still sitting at the same table.

Fitch spoke faster. "You're going to hear that Lori and I used to fight. You're even going to hear that we were quits. It's a load of crap. Sure we had fights. Who doesn't? But we always made up. I bet you and Frank fight sometimes."

"I don't see how this is relevant to the issue, Mr. Fitch." Giulia turned over her wrist to check her watch.

Fitch reached out for her hand, but stopped before he touched her.

"It's the only relevant part of the issue. They're going to say that Lori and I were splitting up. They're going to talk about that stupid restraining order her bitch of a mother talked her into getting. They're going to say our friends were worried about her. Colby's shown me video footage of the prosecutor in action. He'll pick a fact here and an old email there. When he's done cherry-picking, he'll point to me and imply that I'm 'Fitch the Ripper' because of that stupid bar fight Lori and I had the week before my birthday." His eyes never left hers. "I didn't kill Lori. I swear to you. You might not like me too much, Ms. Driscoll, but that doesn't matter, right?"

Giulia didn't unbend. "What does matter to you, Mr. Fitch?"

"Justice. I didn't even consider talking to another private investigator. You're the only one who'd even try to find it at this point." He slid the photograph of Loriela Gil over to his side of the table and stared at it.

Giulia's inner cynic rolled its eyes at the theatrical gesture, despite its kernel of truth. Her inner realist wrote Fitch's entire mess off as hopeless. Her inner bookkeeper catalogued the extra time this case would add to their weekly schedule. Her traitorous hard-nosed inner business owner—a tiny aspect of herself she usually kept squashed under her sensible shoes—whispered that DI could find a reason both Fitch issues weren't a conflict of interest after all.

Her real self, the one controlling all those miniature Giulias, knew she couldn't walk away from this. All of her selves wanted to curse.

She turned to the lawyer. "Mr. Petit, Driscoll Investigations will take this case."

Four

Giulia ran up the narrow wooden stairs to her office as the alarm on her phone signaled five minutes to her first temp interview.

She skidded to a stop on the doormat, dragged her fingers through her curls that she knew looked like Shirley Temple's after a tackle football game, and slowed her breathing. Then she opened the frosted-glass door.

The temp waiting in the chair next to Zane's desk looked like she'd teleported here direct from Harvard Business School.

As though the interviewee wasn't sitting two feet to his right, Zane said, "Your two forty-five appointment is here, Ms. Driscoll."

Only relentless practice kept a smile off Giulia's face as she hung up her jacket. Zane's chocolate-brown eyes didn't waver as he handed Giulia three printouts in a manila folder.

"Thanks." She smiled at the young woman in the gray pinstripe suit. "I'll be just a few minutes."

Safe behind the closed door of her office, Giulia opened the folder and reread the cover letter and résumé inside. Ms. Pinstripe graduated from Duquesne more than a year ago. Ugh, all temp work and nothing really relevant.

The often-useless "Awards and Interests" section at the bottom of the résumé caught her eye. Captain of the debating team. Captain of the women's lacrosse team. Sang the role of Guinevere in *Camelot* her junior year and Maria in *The Sound of Music* her senior year.

Giulia would have to turn in her ex-nun card if she didn't give this candidate a smidgen of extra chance because of that last role.

She buzzed Zane. "Please send in Ms. Reed."

Except Ms. Reed disapproved. Of pretty much everything. The secondhand filing cabinet—the first official piece of furniture Frank bought when he opened the office—received an "are you kidding?" look of dismissal. The more time that passed without Giulia turning to her computer, the more Ms. Reed's incredulous look deepened. Within fifteen minutes, she was telling Giulia the Only Correct Way to run an efficient office.

Within twenty, Giulia showed Ms. Reed to the door.

No good deed goes unpunished, Giulia said to herself as she drew comparisons between Ms. Reed's Fortune 500 style of perfection and her own clothes.

Sidney looked up from her screen. "Why are you trying to smash down your hair? It looks curly and happy, just like it should."

Giulia smiled. "Sidney, you are irreplaceable. I certainly won't choose that Mean-Girl-Who-Dumps-The-Geeks'-Books-In-The-Hall as your substitute."

A noise came from Zane's desk that sounded suspiciously like a laugh. Giulia and Sidney did a tandem double-take in his direction.

Zane choked it down. "Her voice carried through the door. Sidney made faces every time we heard 'In addition...'"

"Serves me right for not going through an agency, I suppose."

Sidney said, "Think of the interviews if you'd have placed the ad on Craigslist."

Giulia crossed herself. "Give me credit for not being that naïve. Okay, I've got half an hour 'til the next interview. Hit save and listen up, guys." She walked to the opposite end of the office and perched on the windowsill so they could both see her. "I agreed to take on the Silk Tie Murder case, and no, it was not because of the excellent lunch."

Sidney put on her most disingenuous expression.

"His name is on the AtlanticEdge list."

"I know. We can do this. The two issues don't overlap. Embezzlement does not equal murder."

A new worry crease appeared on Zane's forehead. "Ms. Driscoll, despite that dichotomy I'm sure there's a precedent."

"Zane, precedents are fine in the mouths of lawyers, but justice trumps legal nitpicking, at least in this office."

The worry crease deepened.

"Zane," Giulia said. "Embezzlement sends people to jail and makes them repay the stolen money. The Silk Tie case is murder and the death penalty is on the table."

"But Ms. Driscoll, even if that's the situation, the amount of statistics we're compiling for AtlanticEdge alone—"

"Zane."

The admin gulped and shut up.

Giulia smiled at him. "I know what our workload looks like. Sidney, don't look all perky. You won't be home playing with your baby for another two weeks. You'll be buried under this with the rest of us." Her phone alarm went off. "Fifteen minutes 'til the next candidate arrives. Here's the scoop. First: I'm not taking this extra work merely to dump it all on you. If anyone puts in extra hours, it'll be me. Second: Yes, I'll be asking both of you to perform more brilliant computer acrobatics and no, it won't break your brains."

Sidney replied with a long-suffering sigh. "Baby Brain is not a twenty-four hour condition."

Zane said, "Ms. Driscoll, the only reason I graduated *magna cum laude* instead of *summa cum laude* was the egregious application of the bell curve theory of grading by the programming professor in my dual major." He cracked his knuckles. "Bring it."

Not a smidgen of guilt disturbed Giulia at Zane's response. A good boss created opportunities for her employees to succeed. This wasn't manipulation. It was Business Owner 101.

"The lawyer's emailing me more specifics. I'll draw up a contract before I meet with him tomorrow morning. Meanwhile, I'm going to look at those Seminarian background checks and write up that report. My goal is to scratch one thing off the to-do list by four o'clock."

Giulia hit "send" on the background check summary at three fifty-one. "They should put us on retainer." She paused with her fingers hovering over the keys. "Retainer. What a beautiful word."

She jumped up and opened the door. "Zane, Sidney, we're going to convince the Diocese of Pittsburgh to put us on retainer."

Sidney looked up.

"Oh." She rubbed her belly. "Mini-Sidney likes that word. It sounds like 'regular income.' What do you want me to do?"

"Make up a spreadsheet with everything we've done for them since the very first commission they gave us. Hours, fees, and importance of projects in ascending order. When you're done, pass it over to Zane. Zane, please crunch the numbers and come up with two different dollar amounts that will get us a decent profit but won't cause the diocesan bookkeepers to throw holy water at me when I bargain." Her phone alarm chimed the imminent appointment. "It's Tuesday. Can you shoehorn it into things for Friday?"

"No problem," Sidney said. "It fits in with all the docs I'm writing up for the temp."

The office door opened.

"Hello? I'm Jane Pierce. I have a four o'clock interview?"

Giulia nodded. "You do indeed. I'm Giulia Falcone-Driscoll. Come this way."

Zane slapped another covering folder into her right hand as she passed his desk.

Jane Pierce's suit was straight out of the lower levels at Macy's. A few tendrils of black hair trailed out from under a plain brown wig. Theater-quality makeup covered the back of her neck.

Giulia forced herself not to try to stare through that makeup.

"Before you ask," Ms. Pierce said as she sat in Giulia's client chair, "yes, my mother's a distant cousin of the fourteenth first lady of the United States. The first-born girl in each generation gets the name. Yay, me."

Giulia said without looking up from the resume in the folder, "Teased in grade school?"

"God, yes."

"Is that the reason for the hair and the neck ink?"

Silence. Now Giulia looked up to catch the interviewee's hand feeling the mousy wig. Jane's body language jumped from nervous to antagonistic.

Giulia smiled.

"Prove to me that this online degree I see here is worth something."

The antagonism broke through the interview veneer. "You want to know what it's worth? Six years of night classes while keeping a full-time job and putting a slimy, cheating ex through med school." She leaned over the desk, stabbing the resume with her left index finger. "I pulled off the third best grade in that degree since the state university system started offering online courses."

Giulia outlined a hypothetical project. Ms. Pierce told her in detail how she'd handle it. Next Giulia threw a different type of project at her and chewed over her solution. Both answers fit in with the way Giulia ran DI.

"Why are you settling for temp work?"

"Because of that blasted hamster wheel employers like to exercise on. You can't get a full-time job without experience. But how can I get experience if no one will hire me so I can gain some of this bright, shiny experience?" She closed her mouth so hard her teeth clicked.

"Been there. All right. My assistant's due date is in two weeks. Her doctor says it's a textbook pregnancy without problems, so she'll be here through the end of next week unless she buys a trampoline or goes for the jumping-jack record." Giulia poked her phone calendar. "Can you come in Friday at...two-thirty to fill out paperwork? Ten dollars an hour but no benefits, sorry. Possible overtime but there'll be warning. Two months full-time and then part-time for four more weeks while Sidney gets used to interacting with adults again."

When she raised her head, fingers ready to type in the appointment, Ms. Pierce was blinking at her.

"You mean it? You're hiring me? Don't you need to think about it or interview ten more people?" She shook herself. "Wait...what am I saying?"

"I know the right candidate when I see one. Ask Zane out there. He still thinks I'm from another planet. So: Yes or no?"

"Yes. Of course yes. Holy crap." She blushed from neck makeup line to forehead. "I beg your pardon."

"No worries. Friday at two-thirty then. Paperwork should take less than an hour." Giulia typed that and opened a new appointment. "Sidney—she's my assistant—gets in at eight-forty-five, so can you start at nine on Monday for her to train you?"

"Good God, yes. The insurance thing doesn't matter. I'm still on the ex's. It was the one thing I bargained for in the divorce."

"Smart. Okay." She finished the calendar entries and stood. "We have a pretty relaxed dress code. No shorts or exposed midriffs or jeans with artsy holes in them." She held out her hand. "As long as your tattoos don't swear or illustrate certain body parts or activities, you don't have to cover them up. Same with the hair."

This handshake gave an entirely different impression. Now Giulia shook hands with a confident, happy woman, all antagonism gone.

"That reminds me," Giulia said. "It seems you can go undercover if we need it. That's good. Sidney's been out of commission for that part since her third trimester."

"I've never acted or anything like that, if you don't count smiling at my ex-mother-in-law when I had to guard against her cleaning out my stuff along with her son's."

"Everything counts." Giulia opened her office door and walked her new employee to the frosted-glass main door. "See you Friday."

Five

Frank's brother, his wife, and their three kids left at eight-thirty p.m. The sprawling Driscoll family had embraced Giulia from that first awkward Christmas party two years earlier and Giulia loved it. Usually. Busy weeknights with impromptu family suppers? Argh. Those nights were the only times Giulia didn't mind that nobody in her own family had spoken to her since she left the convent.

"Frank." Giulia leaned against the closed door of their Cape Cod-style house.

"In here," Frank called from the dining room, where he was attending to a red wine stain on the carpet. "After three kids, you'd think my sister would know not to pick up a full glass when the baby is in Velcro mode."

Frank's voice got louder as Giulia walked through the living room into the dining room. "What are you cleaning it with?"

"I'm still blotting."

"I'll get the baking soda." Giulia did an about-face back into the kitchen. As she mixed the correct proportion with water, she rehearsed different openings for the favor she wanted to ask.

Frank switched positions with her and she covered the stain with baking soda paste. He tossed the pile of reddened paper towels into the kitchen trash, then snagged the remote as he plopped onto the couch.

"There." Giulia sat back on her heels. "I'll vacuum that before I leave tomorrow morning."

Frank clicked 'til he found the Manchester United match replay. "I knew you'd put on a great meal. I'm going to sneak out of bed at midnight and make a sandwich with the leftover chicken and bacon."

Giulia opened the novel she was reading and sat in the corner of the sectional couch, near her husband. She and Frank had celebrated their first anniversary last month and all the cards still made a bright display on the mantelpiece. Their mantelpiece in their house. Their couch and coffee table and just-cleaned wine-stained rug. Life did not get better than this. She knew it because she'd been through much of the worst. Besides, any day she wanted to throttle Frank was one hundred percent better than any day of her final years in the convent.

Even today, when she'd gone into overdrive to get supper and dessert completed on time. Speaking of which...

"Twenty-four hours' notice would be helpful when you invite people for a meal."

"Yeah. Sorry, *muirnín*, sweetheart. Mike really wanted to pick my brain about some financial stuff and the kids love coming here, so I figured supper would be perfect for both." He reached out with his clicker-free hand and pulled her over to his end of the couch.

Giulia couldn't settle in 'til she came clean. "We picked up a new job today."

"Damn, woman, sleep is not an optional exercise." He kissed the top of her curls. "Is it a simple one this time?"

"Not sure. Remember Roger Fitch? He was one of the pianists at the theater."

Frank made a rude noise. "You mean, do I remember the cocky guy who has a thing for strangling people with neckties?"

This wasn't starting out well. "That's him. He convinced the judge that he's the only one who can prove his innocence."

The rude noise repeated. "Only if he's drawn a corrupt judge along with a smooth-talking lawyer. Isn't the judge for his trial Pearl 'Hang 'em High' Ruiz? Nobody's going to sweet-talk her."

Giulia blew out a breath. "You're assuming guilt."

"A result of long experience." He jerked upright and yelled at the TV screen: "No! You moron! Aim for the net, not the crossbar!"

"Roger Fitch won't get a Christmas card from us, but he and his lawyer have a compelling argument. His lawyer's Colby Petit."

Frank stopped watching the match. "Lawyers don't come more silver-tongued than Petit. Did he appeal to your sense of justice?"

"Well, yes."

Frank's head flopped backwards over the top of the couch. "You're going to work yourself to death. How do I know that? Because I know that if things get tight you'll take on all the overtime yourself rather than push your employees too far."

"I can't ask them to take on extra work if I don't do my share of it." She did not want to have this conversation. It was their one recurring argument.

On TV two players cleated each other and writhed like dying fish. Frank hit the mute button. "We've had this case from the beginning, you know. Jimmy made me lead on it when Rao got promoted."

Giulia beamed. "I should thank him, but he'll only try to get me to give up the agency and come work for him, like always."

"He mentions it every couple of weeks. But why does it make you happy?"

"Because I can pick your brain about it, of course."

"No, no, no." Frank banged his head against the couch this time. "I swear, sometimes it was easier sharing the office with you."

"No, it wasn't. You wanted to run it your way and I wanted to run it mine. You were a sleuth long before me. I can't believe you didn't guess that when I got my PI license we'd butt heads like elk in nature films."

A deep, theatrical sigh. "I was blinded by your nun aura."

She leaned away from him, crossed her arms, and raised both eyebrows.

Frank bowed three times, hands flat on the couch each time. "Ex-nun. I know. Ex-nun."

"And don't you forget it." Giulia returned to her snuggle

position. "About picking your brain...I'm meeting with Fitch's lawyer tomorrow to sign papers and make everything official. Shall I call Jimmy to offer information-sharing between DI and the police?"

"Dear God, no. I'll never hear the end of it." He turned the sound back on. "I'll give you a conditional yes on the back and forth between us."

She kissed him. "Teamwork. We have it."

"Persuasion is more like it."

Giulia didn't mention how Fitch was one of their prime suspects in the embezzlement scheme. Driscoll Investigations was her business now, to run as she saw fit. She never wanted to return to those days of arguing about work at work and arguing about work at home. So instead of talking any more, she climbed on top of her husband and started to massage his shoulders.

The next morning Frank had to check ESPN to see if Man U pulled out the win.

Six

On Wednesday at ten minutes to ten Giulia arrived at the Tower of Blinding Glass. Every cell in her body needed coffee. If God was good, this place would have a Keurig with a flavor she hadn't tried.

The receptionist led her to the kitchen.

"Flavored?" Giulia said.

The receptionist smiled. "You have the voice of someone in desperate straits. We've got just the thing." She spun the countertop carousel and inserted a nondescript plastic pod into the machine. "Raspberry chocolate truffle."

"Oh, my." Giulia slid a Styrofoam cup under the spout and pressed the brew button. When the aroma reached her nose, she said again, "Oh, my."

The receptionist laughed. "Everyone I introduce this flavor to reacts like that."

"You are a life saver." She added plain creamer and whimpered when she took her first sip.

"My work here is through for today," the receptionist said with a bow. "I'll take you to Mr. Petit's office."

She led Giulia down a narrow hall patterned in wallpaper the color of lightly buttered toast. After a quick knock she opened Petit's door.

The lawyer nodded at Giulia and waved at his rectangular conference table as he talked on his phone and banged on his keyboard. There was no sign of Roger Fitch to curdle her decadent coffee. From the half of the phone conversation she could hear, it sounded like an involved one. She took out her iPad and opened the files on AtlanticEdge while she waited.

Sipping coffee with her left hand, Giulia worked on a spreadsheet with her right. They'd narrowed it down to a short list of employees, and she named a column for each one: Leonard Tulley, Miles Park, Denise Burns, Autumn Tate...and Roger Fitch.

"It's one of these five," she muttered. "Probably more than one. Definitely more than one."

The company suspected careful, systematic embezzlement, possibly dating back three years. Four weeks into the process of reviewing video footage and data analysis, Giulia, Sidney, and Zane had confirmed that someone—or a handful of someones—were skimming profits. They'd been covering their tracks so well, Giulia was impressed. Zane wasn't, since he still hadn't spotted the clue he was certain existed, the one small mistake that would lead to the altered entry that would point to the falsified purchase orders and onward into book-cooking that was real artistry.

Three corporate heads exploded when Giulia delivered the preliminary report to AtlanticEdge. The anger in that meeting overwhelmed the proposed agenda. So much so, not one of the gathered Vice Presidents kvetched at Giulia's ten- to twelve-day timeline for pinpointing the actual embezzlers. Surprising for a company that claimed to solve every client issue within seventy-two hours or the bill would be pro-rated all the way down to zero. When she left, the lawyers at the table were already salivating over the anticipated prosecution.

Petit's call sounded like it was about finished. Giulia saved and closed the document. Petit hung up.

"Ms. Driscoll. Thanks for being prompt. I see you found the coffee." He brought his Pittsburgh Pirates mug over to the table and took a swig. "Blech. Cold. I'll be right back."

Giulia swallowed more of her new favorite coffee. A couple of extra minutes to add notes. She reopened the Five Embezzlers doc...and Roger Fitch sauntered in the room.

She chastised herself in her best convent manner for putting a negative spin on everything Fitch did. Some people walked like that. It didn't have to mean Fitch had an inflated opinion of himself. Giulia closed the tablet once more. "Good morning."

"Morning." Fitch yanked out the chair opposite and fell into it. "Caffeine gives me migraines. Could use some this morning. Can't even use those five-hour bottles."

"Have you tried a protein shake?"

Fitch snorted. "Once. It cured me forever. Usually I mix up some Muscle Milk, but I ran out the day before yesterday."

Petit returned, French roast in hand. Giulia pinpointed the intense aroma right away.

"Mr. Petit, I've brought our agency agreement for us to sign." She took a nine-by-twelve brown folder and a pen from her bag. "This document is specific to your situation based on the information you emailed me last night. If you look at the bottom of page one, paragraph three, you'll see that I've limited the scope of our services to the two-week period before the scheduled trial date. On page two, paragraph one, I noted the exact amount the judge authorized for this project." She handed a copy to the lawyer and finished her coffee while he read it.

Next to her, Roger Fitch sighed, fidgeted, and played poker on his phone.

Giulia, comfortable with silence and patience, waited without irritation until the lawyer looked up from the last page.

"You'd never make it in the legal field, Ms. Driscoll. This is much too clear and concise." He gave her that jury-winning smile. "Surprisingly, I have no issues with this as-is."

Giulia pretended to look skeptical.

"Not one?"

DI's standard contract often raised eyebrows. She had badgered Frank into retooling it when they set up the business as a partnership. It only took him a month to admit that less obfuscation meant happiness all around.

"Not one." He took it to his desk and picked up his phone. "Jean, can I borrow you for a minute?"

A silver-haired woman in pleated trousers and a green-striped shirt opened the door. "Yes, Mr. Petit?"

"Please make three copies of this."

"Certainly." She returned two minutes later, paper-clipped copies still warm.

Petit brought them back to the table. "Roger, sign all three of these." He handed Fitch a pen and pointed to the appropriate signature line.

"Whatever you say, legal whiz." He scribbled a set of loops and points three times.

The lawyer signed next and Giulia last. He took two copies over to his desk, and Giulia returned one to her folder.

"I'll file this with the court," Petit said. "Now that the easy part's out of the way, let's get to the real paperwork." He brought over from his bookshelf an expandable manila folder crammed with papers and dropped it on the table. "Ms. Driscoll, this is the discovery file. It contains everything we got from the police and the prosecution."

Giulia whistled.

"Let's see what we have to work with." She tipped the contents of the box onto the table. "Police report. Another police report. Autopsy. Glossy eight by ten photos. Lots of them." She contained her initial reaction to the close-up of Loriela Gil, deceased, with a pastel striped tie cutting into her neck. "DNA report. Fingerprints. Affidavits." She shook her head. "I need several hours of complete silence with all of this. Is there anything you want to tell me before I take this back to my office?"

Petit shuffled stapled sets of papers. "It will make much more sense if Roger gives you a timeline of the events leading up to the murder."

Giulia powered up her tablet again. "Go ahead."

Fitch grinned at her, but he lacked Petit's charisma. "Lori and I'd been living together for a couple of months when she wrangled me an interview at AtlanticEdge. I'd gotten pretty fed up with the commission structure at my last place."

Giulia typed as fast as he talked. "Was Loriela in Human Resources?"

"Hell no. Accounting. She had a head for numbers. In charge of the department. Got there because she talked them into overhauling the whole system. Everybody listened to her. She was going places. You know the type."

Giulia nodded, typing.

"Lori got my foot in there, but I proved myself in eight weeks. Pretty soon it was her and me, head of sales and head of accounting. Alpha types, both of us. Strong leaders." He leaned forward onto the table. "Here's where you'll hear shit from her catty friends and her buttinsky relatives. You can't put two alphas together and expect a peaceful sail down a calm brook."

Without raising her head, Giulia said, "You fought. All couples fight."

"Yeah, but we didn't always fight in the privacy of our own place. She liked Long Island Iced Tea and I like single malt. We'd go out to relieve the stress of a hard day. I'd check out a hot babe and Lori'd get all jealous bitch on me. So we'd fight. Not like she didn't stare at a good package in tight jeans, but whatever."

From the corner of her eye, Giulia caught Petit give a facial signal to Fitch. Fitch shifted in his chair.

"So anyway, you'll see in that stack of papers that our nosey-ass neighbors called the cops on us once, and there was this set of emails that got us both in trouble. Sent 'em from work. Stupid, I know, but she said I was screwing around and I said she was and...well, you'll read it all. Cops got printouts from HR."

Giulia finished typing that last sentence and waited. When he didn't speak, she raised her eyes and saw Fitch and Petit making faces at each other.

"Gentlemen, it will be difficult for me to help you if you keep out pertinent information."

Petit looked sheepish. "The way this next part sounds, Ms. Driscoll, it might prejudice you against Roger."

"Mr. Petit, I am not a fragile flower that needs to be protected from the harsh realities of the world." If only he knew what she'd seen since joining DI.

"See, Colby? Told you she could take it. Listen to Uncle Roger when he speaks." Fitch leaned forward again. "My birthday's on April first. We'd made up again and went out to celebrate. Man, we got hammered. Only a twenty in the pockets of the bouncers kept them from tossing us out of the bar. Made it home without running into a cop or a telephone pole—stop looking like that, Colby. Ms. Driscoll, here's where the important stuff starts."

"I'm paying attention, Mr. Fitch." Giulia heard her voice revert to "teacher losing patience."

"I knew you were. Sorry. When we got home we decided to end the night with awesome makeup sex. Best girlfriend ever, you know? I got four of my ties and tied her to the bedposts. Uh...so...skipping to the end. I untied her but left the ties hanging where they were. She was out before I turned off the light and I was out a second later." He shifted in his chair, his voice losing the "great bar story" tone. "My ringtone woke me up. I made it pushy on purpose, see?"

He held up his phone. It played that klaxon alarm from World War II submarines in an emergency dive. Giulia winced.

"Can't remember the last time I got hammered enough to sleep through Lori's phone alarm. She set it up with ocean sounds and birds, because she didn't like loud noises in the morning. When I rolled over to grab my phone, I could tell even with my eyes closed the light in the room was way too bright for it to be our usual wake-up time of seven a.m. My chief underling was on the other end, asking me if I was coming into work that day. I unglued my eyes and it was like the signal for a hangover headache bad enough to make me want to cut my head off. I reached out to shake Lori awake, but her side of the bed was empty."

"What time was it?" Giulia said.

"Ten-something by the digital clock on the cable box. I said I'd be there soon and hung up. That's when I saw the glass door to the balcony was open. My jeans were on the floor, so I dragged them on even though they were still wet from the rain the night before. Didn't want my junk flapping in the wind." He chuckled, but sobered up right away. "I went to the door to get some fresh air and saw the neat little hole in the glass. Turned around and grabbed the phone and called 9-1-1. Reported the robbery, figured it'd save time because if someone knew enough to do that glass-cutting thing it was a no-brainer what they did it for."

Giulia raised her eyes. "Didn't you wonder where Loriela had gone?"

"Didn't think of it—the phone call was instinct. After I hung up, I called out for her—thought she might've been ralphing in the bathroom. The wind blew some new rain in from the open door, so I went back there to close it." A pause. "That's when I saw Lori. She was all crumpled up on the balcony, her blouse from the night before plastered half on her and half against the railing, and one of my ties wrapped around her neck."

"Did you call anyone?"

"Shit, yes I called someone! I called her! I yelled her name and shook her and loosened the tie and tried mouth-to-mouth. Took me forever to hear the cops knocking on the door. When I opened it, I screamed at them to get an ambulance for Lori. Gotta hand it to them, they figured out what was going on in about five seconds flat. But it was too late. The EMTs called it as soon as they showed up."

Giulia stopped typing. "If you altered the crime scene, where did the photographs come from?"

Petit broke into Fitch's narrative. "They asked Roger to return Loriela's body to the same position in which he found it."

Giulia pictured having to do that to a dead lover while police and medical personnel watched. "I'm sorry."

"Yeah, well, I had to do it so the cops could catch her killer." He shook himself. "They took pictures of everything in the apartment and around the balcony. There was a big dent in the landscaping and a trail of brush-type marks toward the street."

"Someone jumped down and ran away," Giulia murmured.

"That's what it looked like. And covered up their tracks.

Despite all that, the fuckers still arrested me." He slugged Petit's shoulder. "Superman here got me out in forty-eight hours. Had to pony up a stupid amount of bail, but he convinced the judge that on top of everything being circumstantial, I wasn't any kind of flight risk. Hell, I wanted to find out who killed Lori more than the cops did."

"Circumstantial in what way?" Giulia said then waved the question off. "I'll read that later." She checked the time in the corner of the tablet and hit save. "It's almost eleven-thirty and I have prior obligations to meet. Mr. Petit, I'm going to schedule several meetings with Mr. Fitch. Will a summary email from each be enough?"

Petit began to stack all the documents and return them to the folder. "Absolutely. I know what you mean by prior obligations."

"Hey." Roger Fitch looked from one to the other. "What about me? I'm the one going on trial for my life in two weeks. My life, people."

Petit held up both hands. "We know. We're professionals. We've got this."

"That's correct, Mr. Fitch." Giulia packed away her tablet and stood. "If Mr. Petit will give me an oversized folder to protect this evidence, I'll look it all over and come up with a plan of action later today."

Fitch looked from Giulia to Petit and back again. "I guess I don't have a choice."

Giulia restrained an eye roll at the pout in his voice. Petit left and returned with a large-sized shipping box.

"This should work. It's good camouflage too."

Together they fit everything into the box and sealed it. Petit turned the smile on her again. "We can do this."

Giulia returned a lower-wattage version. "Yes, we can." Her smile widened. "Why are you quoting Rosie the Riveter?"

His expression became faraway for a moment, then he laughed. "Because she's my hero, of course. Everything a lawyer says is the perfect truth."

"Oh, yes, of course." She left before she said what she really thought of that last sentence.

Seven

Giulia called Sidney from the Glass Tower's parking lot.

"I'm heading back with food from Scarpulla's Deli. What is mini-Sidney craving today?"

"You're a life saver," Sidney said. "Eggplant on wheat with feta, please. It's on their specials menu." Her voice turned sing-song. "Giulia, Zane is making faces at me! Tell him to stop."

Giulia laughed. "Zane is still acclimating. Ask him if he wants me to pick up lunch."

Muffled conversation followed, then Sidney's voice again. "After many pauses and apologetic noises, he says he would like a Reuben."

"Got it. Explain how this works, okay?"

Giulia caught the deli right before the lunch rush. She'd come here the first day they opened a satellite location in Cottonwood thereby making the world a better place.

The owner welcomed her with his usual exuberance. "Ms. Driscoll, I have the perfect sandwich for you on this sunny day." His three chins jiggled as he nodded at her.

"Giuseppe, you've never steered me wrong." Giulia inhaled. "Is the pasta fagiole ready?"

"No, no, not for you today. Today you will try the new sausage my wife makes, yes?"

She caved. "Of course. I have lunch for my staff to order too."

"The pregnant lady, she wants peppers and cheese again?"

"Not this time." Giulia gave Sidney's and Zane's orders.

"*Bene.* Eggplant is very healthy. Good for the brain. Angelo!"

A teenage version of Giuseppe, minus the extra chins, stuck his head around the door from the kitchen.

"Yeah, gramps?"

"One Reuben. One fried eggplant with feta on wheat, dry. One of your grandmother's new sausages on a bun with peppers and onions."

"Got it. Hey, Ms. Driscoll."

"Good morning, Angelo. Spring break?"

"Just started. Next year, France." He vanished into the kitchen and the sound of sizzling came a moment later.

Giuseppe wrapped a whole pickle in waxed paper and then in a Ziploc bag. "That boy, he will be a great chef one day. He promises to make fancy French desserts for me to add to the menu."

"You'll have to beat people away with a stick." Giulia opened her wallet. "Three bottled waters, too, please. What exactly are you giving me to eat?"

He rang up the three orders. "It is lamb and fresh romano and *chicoria.* The spices she will not reveal except to Angelo."

"That sounds wonderful. Now I want to make greens and beans. My husband says he's getting fat."

The bell over the door rang and six people came in by twos. Giuseppe handed over her change. "That is the sign of a good wife."

Angelo came out of the kitchen with three wrapped sandwiches. His grandfather set them in a plastic bag and Angelo handed that bag and the bag with water over the counter to Giulia. "Here you go, Ms. Driscoll. You'll love the sausage."

"Thank you both." Giulia made way for the new customers.

By the time she pulled into her building's small parking lot, her mouth was watering from the mingled aromas rising from the deli bag. She walked up the stairs and into the office balancing both bags in one hand and the box of documents on the other arm.

"Somebody take this food before I eat all of it in front of you."

Sidney tried to leap out of her chair, but the baby foiled that.

"No fair. The baby's sabotaging me. Zane, rescue our lunch?"

Zane stood, took a sideways step, and froze in place. Then with a palpable effort he reached across his desk and took the bags from Giulia's hand.

Giulia pretended to grimace. "Fine. You win. The bill's in the bag with the water bottles. I'm eating at my desk, but remember, you do not have to do the same." She stared pointedly at Zane. "The machine can get any phone calls."

"I'm reading a new thriller on my Kindle," Zane said.

"Excellent."

"I'm working through," Sidney said, "but that's because I have to leave an hour early for my OB/GYN appointment."

"Remind your doctor that you can't go into labor 'til you train your replacement."

Sidney was already unwrapping the eggplant. "I know, I know, or you'll bring her to the maternity ward for instructions." She took a bite. "I totally need to get this recipe."

Giulia shook her head. "Too late. You'd have to marry into the family."

"Rats."

Giulia closed herself into her private office. Before anything else, she unwrapped the sausage and peppers and took a bite.

"*Madonna mia.*" The chicory lent a bite to the lamb and the romano smoothed out the spices. "Angelo will get his grandfather's deli into Zagat's."

Chewing a second bite, she gauged the space on her desk and chucked that idea. She pushed the sausage sandwich and its wrapping nearer the edge of the desk and planted herself on the floor. A drink of water—that last bit had been extra-spicy—and she opened the shipping box.

The photographs she set directly in front of her, face down 'til after lunch. Three years in this business hadn't hardened her to the point of being able to look at certain things while eating.

DNA test printouts at her right. Fingerprint reports at her left. Like a clock face: Photos at twelve o'clock, DNA at three, fingerprints at nine, herself at six. Police report from the April call at one o'clock, documents inventorying similar break-ins in the area at two o'clock, move the DNA reports down to four o'clock and set the autopsy at three. Move the fingerprint pages to six o'clock. Affidavits from neighbors at eleven. From her relatives at ten, from his relatives at nine. More photos, this time of the outside of the apartment. Shove everything on the left down an hour and put the apartment photos at eleven.

"Whoa." Her breath fluttered the fingerprint records. She backed out of her circle of documents and found a bag of butterfly clips in her bottom drawer. When each stack of papers and photographs was clamped together, she groped on the top of her desk for the sandwich and took another bite.

"This is at least ten hours' work. I need Sidney." She stepped over the affidavits and opened her door.

Kitty-corner from the doorway, Sidney was chugging water with one hand and typing with the other. While not too different from the eager college graduate Frank had hired four years ago, this Sidney's skills were sharper with her energy undiminished.

"Pregnant lady, can I borrow you when you have a minute?"

"Be right there." Sidney typed for another few moments and stood. "We're at your service."

"Zane," Giulia said, "when your lunch hour's over, can you join us?"

Zane nodded, eyes on his Kindle.

Sidney stopped in Giulia's doorway. "Whoa."

"That's what I said. This is going to take more time than I thought, so can you give me a rundown of where we're at with AtlanticEdge?"

Sidney handed Giulia seven dollars and leveraged herself into Giulia's client chair. "Here's for my lunch. I love being pregnant, but I'm ready for mini-Sidney to vacate the premises. Did you know that alpacas are pregnant for almost a year? No wonder they spit when they're cranky."

"Jingle didn't spit on Olivier again, did she?"

Sidney hung her head. "She did. It's a good thing our condo lease was up three months ago, because Olivier wouldn't set foot near Jingle or Belle again if we weren't living in the cottage."

"You'd think the girls would accept him because you're married."

"It's the exact opposite. I raised both of them and they're wicked jealous." She rubbed a sudden bulge in her stomach. "God knows what they'll do when the baby's born."

"They're both moms too."

"I guess. Olivier's threatened to paper the inside of their barn with pictures of rump roasts and fried chicken legs if the girls spit on the baby."

Giulia snorted. "Isn't that a little passive-aggressive for a psychologist?"

"You think?" Sidney belched. "Gah. Sorry. The tenant just punched that tiny place she shoved my stomach into." She shifted position. "Okay, AtlanticEdge. I've organized it so it makes sense to me, but not to anyone else yet. Can you open my files and I'll explain?"

Giulia clicked the icon titled "Sidney" and then the "AtlanticEdge" folder. Sidney scooted her chair next to Giulia's.

"Now the Word doc labeled 'Week of March 2' and the Excel doc labeled the same."

Giulia opened both and a kaleidoscope of colors filled her screen.

"Okay. Page one of the spreadsheet has seven columns, one for each of the employees I think is a likely thief."

"Wait a sec." Giulia turned on her tablet. "I started one of these this morning at the lawyer's office." She checked hers against Sidney's. "Yes. Yes. Yes. Him? I didn't think he was that suspicious. Yes. Yes. Really? Why her?" Giulia pointed to the last column.

"She's heavy into online gambling. I found video footage of her checking one of the biggest sites on her phone while she was at her desk. I didn't need to be able to read lips to see that she was losing."

Giulia typed onto her tablet.

"Okay, she's added to my list. But why the box of crayons guy?"

All the names on Sidney's spreadsheet had photos from their employee passcards next to them. Only the fourth one made Giulia cringe.

Sidney wrinkled her nose. "I know, right? I'm secretly hoping he's stealing money to buy clothes that actually go with each other." The bald man in the picture wore a purple shirt, green plaid tie, and orange checkered pocket square.

"I just get a weird feeling about him," Sidney said. "Like if this was a horror movie he'd be the guy training an army of rats in his mother's basement or making sculptures out of dead bodies."

"Both hobbies would take significant funds," Giulia said, crumpling her sandwich wrapper and tossing it into the trash can. "Plus, either scenario would be easy to trace. Massive plaster purchases or antibiotics and bandages."

"I guess. Okay. Page two."

More colors.

"We organized two years of sales and returns and bonuses and all that stuff. Zane helped me a lot with this."

"What did I do? Whoa. What's with the conjuring circle?" Zane stopped in the doorway, money in hand.

"It's all the documents from the lawyer with related information grouped together," Giulia said. "Bring in a chair and squeeze around everything, please."

"I'd rather stand. Thanks for picking up lunch." He placed the money in Giulia's in-box and came around to her other side. "Oh, the books."

Sidney pointed to the cells highlighted in yellow. "These are the retail software sales. Green is consulting, pink is monthly contracts, blue is big corporate sales. The blank column is only there to separate income from outflow. Light brown is sales staff expenses, gray is bad debts, red is manufacturing, purple is advertising. We used light green for paychecks and pale yellow for bonuses."

Giulia leaned back in her chair. "I am officially impressed."

Sidney jerked a thumb in Zane's direction. "He showed me how to organize it so if I got hit by a semi someone besides me would be able to figure out what I did."

"Sidney."

She grinned at Giulia. "Don't worry. It's the hormones. It'll pass once I evict this one." She patted her stomach and got kicked in return. "Brat. Don't beat up mommy. My desktop has the link to the company surveillance footage stored offsite. I'm spot-checking it against dates where Zane found what he thinks are small discrepancies in the books."

"These guys are slick," Zane said. "They're not using an easily detectable pattern. What's ticking me off is how long it's taking me to pin down their pattern. It's mimicking complete randomness, which is just another way of saying they think they're smarter than everyone else."

"Guys," Giulia said, "we've had the job just under four weeks. The company employs a thousand people."

"Eight hundred seventy-three full-time, ninety-six part-time."

"Zane," Giulia said.

He turned away from the monitor to look at her. Giulia didn't say anything else as she watched his face. When everything slid into place behind it, his pallid skin lost all traces of color.

"Ms. Driscoll, I apologize. It was never my intent to be disrespectful." He placed his palms together before his face and bowed.

Giulia waited a few seconds for him to move. When he opened his hands, she smiled at him.

"Zane. I'm not your teacher or your spiritual leader. I'm your boss. You're still learning the boundaries between college and a real job. Like, for example, not correcting the boss when she chooses to use a rounded number."

A touch of color returned to Zane's face. "We were expected to challenge our professors at MIT."

"Of course. And at PayWright you were sat on like suitcases 'til you were latched and stuffed into your slots."

He nodded. "We got written up if we had any conversations on shift that weren't directly related to a call." He gave her a crooked smile. "I got written up on average once every twelve days."

Sidney made an indefinable noise. "Why didn't you go into computer programming like you got your degree in?"

He gave her a one-shoulder shrug. "I like the analysis but I didn't want to sit at a desk staring at a screen all day. My student loan grace period ended and I had to do something. The call center was half a step up from cleaning portable toilets for a living, which I actually considered, since I can't cook and don't know how to bartend."

"Portable toilets." Giulia shivered. "That beats any cleaning job we got stuck with in the convent. And that's saying something."

Sidney stretched her back. "You people are making me dread diaper changes, and I've cleaned alpaca poop for years."

"Zane," Giulia said, "I'll give you the two extra employees that aren't on my list. You and Sidney give me reasons to keep all seven or to narrow it down to five or fewer by Friday morning."

"Deal."

"All right, go away. I've got piles of police reports and evidence and photographs to plow through."

"You used to be all shy and soft-spoken like a nun in the movies. Power has gone to your head." Sidney's voice broke on the last words and she giggled 'til she got the hiccups.

Giulia face-planted on her keyboard and then made a big show of typing up a fake "Termination of Employment" notice. Zane ran to the bathroom and returned with a cup of water. Sidney choked it down, reduced the frequency of the hiccups, and hit the escape key on Giulia's keyboard.

Zane's reaction to Sidney's audacity ruined all her efforts to eradicate the hiccups. Only deep-breathing and determination kept Giulia from catching them.

Eight

Two hours later, her butt numb and her fingers cramping, Giulia set down the police report on break-ins similar to the one at Fitch's apartment. Bulleted lists filled three pages of the legal pad on her lap. Multi-colored fluorescent Post-it notes fattened the report's right-hand side. She got to her knees to relieve the muscles in her thighs and picked up the autopsy report. The crime scene and autopsy photos, too, since lunch was long digested.

The top photo: Loriela mostly naked and strangled on the small apartment balcony. The next, a close-up of her face and neck. The pathetic image of the soaked, draggled blouse and hair—brown according to the autopsy but looking black in the early morning rain—made Giulia's throat close up. So vulnerable. So final. And according to the information they'd gleaned from AtlanticEdge, Loriela Gil radiated confidence and energy when she was alive.

Frank would lecture Giulia about getting too involved with the case, with emphasis on her bleeding-heart tendencies.

"Guilty. So what?" She bit back a smile. "Now I'm copping attitude."

Several more photos of Loriela's body from different angles. Giulia divorced herself from the pathos of it and put on her detective hat. She treated the imaginary fedora like an actor putting on a costume: When she wore it, Giulia Falcone the ex-nun who was still a Franciscan at heart up to, and including, working with homeless humans and animals, took a vacation. Giulia Falcone-

Driscoll, who'd started as DI's admin and now ran the business, took her place. Professional Giulia fought for justice and made a living doing it.

She stepped over the circle of documents and spread out the eight-by-ten photos on the floor beneath the window. If she treated them more like a PowerPoint slide show than a puzzle...

Starting at the upper left-hand corner of the narrow end of the office, she sat on her heels and placed the photo taken at the farthest point away from the apartment. Then, as though she was walking alongside the apartment building, the photos of the footprints, of the broken barberry bushes, of Loriela's shirt and hair drooping off the edge of the second-floor balcony. Then, as though she too had used the bushes as a stepping stone up to the wrought-iron railing, Loriela's body lying in the corner, the open glass door, the neat circle cut from the glass above the deadbolt. In the third row, the soaked carpet from where the rain had blown in when the killer had opened the door to steal, according to the police report, wallets and laptops.

The footprints on the carpet trailing mulch and bits of grass. The rumpled bedcovers. The open purse on the kitchen counter. In the office-slash-den, two rectangles of dust-free table where two laptops used to be.

The rest of the photos covered the square footage of the entire apartment. Master bedroom, hall, spare bedroom turned into the den which still contained an Xbox and flat screen TV, kitchen with marble-topped island and dining space, living room with another flat-screen TV. Walk-in closets in each bedroom, one and a half bathrooms, a tiny laundry room off the kitchen.

"Their rent must be as much as our mortgage."

A knock and the door opened. "I'm heading out to my baby checkup," Sidney said.

"It's four o'clock already? No wonder my muscles have locked up." Giulia un-knotted herself. "See you tomorrow."

"I promise not to drive over any railroad tracks." Her slower than usual footsteps retreated 'til the main door closed behind her.

Giulia twisted left and right, easing her back and shoulder muscles. So much left to read. She'd filled seven and a half pages of the legal pad. At this stage she liked to scribble and rewrite and draw lines between connections rather than type into her tablet.

She'd had to keep the window closed so the papers wouldn't blow all over and the air in her office was dead. Plus she didn't want to spend the night on this hard floor.

That settled it. She stacked the photos in reverse order and slid them into their envelope. Returning all the documents to the shipping box went much faster now that she had a handle on their order. Her first action after closing the box was to open the window.

"Brr. False spring lived up to its name." She inhaled the fresh air.

When she opened the door, Zane's right hand flailed at her. Her evil imp whispered that she ought to buy a hand-held flag at the dollar store for him to wave. Her good angel whapped the imp with its wing. Zane was sloughing off the insanity of his year in telemarketing, but it wouldn't help to push things too soon.

"Yes?" she said to him.

"Ms. Driscoll, check this out." He turned his monitor toward her. "The dumbed-down version of their proprietary software, the one sold online and in stores? There's something off with the numbers."

Giulia grinned. "Excellent. Do you know what?"

Zane's shoulders slumped, emphasizing his weightlifter's neck muscles. "No. But I will."

"I have perfect confidence in you."

Her admin looked up, his eyes studying her for sarcasm.

"Yes, I mean it. I'm heading home for a quiet evening with cinnamon coffee and DNA reports."

"I can stay—"

"No. We're not on deadline with this job yet. Let it percolate."

His shy smile appeared. "I was hoping you'd say that. I've got a date."

Nine

"Are you going to work all night?" Frank's voice hovered between plaintive and annoyed.

"It's only nine-thirty," Giulia said from their living room floor. "I want to get a better handle on this DNA report."

With a deep sigh, Frank sat beside her. "Let me see it."

"I knew you'd say that."

"I have an ulterior motive," her husband said as he studied the graphs and numbers. "I want dessert."

Giulia batted her eyes in the best cartoonish manner. "I've lost my allure so soon?"

"Your espresso cake hasn't." Frank looked down at her. "I'm joking. Don't look like that. But seriously I want a honking big piece of that cake before I take you to bed, wife of mine."

"Then reveal some secrets to me so I can fit it in with these photographs and other reports."

Frank unstapled the pages. "Come closer, my child, and let Papa Driscoll explain forensic DNA to you."

Giulia sat cross-legged next to him. "My spirit is open to absorb your wisdom."

Frank's eyes skewed sideways at her. "Don't use your Sister Regina voice. It freaks me out."

She kissed his cheek. "All part of my plan to keep our marriage fresh by keeping you slightly off-balance. *Cosmo* says so."

"I don't trust that magazine."

"Focus, Mr. Driscoll."

"Right. DNA. Let's start with this table of alleles for a nasal mucus sample."

Frank took her through alleles and loci and short tandem repeats. "STRs. Easier to say and most cops and lawyers know what they are nowadays. This table shows samples from—damn—eight people—the dead girlfriend, the suspect, the cleaning lady, the apartment building manager, the landscaper, and one—two—three other names, probably the friends who hung around most."

"Those suspects are so obvious they're cliché."

"Don't knock every cliché. There's a reason the obvious suspects became cliché."

"Yes, O guru."

"Stop it. Okay, see where the numbers of the dead girlfriend are the only ones that match the mucus sample exactly? Sometimes the chart shows matches that are too close to call, but not here. See how it says that sample two—the piano player—is 'included' and everyone else is 'excluded' as possible matches?"

Giulia raised her finger from the page where she had been following Frank's explanation. "All right. I've got the basics of this chart. What about the electropherograms over here?"

Frank described peaks and "off-ladder" loci and ambiguities. "There's also what's called 'noise.' You've got a little of that here in this urea crystal sample on page four." He picked up three different pages from the initial charts and after that two more pages of electropherograms. "None of the samples appear to be degraded. That'll make things easier for you."

A few minutes later, as Giulia was repacking the shipping box, she gave Frank her best "stop the erring student in his tracks" stare.

"You're giving up much easier than usual."

Her husband's eyebrows raised in comic innocence. "What do you mean?"

"Come on. Recall last year when we ran DI together. How many times did we argue over method versus means?"

"Forget that. What about justice versus logic?"

"Exactly." She set the box on the hall table. "So allow me to rephrase my observation: Why are you so calm and cooperative tonight? Yesterday you treated this case like it was a joke whose punch line I didn't get."

"Oh, *muirnín*. I'm sorry." Frank jumped up from the couch and wrapped his arms around her waist. "I have a mouth like an *asal*."

Giulia snorted before she could stop herself. "You are not a jackass. You do, however, lack a reliable internal censor."

Frank turned her around and kissed her. "Then I won't mention how unladylike it is to snort." Before Giulia could protest, he said, "Seriously, you know I'm all for giving you any advice or bits of knowledge I have if it'll further DI's reputation. Gotta keep my reputation for incisive sleuthing intact."

"*Your* reputation?" Giulia's voice jumped half an octave.

Frank wrestled her onto the couch and tickled her into gasping submission.

Ten

Roger Fitch arrived at Driscoll Investigations at nine o'clock Thursday morning dressed in jeans and a Steelers jersey under a leather jacket. He clutched a V8 energy drink like it alone could drag him into communication with his fellow human beings.

"Good morning," Giulia said, mentally contrasting his hangover-chic to her neat brown wool trousers and jade-green sweater. "Please have a seat. I'll be with you in a minute." She indicated Zane's client chair.

Sidney disappeared into the bathroom for the second time since eight-fifteen. Fitch ignored Giulia's invitation and paced between both desks, drinking and staring first out the window, then at Zane and Giulia, then at Sidney when she emerged from the bathroom.

"Zane, can you give more reasons to justify items *b*, *d*, and *g*? I don't want to give Monsignor Jerome any reason to cut us off before we complete the presentation."

"Yeah. I'm pretty sure." He added notes to three header cells in the spreadsheet on his screen.

Sidney eased herself into her chair, both she and the chair creaking.

"Ready to pop, huh?" Fitch said.

Sidney gave him an excellent imitation of Giulia's "frost in July" smile.

Giulia inhaled sharply enough for Roger to hear her. He

turned, but Giulia's face showed nothing but polite welcome. As recently as last year, she would've laughed out loud at Sidney's mimicry. Now? Not a chance. One, she liked Sidney too much. Two, it wasn't professional. Three, it was an excellent imitation of Angry Giulia and she wanted to see more. So she cut Roger off before he could do any real damage.

"Thank you for waiting, Mr. Fitch. Please come into my office. Zane, I can take calls." She closed the door behind them.

Roger dropped into Giulia's client chair and slugged more of his V8. "Okay. Thirteen days 'til my trial starts. What's the strategy?"

Giulia's professional mask never cracked, even as she catalogued Fitch as a typical problem child. Well, she didn't spend ten years teaching high school students in challenging settings to allow a client like this to disturb her equilibrium. Besides, the attitude was most likely slapped on to cover his fear of that looming antiseptic death chamber with its poison-filled needle.

Out loud, she said, "I've worked up a multi-step plan. It's labor-intensive, but the time constraints give us no choice."

"I knew it. Laid in a stock of these V8s and single malt and steaks to get me through."

She opened her spreadsheet on her desktop rather than the tablet, for the sake of using her ergonomic keyboard.

"I want to go over some of the ground that the police have already walked."

"Good God, why?"

"Because my team will look at it in a very different way than the police did. See these DNA reports?" She handed those papers out to him.

He made a puking noise. "I remember those giant Q-tips they stuck in my mouth and in Lori's."

"They're going to be just as much use to us as they are to the prosecution. So are the police reports and all the crime scene photographs."

A shrug. "You're the boss."

"True. First of all, I would like more background on you and Loriela. Specifically, the restraining order."

Fitch's eyes narrowed. "Scheming bitch. Lori's mother, that is. Ever read up on Alexander the Great? His mother was a real piece of work. Pushed, pushed, pushed; killed off rivals; thought up more schemes than contestants on reality shows. Lori's mother could've been her star pupil."

Giulia typed it all up with a straight face. "And?"

"I wasn't good enough for Madre Cassandra's little princess. Forget the fact that Madre Cassandra raised her princess in a two-room welfare apartment because Madre Cassandra spent her career cleaning second-rate office buildings."

"There is nothing demeaning about working with one's hands," Giulia said.

"Yeah, yeah, I know. Honest wages for honest labor, yada yada. Lori got a full ride to Temple because of her kickass grades combined with Madre's extremely limited income, so it all worked out." He shook the V8, drank the dregs, and tossed it dead-center into the trash can. "Oh, no," Fitch continued. "Nothing less than a CEO was good enough for the princess. Of course Lori wasn't like that. If she was here, she'd tell you I was the guy that made her get a clue." He stood up and started pacing the narrow space. "Lori inherited two things from her mother: legs up to here—" he stopped pacing and gestured at the level of his lowest ribs—"and love for the bad boys. She broke a guy's nose in high school and brought a successful sexual assault suit against a guy in her junior year at Temple."

Without breaking her typing rhythm, Giulia headed up a new column for the college incident.

"Madre Cassandra conveniently ignored her own tastes in male companionship and became suspicious of anyone who wanted to date her daughter. Lori moved into a better neighborhood and started her own catalog of Bad Choices. Thought she could handle anything when AtlanticEdge recruited her right out of college."

Fitch leaned on the windowsill and stared out.

"They got decent pizza at that place across the street?"

"Yes, they do. I gather you're about to tell me Loriela made some poor choices when she started out on her own."

With a brief laugh, Fitch faced into the room again. "You're right. I don't have time to get distracted. Lori hooked up with a bartender with baby-blue eyes and a head full of muscle. Lots of muscle on the rest of him, too. Lori found that out fast enough."

"Name, please?"

"Jonathan Stallone, no lie. 'Yo, Adrian' and all that. Cops should have his address. He only called Lori once when I knew her, and she shut him down pretty fast." He waited for Giulia to finish typing. "The guy I shouldered out of her life hates my guts, but who cares? He thought he was tough 'til I kicked his ass. Then there's the other manager who got passed over for promotion when Lori was named head of bookkeeping. She got transferred to the unemployment line." He spelled out both names.

"Thank you." Giulia stretched her arms above her head. "Mr. Petit mentioned a restraining order against you."

"Didn't think you'd forget about that." He put on an air of repentance. "Happened when Lori took me to stay with Madre Cassandra our second Christmas together. Couple days after Christmas, I got bored, Lori started arguing with her mother, with me, with the nosy neighbors across the hall. So I bailed and got wasted at the corner bar—real trash heap, but good beer. Lori came after me. I didn't want to go back to that rat-trap of an apartment. Then, would you believe it, her mother followed her to the bar. Started nagging Lori, who started nagging me. Who the hell needs that?"

Giulia typed it all as though she was transcribing nothing more interesting than a term paper.

"I had at least three boilermakers in me. Wasn't at my best, you know? Lori grabbed my arm and dug her pointy nails into my skin. I shoved her off me and she crashed into a barstool. Cut her scalp. You know how head wounds gush blood. Her mother screamed and cussed at me in Spanish. I helped Lori up, the bartender handed me a towel and some vodka, and I cleaned her up. Hurt her like hell. She said a few choice words to me, too."

Giulia reminded herself not to judge.

"We ignored Madre pitching a fit and headed back to the apartment together. I patched Lori up and we had a heart-to-heart." He walked behind her desk and read over her shoulder. "Open up YouTube, will you? Type in 'Mother-in-Law Trouble.' There it is. Third from the top."

Giulia clicked the link. A shaky video began. The ceiling lights reflected in the mirror behind the bar showed the standard row of hard liquor bottles, a line of bar stools, several beer bottles on the bar itself, and a few tables off to the right and left. Something by Metallica played in the background, but Giulia couldn't tell which song because of the full-volume brawl in the foreground.

A tall woman with blonde-streaked black hair screamed Spanish curses in a progressively higher voice. Fitch stood opposite her, arguing with both her and an equally tall woman with short auburn hair. Giulia recognized Loriela Gil from the police photos. Loriela's voice was pitched lower than her mother's, but every so often it jumped up and the two sounded identical.

Fitch's lines cycled through "Shut up!" "Leave me alone," and "Fuck this. Just fuck this."

Then Loriela grabbed Fitch's arm and he cursed louder. When he shoved her off, five circles of blood appeared on his t-shirt sleeve. A crash and several gasps and noises covered the music. The camera swung left. Loriela lay on the floor, a bar stool on top of her and two more rolling away in opposite directions. Her mother's voice reached new heights. Loriela held one hand to the back of her head and told Fitch exactly what she thought of him with the middle finger of the other.

Male laughter much closer to the camera drowned out all the other noise for a moment. Fitch's back filled the screen and then he was helping Loriela onto one of the still-upright stools. The bartender handed him a towel and a vodka bottle. Fitch wet the towel and wiped Loriela's hair. It came away covered with blood.

"Ow! Asshole." Loriela took the bottle and gulped from it.

Her mother hadn't stopped yelling. One of the closer male voices translated, "He's the son of a whore, she'll cut his *cojones* off if he ever touches her daughter again, he's lower than a fly on a dung heap, and back around to his questionable parentage."

Fitch took Loriela by the waist and together they walked around her mother and out the door. The camera followed them until Loriela's mother's furious face filled the entire screen.

"You have recorded this? You will send it to me, yes?"

"Uh, sure, lady." The voice tried to be soothing.

Her mother shook Loriela's bloody towel at the screen. "I will make him pay for this."

She ran out of the bar. The male voice said, "Should've checked out the mother before he married the daughter." The video ended.

What Giulia wanted to say was, "Could you possibly make this any more difficult?" What she said was, "The restraining order followed directly after the incident in the video?"

"Yeah." Fitch took two folded papers out of his back pocket and spread them on Giulia's desk. "I brought it for you to see. Colby has the original. He wasn't going to give it to you because he said it put me in a bad light. Heh. Like you couldn't find this out on your own."

She read through them. "Based on the Affidavit and Petition for an Order for Protection in this matter, an Order for Protection should be issued...Refrain from assault, stalking, harassment..." She looked up at him when she finished the second page. "Since your relationship continued, what exactly happened with regard to this?"

"Len Tulley, he's one of Lori's co-workers, sent me the YouTube link. Don't know how he saw it and didn't care. I went straight to my VP at eight the next morning. It helped a lot that he and I were regular drinking buddies and spotted each other on weights at the company workout room. I put a good spin on it and got Lori on speakerphone. What saved my bacon is we never used each other's names on the video. Nothing searchable linked me or the company to the bar fight."

Giulia allowed her skeptical expression to speak for her.

"No, no, really. My VP took it to Lori's VP and they took it together to the weekly steering meeting. Management always likes proactive rather than reactive plans. 'Course, what really helped is that Lori and I'd posted increasing ROI and on-budget projects for the past seven quarters straight. We both got an official warning with a copy in our employee files."

Giulia typed like a machine.

"A cop showed up at my apartment with a summons a couple of days later. Lori went with me to the hearing and totally took my side against Cassandra." Triumph filled his voice. "The judge tossed it out. Cassandra cursed at me, but the judge threatened to charge her with contempt or some such, and she shut up. It was funny."

Giulia pressed her lips together. She saved her working document and reminded herself, again, not to judge the client.

Eleven

Giulia heaved the delivery box onto her desk and extracted a gray folder labeled "Fitch/Gil correspondence" and the case number.

"Let's move onto the emails you and Ms. Gil exchanged at work."

Fitch dropped into her client chair exactly like a marionette whose strings had been cut.

"You're a woman. Tell me what it is with you women and drama."

Giulia's back stiffened. "I beg your pardon?"

"You know. The angry texts. The weepy voicemails. Emails like these. Did you read them?"

"Yes."

"Then you know what I'm talking about." He pulled the folder toward him and opened it. "I mean, come on. '*Mi querido*, I wept into my pillow half the night after you left. Why do you say such cruel words to me, who you have called the queen of your heart?'"

Giulia tried and failed to imagine Roger Fitch saying those words to anyone. "What did you say to Ms. Gil to cause her to send you such a personal email on the work server?"

Fitch grumbled. "I don't remember. I probably saw a babe in a short skirt and said she looked better in it than Lori would. If anything could set her off, comparing her to a hot blonde cheerleader was number one." He wagged his eyebrows. "Nothing beats a pair of long legs in a short skirt."

All he needed was a cigar and a greasepaint mustache and he'd be Groucho Marx.

"If Ms. Gil disliked hearing such remarks, why didn't you keep them to yourself?"

"Seriously? Jeez, women are insecure. Guys don't give a crap about being compared to other guys, not if they're confident in their own prowess. Lori was gorgeous, sexy, and had *cojones*. She should've known I wouldn't dump her for some blonde bimbo."

"That's why you replied—" Giulia retrieved the folder and checked the time stamp on the next sheet— "four minutes later, also on the company server?"

"Ah, company email use is flexible. The VP of Research runs two outside football pools on his, plus the office one. So yeah I answered Lori right back. Upper management loved us. I wasn't worried."

Giulia skipped the next two pages. "Not even when, two replies later, you described in detail your plans for your makeup evening?"

He spread his palms out. "What? I said I'd take her dancing at her favorite club."

"Mr. Fitch, please don't sham disingenuous. I'm referring to the paragraph after that, in which you detail what she should wear under her miniskirt and spandex top and how you planned to end the evening."

One side of Fitch's mouth curled in a salacious half-grin. The ruler in Giulia's desk was begging her to use it to rap his knuckles.

"Yeah, well, Lori'd get into this 'I'm not white and blonde and perfect' funk. I knew how to snap her out of it." He flicked the open folder. "Management likes happy employees. Happy employees perform better. I made Lori happy, which made me happy, which made me a better salesman. Simple."

Giulia flipped to the last page. "Then this rebuke from management to both of you meant nothing?"

"Pfft. A speed bump. Nah not even that. A pebble. You check my sales figures for that month. I guarantee they were up."

Giulia squeezed her forehead with her thumb and index finger.

"Nevertheless, these emails are an indication your relationship was volatile."

Fitch stood and walked away from the desk. "Oh, come on. Everybody fights. The cops tried to make me admit that Lori and I were unstable and, yeah, volatile. Stupid word. We kept our relationship interesting." He swept his arms wide, encompassing the room. "We were nothing like this room, all pale and boring. We were bright colors and loud music and excitement."

"That's quite poetic. I'll keep it in mind as I gather information about your case." She clicked a blank page in the spreadsheet. "As part of going over the same ground as the police, I'd like to talk to some of the people they interviewed, if that's all right."

Fitch resumed his circuits of the office. "If it'll get me closer to freedom, I'm all for it."

"Thank you for being so cooperative."

He shrugged. "Why wouldn't I? Most of my dirty laundry is going to get paraded in front of a jury in two weeks. You're only one person. I can handle you knowing my sordid side."

He dictated names, addresses, and phone numbers for Loriela's mother, the bartender Loriela dated, the co-worker who told him about the video, three of their neighbors, and Loriela's former co-worker who got passed over for promotion.

The clock in her icon tray read 11:10. Giulia stood. "Mr. Fitch, that's plenty for me to work on for the next day or two. You've been suspended from your job for the time being, correct?"

"Yeah. What else could they do? They can't fire me because it'll be bad for their image when you and Colby prove I didn't do it. But they're—quote—giving me this time off to prepare my defense—unquote. With pay, since it's a small risk for them."

"You're cynical."

"I'm realistic. For the past year I've been working exactly as hard as I did before all this started. This way they don't have the aggravation of training a new employee. When I'm cleared, they welcome me back all smug and self-righteous. They're also thinking that just in case I'm guilty, they come out of it pure as the driven snow and all that crap because they kept faith with their employee no matter what."

Giulia opened her door onto the main office. "I wish I could find an argument against all that."

Zane said into the phone, "Certainly we won't contact you via email if you prefer we call your cell number."

Sidney pounded her index finger on her keyboard. "I said add a page number *and* a header, you ridiculous machine!"

Giulia walked Fitch to the main door. "Expect to hear from me late tomorrow. It could be very late, so don't be concerned if I don't call you by five o'clock."

Roger Fitch, suspected murderer, possible embezzler, violent yet ego-driven charmer, turned his charming smile on Giulia.

"If you'll forgive a cliché, my life is in your hands."

Giulia turned Bambi eyes on him. "No, I really can't forgive anything as obvious as that. I'm sure a top salesman like you would never resort to canned phrases."

He laughed. "You win that round. I'll stop playing the 'poor me' card. All business from here on."

Twelve

Giulia closed the door behind Fitch and sagged against it.

Zane covered his phone. "Ms. Driscoll? Are you okay?"

Giulia waved at him to continue the conversation.

Sidney's fingers didn't miss a key. "Let me start a list: Number one, his ego. Number two, his ego. Number three, his ego. Want me to lure him out to the farm so Belle can spit on him?"

Laughter burst from Giulia's mouth. Zane huddled over his phone. Giulia tiptoed over to Sidney's desk and sank into her client chair.

"I do not like that man."

Sidney giggled. "I don't think he realizes it. I bet he thinks he's bamboozled you into believing everything he says, even though I can tell you were grilling him in there. Olivier could write an article for *Psychology Today* about him. He's been published in smaller journals, but he's still trying to get past *PT's* form rejections."

"Olivier is welcome to him after the trial, when he's fair game."

"Cool. I'll tell him tonight." Sidney grunted and shifted in her chair. "Mini-Sidney is not Zen today at all."

Giulia moaned under her breath. "Sidney, if you need to leave…"

Sidney got herself resettled. "Huh? It's not even noon. I don't have much room for lunch these days anyway."

"No. I mean if you need to start your maternity leave today, you should do it. I don't want to guilt you into staying if it's not good for both of you."

Sidney patted Giulia's hand. "You'll never get a reputation as a cold, evil boss if you keep being all concerned and kind like this." She leaned closer. "I'm fine, honest. My doctor says I'm in great shape."

"If that changes, you tell me."

"Yes, ma'am." Sidney giggled, but regained her serious expression a moment later. "You haven't really fallen for that guy's act, have you?"

"Give me credit for functioning brain cells. He ought to have one of those red bisected-circle 'NO' signs tattooed on his forehead." Giulia stretched the small of her back. "Fortunately for him, I don't have to like or trust him to make sure I do everything in my power to discover his guilt or innocence."

Sidney's phone rang. "Now who's talking in clichés?"

"Ick. You're right. I'm going out to clear my head."

Giulia parked the Nunmobile in Precinct Nine's side lot. Two patrol cars passed her, the drivers giving her a quick wave. A chunk of cement was missing from the second step leading to the front door and some shiny new scrapes decorated the railing. A screaming male voice hit her like a rock as soon as she turned the door handle.

"I'll sue you for false arrest! My lawyer'll ram that bullshit warrant down your throat, you dirty bastards!" Clanking metal and high-pitched rasping noises accompanied the voice.

The Bond Girl wannabe at the reception desk rolled her multi-shaded eyes at Giulia.

"You know what I love about this job? It's so peaceful." She pointed a turquoise nail toward the noise. "You take karate lessons, right? Detective Driscoll might want to borrow you."

Giulia walked into the central office space. Two of the six desks were shoved against each other and one computer monitor lay on the floor surrounded by its shattered frame. A scarecrow in camouflage jerked against the handcuffs locking his hands and feet to the legs of one of the desks. His long, greasy hair kept getting caught in his mouth as he cursed everyone in the room. Giulia walked around the perimeter, as far as possible from the prisoner's stinks of body odor and stale weed.

She spotted her husband typing on a keyboard at a desk not his own. His charcoal gray suit and dark blue shirt were unrumpled, his short ginger hair looked as startled as it always did. Only the jagged rip in his striped tie marred his appearance.

His partner's suit...ouch. One sleeve ripped at the shoulder, tie shoved into his flapping pants pocket, a bruise forming on his left cheekbone, and an open cut on his forehead.

Giulia made her way to her husband's temporary desk. The curses from the handcuffed prisoner got more colorful when he caught sight of her.

Frank looked up from the keyboard, took in Giulia, then took in the prisoner's line of sight. "Hey, Weed Boy! Shut up before I stuff a dishtowel in your mouth."

"Come over here and try, pig!" More invective followed.

Three different detectives yelled into their phones over the shouts. One uniformed officer pounded a keyboard at the unbroken monitor next to the desk housing the prisoner. The cop's nose wrinkled every time the prisoner opened his mouth.

Captain Reilly came to the doorway of his own small office. "I knew I should've taken today off—Giulia!" He snatched her off the floor and embraced her. "I apologize for the idiot over there. If you come work for me, I promise nothing like that will ever happen again."

"Jimmy, what did the nuns teach you about where liars go when they die?" Giulia said when he let her down. "Your Saturday confessions must be very interesting."

The prisoner scraped the desk across the linoleum. Everyone winced.

"Think of the good influence you'd bring to this godforsaken place."

"Jimmy, stop tempting my wife," Frank said. "She owns her own business now. Why in God's name would she chuck it all to work here?" He saved the document and pulled Giulia over to his desk. "Hey, honey. What's up?" And he kissed her.

Giulia ignored the "ooohs" and whistles. When they separated, she said, "You look good."

"So do you. I like the way you fill out that sweater."

More "ooohs."

Giulia made a face at him. "Thank you, darling. Who's the sweetheart on the floor and can we bill him for a new tie?"

"We could sell a tenth of his hydroponic basement garden and outfit everybody in the room." Frank jerked his head toward his partner. "VanHorne here really does want to thank him for the injuries."

"What? Why?"

Frank winked. "He's got a date tonight. Chicks dig scars."

"Screw you, Driscoll," his partner said. "Apologies, Giulia."

"No worries, Nash. Are you still seeing the pharmaceutical sales rep from Christmas?"

"Yeah." His roughed-up face reddened a little. "We had a pregnancy scare last month. You know how it is: The one time we don't use a condom, and sure enough, she's late. Turned out to be only a scare, but it got me thinking that we would've had to get married." He broke off and yelled over to the prisoner, "Close your mouth, druggie. Your breath is stinking up the place." He smiled at Giulia. "Then it got me thinking that marrying her wouldn't be such a bad idea."

Giulia grinned. "Does she have the same idea?"

"I think so." His smile became shy.

Frank still typing, said, "Go on. Show her the ring."

The younger detective took out his wallet and removed a folded white handkerchief. He draped the corners of it over his open hand and revealed a plain gold band set with a square-cut sea-green stone.

"It's lovely," Giulia said. "That's not an emerald, right?"

"I knew you'd pick up on that. None of the Neanderthals in this joint did."

A chorus of grunts and cartoon caveman noises came from the other desks.

Nash ignored them. "It's a green sapphire. She's into greens— the color looks good with her blonde hair. She's got nothing like this, though."

"So go get that cut looked at, Mister Romance. Who knows what germs are crawling around the Screaming Wonder's skin." Frank closed and sent the report.

"Yeah, yeah. I got a mother back in Cleveland, you know."

Giulia folded the handkerchief back into place. "Ignore him. I could tell you a ton of stories about the adorable romantic surprises he's cooked up for me."

Jimmy guffawed. The detective at the desk behind Frank got a case of the coughs.

Frank raised two fists to the ceiling. "Woman, why do you emasculate me in front of my brethren in arms?"

Giulia winked at Nash.

Jimmy said, "See how you mother everyone in here? What can I do to bring you into our fold, Giulia? There must be a way to tempt you."

The desk near the door screeched on the linoleum again. "Unlock these cuffs, you bastards, or I'll sue you for police brutality!"

All four of them turned their heads to gaze toward the other side of the room.

Giulia made an expressive open-hand gesture and paired it with a rueful smile which clearly indicated "Not going to happen."

Jimmy hung his head. "If it were legal, rest assured I'd take my desolation out on that idiot on the floor."

"I could recommend a good lawyer," Giulia said. "Speaking of lawyers, may I borrow my husband for a few minutes?"

Nash said, "Sure, go ahead. I'll get Anderson to help me wrestle our guest into a holding cell."

Frank escorted Giulia into one of the interrogation rooms. "These cinderblock boxes give me the creeps."

"Aha," Frank said. "What guilty secret are you hiding, Mrs. Driscoll?"

"You wish. It's just that they remind me of one of the less pleasant convents I lived in." She shivered. "Can you really handcuff someone to a desk like that in the twenty-first century?"

Frank's smile vanished. "We can when he is awake, not under the influence of any substance which would cause him to injure himself or choke on his own vomit, does not have any physical impairment which would cause him injury, and when the alternative is for one of us to take that computer monitor he busted and smash it over his head. Okay, I made that last one up. Nash and I had a hell of a time getting him from our car into the building, and he went berserk when he saw that the only other exit from our main room leads deeper into the building. Took four of us to get him on the floor and cuffed to the desk like that." His smile reappeared. "Weed Boy in cuffs is the culmination of five months' work. Idiot should've opened a legitimate hydroponic garden store instead. His setup was genius." He flopped into the chair behind the small, square desk. "What's up?"

"I'm going on an interview binge starting now and lasting through tomorrow night. You're on leftovers for the duration. My goal is to snag seven of the Silk Tie case's neighbors, co-workers, and ex-girlfriends."

"I'd say you were wasting your time, but since you're getting paid, good luck with it."

Giulia poked his ribs. "You, sir, are the poster child for cynicism."

"Nope. For realism. You don't really think this guy is innocent, do you?"

Giulia considered her answer. "Honestly? I think the odds are six to one he's guilty and three to two he's an accessory and someone else really strangled the victim."

Her husband stood, leaned his hands on the desk, and loomed

over her. "And I'm stuck eating nuked sauce because of those lousy odds?"

Giulia gave him her most beatific smile. "We all have our crosses to bear."

"Oh, God." Frank reached over and shuffed the top of Giulia's head. "Whew. Despite indications to the contrary, no invisible veil perches atop my wife's hair."

She laughed. "I apologize for freaking you out. Sometimes the old me peeks out before I can squash her." She stood. "To distract you, I have a relevant work question. Did whoever was in charge of the Silk Tie investigation get surveillance footage from the apartment building?"

"I'm sure they did. It's routine. That lawyer didn't give it to you? He must have a copy."

"No. He also withheld some information from me that Roger Fitch gave me on his own. Apparently the lawyer thought it'd prejudice me against my client."

They looked across the little desk at each other.

"Really," Frank said.

"Really. Before you ask: Yes, he's now on my list of suspects. He's not high on the list, but he made a rookie mistake, and he's not a rookie."

"A lawyer keeping secrets. What a shock."

"Indeed. Now, sir, would you be so kind as to check on that footage while I make a few phone calls?"

Thirteen

Fortified with a burger and sweet potato fries, Giulia pressed the entry button labeled Asher, Geranium. A few seconds later, Fitch's next-door neighbor buzzed her into their apartment building.

The place surprised Giulia. From Fitch's attitude, she'd expected a live-in Westin Hotel with a doorman and a concierge. What she walked into was a higher-end apartment building with decent carpets and no stink of boiled cabbage in the air. The beige paint on the walls wasn't too badly scuffed. The imitation wood-paneled elevator didn't creak and moved at a pace faster than an asthmatic snail. A ghost of cigarette smoke lurked in the second-floor hallway, but no dust coated the artificial flowers in a bowl on a narrow table near the elevator doors.

The door to apartment 210 opened the three inches allowed by its chain. A long, narrow face came forward just enough for Giulia to see that its owner's eyes were a washed-out brown and its shriveled lips were once full and used to smile a lot.

"Mrs. Asher? I'm Giulia Falcone-Driscoll."

The face remained in its noncommittal position. Giulia stayed a step away from the door. Without warning, the face pushed right up to the gap.

"Young woman, cover up that mop of hair."

Giulia hadn't expected that. "I beg your pardon?"

"You heard me. Take your two hands and cover your hair right up to your forehead."

Giulia covered her head as requested. The sooner she complied, the sooner she could write this one off and work on her questions for Fitch's video-surfing co-worker.

Seconds ticked by. The woman had seen Giulia through the camera installed above the row of buzzers in the vestibule, so what was up with this extra inspection?

"May I put down my arms now?"

"You're not Giulia-whatever-you-said. That's the wrong name. I can't remember it right now, but it'll come to me. Where are your veil and your black dress?"

Giulia got it now. She dropped her arms and said with her brightest smile, "Yes, I used to be a nun. My name back then was Sister Mary Regina Coelis. But it's been—"

"That's it!" The door closed and the chain rattled free. When it opened again, a tiny old woman in black yoga pants with orange piping and a matching orange t-shirt stood aside to let Giulia in. "You taught both of my granddaughters Sexual Education. Their mother was scandalized—my daughter gets a pole up her behind sometimes—but my granddaughters said you taught it like a real person, not like someone locked behind convent walls all her life. Come in, come in. Can't talk in the hall. Some people," she raised her voice and spoke to the closed door opposite, "have nothing better to do than spy on the neighbors all day." She closed the door and replaced the chain. "You sit down on the couch and I'll make us some coffee."

The bright blue walls and blue-patterned carpet contrasted with the brown sofa and gold curtains, but in an eye-catching way. Not that Giulia could see much of the walls. Photographs of three children from birth to adulthood and then five more children paired with them covered three-quarters of the available space. Kids skiing, kids creating science projects, kids holding cheerleader pompons; in football gear, in hockey gear, graduating high school and college, in formal wedding portraits. Giulia looked longest at the sepia toned photograph of a tall, serious black man and petite, equally serious black woman in stunning period clothes.

Geranium Asher kept talking from the kitchen over the clatter of plates and silverware. "Those are my grandparents back in nineteen ought four."

"Her wedding dress is gorgeous."

"Isn't it, though? The cathedral train ripped clean off when she got out of the car to go change into her traveling clothes. Her mama made it into a christening gown. We all wore it. Real satin, it was; you should have felt it running through your hands just like water."

"My wedding dress was an antique, but not as lovely as hers."

"You have to tell me how a smart young sister turns into a smart young detective, Mrs. Driscoll. Now, I got one of those Keurigs last Christmas and I don't know how I lived without it. What can I make for you? I have French roast, hazelnut, cinnamon, and Irish cream."

"Irish cream, thank you."

"Me too. I'll just be another minute. You set yourself and get comfortable."

Giulia obeyed, out of both politeness and the overall goal of getting as much information she could out of this witness.

The aroma of strong, sweet coffee filled the apartment. A few minutes later, her host brought in a hand-painted floral tray set with two mugs, a creamer, a sugar bowl, and a plate of jam-filled thumbprint cookies rolled in crushed nuts.

"All right now. I made these cookies and I guarantee you will love them. There's half and half and sugar for the coffee if you take it. You dig in."

Giulia declined both but chose a cookie with raspberry jam in its center. "Just like Christmas," she said after the first bite.

Geranium accepted the homage like a queen. "I have never met a person who didn't like my thumbprints. Now, Mrs. Driscoll. I know you came here to ask about that horrible murder from last April, but we're going to do some bartering. I'll tell you everything I can about Mr. Fitch and poor Miss Gil, but first you have to tell me how my girls' teacher is sitting in my living room as a detective and not a Sister."

"That is more than fair." Giulia gave the "for public consumption" version of her last few years in the convent. This version, similar to the Bowdlerized Shakespeare editions of the early 1800s, omitted the despair, the backstabbing, and the confessional attack by the popular priest. Instead, it focused on the humor at her own expense: Having only underwear and a single pair of jeans and a t-shirt to her name afterwards. Learning how to put on makeup, trying to walk in two-inch heels. One of her first, disastrous dates.

Geranium laughed hard enough to soak one of the square cocktail napkins with tears.

"You poor thing," she said between gasps. "I'm so sorry for laughing, but you ought to be on YouTube."

Giulia laughed with her. "I'm very glad no one was around me with a camera phone those first months."

The old woman patted Giulia's knee. "So now you're married and in charge of your own business. You are a strong woman. I'm sure going to use you as an example for my granddaughters. Just look at what they can do if they put their minds to it."

"I'd be honored." Giulia finished her cookie.

"Before you work on a polite way to ask me to get to the whole point of this visit," Geranium winked at her, "you tell me what you want to know about last April."

Giulia breathed easier. That was exactly what she'd been about to say. She had two other interviews to get to today and it was already after one o'clock.

"First I'd like to know what you thought of both of them, Fitch and Ms. Gil." Giulia slipped into her mnemonic memory space. People always talked more freely when she didn't bring out a tape recorder or pen and paper.

"They liked their battles, those two. At least once a week they'd be yelling about this and arguing about that." Geranium's eyes rolled up beneath her wrinkled eyelids. "Money, sometimes. Roaming eyes, most of the time. Mind you, I don't think either of them cheated on the other, but they liked to pretend."

"They actually enjoyed fighting?" This didn't surprise her, despite her appearance that it did.

"Well, if you'll pardon the expression, I think what they liked was the making-up." For a moment Geranium appeared embarrassed. "The walls in this building could be thicker, if you get what I mean. Those two had...stamina."

Giulia nodded. "I get what you mean. Do you know anything about the police being called during one of their fights?"

"Darn right I do. I called them once, and Nosy Nora across the hall called the police twice."

"Three times in two years? They sound like the floor's personal reality show."

Geranium held up a hand. "It wasn't as bad as it sounds. The first time I called the cops, the two of them were cussing and throwing dishes or some such. Crash! Cuss! Smash! It got so bad me and Sue Ann and Katsuo stood out in the hall waiting for one of them to bust through the door. Finally Old Man Vandenburg knocked on their door loud enough to shut them up. That Fitch opened it and cussed him right to his face, and Vandenburg's old enough to be his grandfather."

"And yet Fitch always seems so charming."

Geranium's laugh sounded more like a cackle. "Never trust the ones who can turn that charm off and on like a light switch. Anyway. After Fitch slammed the door in Joe Vandenburg's face, I went right back into this apartment and called 9-1-1. They got here pretty fast. It's nice to live in a higher rent district." She grinned.

Giulia returned the grin and the sentiment. She'd lived in some places where it wasn't safe to go out in the daytime, let alone after dark.

"What did the police do?"

Geranium rubbed papery-sounding hands together.

"Oh, it was a show. The cops banged on the door too, and all the while the screaming and breaking noises still came through, but not as often. Finally Fitch opened the door and opened his mouth like he was about to say something that would've made his mother slap him silly. Then he saw it was the cops. He choked on whatever had been in his mind to say, and called to poor Miss Gil calm as you please. Said something like the police were there, honey, and could she come talk to them with him."

"What did the police do?"

"They stood in the hall and talked to Fitch and Miss Gil together. Said they'd gotten a report."

Giulia recalled Fitch's quick-change personality in her office. "Could he always shut off his anger that quickly?"

"I couldn't speak to 'always.' Most times I've seen him, he's talking into his cell phone. As long as they lived here, they never took their fights outside of their apartment. They knew how to keep the right face on in public."

"What did they say to the police that night?"

"Some bold-faced lies about him dropping the dish that was her mama's favorite dish, so she broke his favorite coffee mug."

"The police believed it?"

"Not much else they could do. Miss Gil said everything was just fine now and Fitch backed her up. Her hair and clothes weren't mussed, she didn't have a mark on her, and neither did he. They both laughed about the old biddies who liked to pry into everyone's business. Finally the police asked them to keep the noise down and left."

"And they winked and laughed and said they'd do their best?"

Geranium nodded, chomping down harder than necessary on her soft cookie.

"Why do you think they were together if they fought so much?"

Geranium studied the rest of her cookie with a critical eye. "I prefer the blackberry jam to the raspberry. You try one and tell me what you think. As for those two next door, they loved each other, far as I could tell. But they both wanted things their own way too much. Especially about money. Lord, did they fight like cats and dogs about money." She washed the cookie down with the rest of her coffee.

"How do you know, if you didn't talk to them much?"

Her host chewed the inside of her cheek. "Well, you see, I'm retired and I don't watch much TV. All those greedy people screaming and fighting or hopping in and out of bed like it was an Olympic event."

Giulia bit into a blackberry cookie to conceal a smile.

"I can tell you this, because you were a good influence on my granddaughters back when you were a nun. People don't change, not deep in their bones. So you won't look down on me like Miss Nosy across the hall."

"Of course not."

Geranium nodded once, a sharp movement. "I knew it. You see, they were loud and the walls are thin, like I said. So when things got interesting on the other side of the wall...I scooted a chair right up to it and listened."

Giulia held up the remaining half of her cookie. "I see what you mean about the blackberry. Now, since you had a front-row seat, you can help me find justice for Ms. Gil."

"Oh, yes. That poor thing needs peace. And her mother, too. I only met her once, but she sure left an impression."

It took a lot of restraint for Giulia not to lean forward, to stay sitting quite straight as though this upcoming information was no more or less important than everything else she'd learned this afternoon.

"Like I said earlier, they fought about money and each other's roaming eyes. The worst fights they had, though, were about wanting things. He wanted a bigger TV, a faster car, pricey liquor, things like that. She wanted stuff too, but what she really craved was power. There she was, young and pretty and head of the bookkeeping at that huge company, but it wasn't enough."

"And Fitch didn't want power?" Giulia's posture still didn't alter.

"Not that kind. He used to lecture her like a preacher on Sunday. He liked working for someone with power so he could sell things when he wanted and play when he wanted. It was all what he wanted and to the devil with anything in his way." Geranium studied Giulia the same way she's weighed the finer points of the cookie. "But I'm not telling you anything you don't already know."

"I'm trying to keep an open mind."

"That's what you're supposed to do, I guess." Geranium made a face. "Me, I don't have to play nice. That Fitch is a real piece of work. Mind, I'm not saying he's a killer. I wouldn't want anybody, not even my mother-in-law, God rest her wicked soul, to be wrongly convicted for murder. Nobody gets a do-over for the death penalty."

A black-capped chickadee whistled from the kitchen. Giulia started. Geranium chuckled.

"That's my bird clock. I have a Christmas carol one that I keep up from November through February. The birdsong clock makes me think of summer."

Giulia stood. "You've been wonderful, but I have to run. Two more interviews are waiting for me."

"Then I won't keep you. This has been the nicest surprise." Geranium stood and ran into the kitchen, returning with her cell phone. "Tell me you don't mind taking a picture together."

"No, not at all."

"I'm so pleased. My granddaughters will get such a charge out of this." Geranium held the phone at arm's length and put her curly gray head next to Giulia's curly brown one. "Three—two—one— smile!"

Blinded by the flash for the moment, Giulia blinked several times while Geranium checked the photo.

"Perfect. All right, Mrs. Driscoll, I'm done taking up your time. You catch whoever murdered that poor thing, now."

"That's what I plan to do," Giulia said as she shook her host's hand.

She walked steadily down the hall to the elevator, thinking about nothing, then to her car, still thinking about nothing, right up to the point where she locked herself in and opened the voice message function on her phone. Staring at a spot in the distance and unfocusing her eyes, she dictated everything she remembered about the interview. Every word, every impression her mind retained went into the memo: what the apartment looked like, what the cookies tasted like, Geranium's facial expressions and tone of voice as she described Fitch and Gil and the night she called the cops on them. All the denials that she was nosy and all the details from her eavesdropping sessions.

Twenty minutes later, she saved the memo.

"Mnemonics rule." She rubbed her eyes and saw the word around her again. "All right, Leonard Tulley, let's talk about why you set up a Google search for your boss' boyfriend." A new idea struck her. "Or for your boss. How much of a stalker are you?"

Fourteen

Leonard Tulley worked Monday through Friday from seven a.m. to three p.m. in the accounting department at AtlanticEdge. Tuesdays, Thursdays, and Saturdays from six p.m. to nine p.m. he became resident brewmaster at Long Neck, the trendy downtown microbrewery.

Worked for Giulia. She rang the doorbell of his condo at 3:45 on the dot.

The man who answered the door reminded her of about five different people. Bruce Willis, if the actor had been black, stopped working out, and added fifty pounds, mostly in the gut. Samuel L. Jackson and The Rock and Vin Diesel, with the same body issues. Charles Barkley and...that was it. Charles Barkley in his sports announcer job. Flabbier and with a beer gut Giulia's great-grandfather would've been proud of.

"You're Ms. Driscoll, right?" His smile didn't reach his eyes. "Come in."

The whole place was a monument to college football. Group photos of teams and beefcake shots of a younger Tulley hung everywhere. A framed jersey dominated the wall above the living room couch. Trophies sat on top of the entertainment center, crowning the 42-inch TV like castle turrets. An entire row of sports and war games for the Xbox lined the bottom of the sectioned wooden structure, the Xbox itself in a narrow vertical slot next to the games.

Giulia took note of the doors and windows as he led her into the dining nook. This accountant gave her a definite impression of someone not to be trusted. Foolish, really, since she had no reason to doubt he was exactly what he appeared to be: An ex-jock gone to seed.

The Scoop's daily half-hour of rumor and mud-flinging blared on the TV. Giulia turned away from the screen.

She and Tulley sat opposite each other at the octagonal table, between them a football-shaped Lazy Susan stacked with condiments.

"So what do you want to know about Roger?" His flat voice challenged her to convince him she was legitimate or else he'd toss her out onto the landscaping.

"In your case, Mr. Tulley, I'd like some information about the video of him you discovered online." Giulia kept her voice efficient and bright, but not perky.

"Huh? Why?"

"It's part of the investigation Mr. Fitch's attorney hired us to do. In the first place, how did you happen to notice it? The web is overflowing with videos of people's dirty laundry."

His wheels turned, but at a slug's pace. Giulia, watching his eyes, wondered if he was drunk. Then she wondered if he was punch-drunk. A thirty-four year old former defensive tackle—she'd seen that in the photos—would've played in the pre-concussion awareness years.

"I was bored," he said at last. "Nothing on TV, nobody online to play Madden." His eyes slid to her right. "You know how that is. You sit there and surf the web." His eyes slid to her left.

Liar, Giulia thought.

"We all do that," she said with a smile. "I'll start looking at cat pictures and the next thing I know an hour's disappeared."

One corner of his mouth curled up. Giulia couldn't tell if it was the beginning of a smile or a sneer.

"Yeah, you don't look like the online porn type. It was like this: I've got a few search strings I use whenever I think I've been a bachelor too long. Nagging wives, screaming in-laws, kids from hell. Everybody uploads their sneaky videos." His eyes didn't shift as much during that confession.

"And?"

"And I could've sworn I started watching some streaky-haired broad ripping Roger a new one. I blew it up full-size and sure enough, there was Roger and Loriela and, according to the description, Roger's 'mother-in-law,' all of 'em looking like an episode of *The Jerry Springer Show*. You remember that one? Back when they used to throw chairs at each other and the bouncers would wrestle the idiots to the floor."

Giulia nodded.

"Loriela's mother kept switching from English to Spanish but I got the gist of it. Especially the cursing. That broad can cuss with the best. Then a barstool went flying and Loriela was bleeding and things got even crazier."

"I've seen the video."

"Roger showed it to you? He's got balls."

With an effort, Giulia refrained from reacting. Tulley appeared to be trying to get her to rise to his locker-room language. The longer she kept her interested face on, the more it ought to goad him into revealing something juicy. If Giulia could play one part well, it was the proper lady.

She said, "He recognized that concealing information I could find out on my own would be counterproductive to our investigation."

That did it. Tulley's eyes rolled back in his head before he caught himself.

"Yeah, whatever. So Roger's baring his soul to you to keep his butt out of the death chamber. Always said he was the smart one." He tilted his chair back and twisted his head to the left. "It's after four. I gotta get to the brewery soon. You need anything else?"

Giulia thought fast. "I'm going over some of the ground the police already covered, if you'll bear with me. Did Mr. Fitch or Ms. Gil have any enemies that you knew of?"

A snort. "You serious? Loriela stepped on a bunch of heads to get to the top of Accounting. Roger's broken a bunch of hearts and pissed off a lot more. I heard he dumped one of his pieces when she got pregnant, but he'll deny it."

"I'll check into that. Thank you. Would you consider any of those people capable of murdering Ms. Gil out of revenge or out of a desire to frame Mr. Fitch for the killing?" Giulia didn't move when she asked this crucial question, just like she'd kept still in Geranium's apartment.

The sluggish eyes dropped their glaze and came into tight focus on her. Giulia kept her own camouflage in place: The precise, pedantic investigator, checking off points on her invisible list.

"That's what you think?" Tulley said. "Or is that what his lawyer thinks?"

"I'm exploring every possible angle. We have less than two weeks until the start of the trial."

"Damn, you're twisty. Roger told me you were a pushover because you used to be a bleeding-heart nun." His grin turned hard. "I think I'll let him find that out for himself." He stood. "All right, Ms. Driscoll, point to you. Here's who I've got money on: One, Loriela's ex—the bartender, not the actor. Two, Roger's apocryphal baby mama. Three, Roger's hotshot lawyer. Four, Roger."

Giulia stood and pushed in her chair. "You surprise me."

"No smoke without fire. Did you know that Roger and his lawyer went to high school together? Big sports rivals, but all friendly and best buds. That is, 'til they got to fighting for the last starting position on the basketball team. They'll say they're over that high school rivalry now, but what man ever lets go of the sports glory he thinks he should've had?" Tulley pointed to his knees. "I was second string All American. All set for the NFL draft 'til I blew out both knees. Trust me when I tell you I've never forgiven the bastards who ruined my career with a deliberate below-the-belt tackle."

He opened the door on another ex-jock type whose finger stopped short of the bell.

"Dude. Gimme a ride?"

"Sure. Come in for a minute." Tulley shook Giulia's hand. "Roger and his lawyer haven't forgotten it either. That lawyer's big on justice and second chances and all that, but you ask him about the season Roger got the last starting position and the lawyer warmed the bench."

He closed the door on her.

Giulia took a deep breath and walked straight to her car. She opened the voice memo function on her phone and talked.

Fifteen minutes later, she saved it and sank back against the headrest. "I need an extra-large glass of red wine."

Fifteen

Red wine and driving being incompatible, Giulia drove to her last appointment instead.

Cottonwood was a mere twenty minutes from Pittsburgh, on a good day. A good day not at rush hour. Giulia maneuvered the Nunmobile off bumper-to-bumper route 376 much too soon for the GPS on her phone, which shut up in the middle of a word. Giulia stuck her tongue out at it.

Her detour saved her eleven minutes. She reached Cassandra Gil's apartment building four minutes early and found a narrow slot labeled "Compact Cars Only" in the parking lot.

Theories and interview plans spawned by Tulley's quick-change revelations jostled each other for headspace. This interview would be a waste of her time if her mind wasn't clear.

Last year, Sidney discovered Kundalini yoga. Giulia had let herself be dragged to a few sessions, but she preferred attacking an elliptical machine or a circuit training session. She did find the breathing exercises quite useful. Sitting in a bucket seat was pretty much the worst position, but Long Deep Breathing was what she needed.

She closed her eyes and corrected her posture as much as possible. Inhale...fill the abdomen...expand the chest...fill the lungs...hold it...contract the diaphragm and force out the air.

Four of those and her head cleared. She checked her hair—like it made a difference—and headed to apartment 517 to meet the mama bear in that bar fight video.

Mama bear must have been on the lookout, because her door popped open when Giulia was still five feet away from it.

"Mrs. Driscoll, I am very happy you are here. Please come in. Thank you for arriving on time. Not everyone remembers to be courteous to old women."

Giulia said something polite and followed her in. The blond-and-black streaked hair had been replaced by plain black speckled with gray. She was still rail-thin, but her shoulders stooped a trifle now and frown lines marred her otherwise flawless skin.

The apartment was smaller and darker than Geranium's. It also had signs of more than one person occupying it. A well-used recliner faced the TV on one side of a low table and a slider rocking chair faced it on the other. Two cell phones lay on the kitchen counter, and when Giulia came all the way into the kitchen, she saw a laundry basket with lacy bras and tightie-whities on top of a pile of clothes. The sound of a running shower reached her from somewhere to the left.

"Come and sit down, please. Would you like coffee? A beer?"

"Thank you, no. I'm fine."

Cassandra sat kitty-corner to Giulia, hands interlaced before her on the table. "Why are you working for the piece of *mierda* who murdered my Loriela?"

Giulia blinked. "Because there is a chance he didn't. I'm going to find out who's responsible, whether it's Roger Fitch or someone else."

A sharp nod. "You are a fair woman. I will prove to you he is the killer so I may watch his execution and drink a glass of champagne at the moment he dies."

Before Giulia could form a neutral yet encouraging response, the shower turned off.

"George!" Cassandra called into the silence, "We have company. Put on pants if you are coming out here." Her voice modulated for Giulia with the next sentence. "He works seven-to-three at the nursing home. Sometimes he's so tired he comes out in nothing but his underwear and drops into his chair for a few hours. He is a hard worker."

Giulia answered the pride in Cassandra's voice. "Hospital work can be grueling. A friend of mine is an emergency room nurse. The stories she tells make me tired just listening to them."

Cassandra perked up. "George is a nurse too. I thought it was strange, a man being a nurse and not a doctor. Then he told me of the muscles it requires to lift the old people who cannot walk and I told him that I am not too old to learn something new." She resettled herself. "Where do you want to start?"

"Tell me about the restraining order."

Loriela's mother indulged in several unprintable Spanish words. Giulia had heard worse in her years of teaching high school. A tall man with long, wet hair in a ponytail walked into Giulia's line of vision. Wearing (*oh, good*) pants and a t-shirt.

"Cassie, stop it." He kissed the top of her head. "She knows you're angry. Use it." He held out his hand to Giulia. "I'm George Barras."

"Giulia Falcone-Driscoll." She shook his hand, if her own hand disappearing completely in his gigantic muscled fingers could be called a legitimate handshake.

"I'll leave you two to business. The TV volume won't disturb you, I promise." He snagged a Bud from the refrigerator and settled into his recliner.

Cassandra pressed the heels of her hands into her temples. "George is right. I apologize. What do you want to know about the restraining order?"

"Let's start with the video someone took at the bar."

More Spanish invective.

"He and Loriela stayed here that Christmas. She wanted me to meet him. I told her he was bad business, but she told me I had made too many bad decisions to throw stones at her." She pressed her lips together and breathed deeply. "Loriela preferred dangerous men, like I used to. I could have wished she took after me in keeping to a household budget instead." A small smile.

Giulia returned it, but didn't interrupt the flow of words.

"That man lounged around for four days, complaining that he was bored. Then he would go drinking and return after midnight. He disliked my cooking and argued with Loriela and tried to ignore me. I might as well have sold tickets to the neighbors. Every time I opened my door all the other doors in the hall closed much too fast."

Giulia made a sympathetic noise.

"The last day, all three of us had had enough. We said out loud everything we had been thinking all that time. He walked out. Loriela and I said terrible things to each other before she walked out after him." Her bony hands twisted together on the tabletop. "I saw through his charm and he knew it. Loriela might have, because she was smart and also beautiful, but she loved him so it didn't matter to her." Another small smile. "I made use of the neighbors for once. After she left, I knocked on Mrs. Harper's door at the end of the hall because her windows look out onto the whole street. Her face was a picture. I asked her where Loriela went and she told me."

A laugh track from the TV filled the momentary pause.

"Sorry," George said.

"That bar is not a good place for women. When I walked in, he and Loriela were still arguing. I could see he was halfway to being drunk. The words he said to my daughter in such a place made me so angry that I returned to my days in the barrio. You would be surprised, Mrs. Driscoll, at the language that came from me, a mother who raised a successful businesswoman. But you have seen the video, so you know. Do you have children?"

"Not yet."

Cassandra nodded. "But you will. Then you will watch that video and understand. The drinking men sat there and laughed at Loriela and I fighting like cats in the street. I do not know how it would have ended, but then Loriela grabbed her man's arm and her man, who should have protected her, threw her away so she injured herself on a barstool." Her smile wasn't pleasant this time. "They left the bar together, but I had the man who filmed it send a copy to me. I took that to the police officer who patrols this neighborhood and he went with me to his father the judge."

"You have connections."

Cassandra shook her head, her hair swinging across her face. "It is not that. Loriela grew up here. Everyone knows her. The judge's sister is the nurse who delivered her. She went to school with the police officer. We take care of each other, especially now the neighborhood is older and the crime rate is rising. The judge watched the video and listened to my stories of what happened over Christmas and issued the Order of Protection." Another unpleasant smile. "Loriela called me the night it was delivered to him. I heard him cursing in the background. She took the telephone out onto her balcony. She was angry that I had interfered, but she did not say evil words to me."

Giulia risked interrupting the narrative flow. "I understand the order was vacated later on."

Cassandra's fingers knotted themselves together again. "She allowed him too much control. I did not care that she loved him. He was bad for her. They demanded a hearing. By that time, he had wormed his way back into Loriela's heart and mind. At the hearing, he established a rapport with the judge, a man, right away." A pause. "Loriela took his side against me. The judge vacated the order. I lost my temper and said regrettable things until the judge threatened me with contempt. Roger Fitch strangled my Loriela one year and three months later."

Her toneless voice, so animated earlier, said much more than her words. Giulia let the accusation slide. Only an idiot would mess with the transient bond they'd established. Giulia was not that idiot.

"Do you know of anyone else who hated your daughter? Anyone who considered her their enemy?" Cassandra opened her mouth and Giulia held up both hands. "I know you think Roger Fitch killed her. That may be the case, but it's my job to research every possibility."

Cassandra frowned. "You said that earlier. I understand it with my head, but my heart says you are wrong. Let me think—George, we need your help."

He stretched out of the recliner and came over to the table. "Yes?"

"What enemies did Loriela have?"

He looked from Cassandra to Giulia with surprise. "There was that actor. You remember him. The one with more ego than talent."

"Oh. Roger Fitch protected Loriela from him. That is right." She gave Giulia an innocent smile. "You see? I too can be fair. The actor was a dangerous type. Attractive and forceful and charming, like Roger, only Roger's charm masks those traits much better."

"What did the actor do?" Fitch hadn't mentioned that one.

"He tracked Loriela to work and waited in the parking lot for her. As though threats would make a woman change her mind about a man. She and Roger Fitch were driving to work together, although they were still living separately. The one good thing Roger Fitch did was to send that actor away with a black eye."

Giulia made a mental note to find out his identity, just in case.

"I heard about a bartender, too." Giulia couldn't recall the name Fitch had given her—something to do with a movie actor— and she'd left her tablet in the glove compartment. Not that she was about to do anything to bust up this interview.

George crossed his arms. "He thought he was something."

Cassandra looked up at George.

"Loriela should have found a man like you." She said to Giulia, "Loriela had dropped the bartender long before Roger Fitch, but the bartender called me for her new phone number a year later. He had no experience with mothers of young women. I told him that he was a leech and should be squashed under my shoe. He found out her number somehow and called her. She told him exactly what she thought of him and threatened him with the police. Ironic, no? Between both of us we got through to him. He left her alone after that."

"Mrs. Gil, I appreciate everything you've told me. I won't take up any more of your time today." Giulia stood. Cassandra stood with her. George headed for the door.

"You will call me, please, when you learn that I am right." Cassandra shook Giulia's hand. "I promise I will not say 'I told you so.'"

"Cassie," George said. He opened the door.

Giulia shook George's hand. "Thank you for your help. I'll certainly call within ten days. We have to finish our investigation before the trial starts."

"Yes, I know all about the trial. I have been subpoenaed." She patted George's arm. "He reminds me at least once a day that I must be calm and detached when the lawyers ask me questions. I am practicing."

"We'll make her a model witness," George said.

Giulia tried to keep her mind blank in the elevator, but one thought squeezed through: If Fitch's trial were televised, it would eclipse NCAA March Madness.

Sixteen

Giulia performed the same memory trick in the car. Only when she saved the twenty-three minute recording did she look at the dashboard clock.

"It's after seven? No wonder I'm starving."

She dialed her husband and got his voicemail. "Frank, I'm on my way home. If you're in the shower, please make salads when you get out. I'll pick up pizza. Be there in forty minutes or so."

Forty-two minutes later, she pulled into their two-car garage—the true selling point of their small house. Her car smelled of sausage and black olives and right now she could've happily gnawed through the cardboard box and called it extra fiber.

When she entered the house, Irish fiddlers played on the stereo and the kitchen table was set with salads, plates, silverware, and red wine. All the day's tension evaporated from her shoulders.

"Attention, Mr. Driscoll! I will be calling your mother after supper to tell her that she raised you right."

Frank appeared in his PAL Basketball warm-ups and took the pizza box from her.

"My mother will preen and my grandmother will tease my grandfather that I take after her and not him. Result: Happiness all around. Did you remember black olives?"

"Of course. Did you put extra cucumber in my salad?"

"Of course." He kissed her. "I'm starving."

She tossed her coat and bag on the couch and beelined for the kitchen. "As soon as I eat I have to sync the interviews to my iPad."

Frank transferred two pieces of pizza to each of their plates. "Food first. You look like a ravenous wolf."

"I feel like one. It's a good thing I'm not obsessed with my looks."

"Sit. You know that's not what I meant."

They scarfed down pizza, wine, and salad for seven minutes by the clock before any more conversation occurred. When Frank got up to refill the wine, Giulia said, "I've been longing for a glass of this since my second interrogation."

"Embezzling employees or Silk Tie suspects?"

"The latter," Giulia said and chomped down on the crust of her second slice of pizza.

"You need me?" Frank liberated his third slice from the box.

"Yes. I need a neck rub." Giulia gazed at him over the rim of her wineglass. "Don't pout. It isn't professional. I'll need you to bounce ideas off of and help me weed the useless from the potential. But not 'til I transcribe all the interviews and stare at them 'til my eyes bleed. No, no more pizza."

"Would it please you if I said there was rocky road ice cream in the freezer and spray whipped cream in the fridge?"

Giulia pretended to be overcome. "What did I do to deserve you?"

"I could start a list." Frank tried and failed to look humble.

"Nuh-uh. We're not going to play one-upsmanship on which of us got the better bargain. I'll have your father be the judge of that."

"And I'll counter with my mother...never mind." Frank sighed in his best dramatic fashion. "She'll lecture me on how you've improved my life."

"We'll call it a draw. I'll clean up before I recharge and sync my electronics."

"You're not going to transcribe those interviews tonight?"

"Good Heavens, no. My brain is fried. Besides, that's what I have Zane for." She gathered plates. "Did I tell you I found a temp for Sidney's maternity leave?"

* * *

Giulia slipped out of bed at five-thirty the next morning without waking Frank. A quick shower and she headed for the Caribou Coffee where Loriela's bartender had agreed to meet her.

Jonathan Stallone walked in as she found a table in the far corner with her coffee and cinnamon roll. She stood by the table 'til he looked her way and then raised her hand. He nodded and got in line, towering over everyone else by a minimum of six inches. Broader than most of them by the same dimension. Giulia couldn't stop herself from humming the *Rocky* theme.

Over the phone, he'd said he worked two jobs now—bartending nights at the same place he'd met Loriela and teaching a series of morning kickboxing classes at a local gym. Thus this too-early-o'clock meeting.

He came to the corner table with an extra-large coffee and two egg and cheese biscuits; one with sausage, one with bacon.

Giulia inhaled. "I should've gone for the bacon."

"Get a couple for lunch on your way out. I do that all the time." He took a Hulk-sized bite of the sausage biscuit. "What do you want to know?"

Giulia avoided the spray of biscuit crumbs from his mouth. "I'd like to know about your relationship with Loriela Gil."

His lip curled. "You mean you want the gory details on how she cut off my balls with one phone call."

Giulia sipped her coffee. "I wouldn't have put it that way, but yes."

A hearty slug of coffee followed the Hulk bite. "Why?"

"Roger Fitch's murder trial starts in less than two weeks. He maintains his innocence. I've been hired by him and his lawyer to find evidence which backs up that claim."

He choked with laughter on his new mouthful of food. This time Giulia's cinnamon roll got a hail of crumbs and sausage bits. She pretended not to see it.

"Sorry." He attempted to stifle his laughter with more coffee. It worked, more or less. "That guy could sell fleas to a dog. You're not telling me you believe him?"

Giulia became Sister Regina, the English teacher feared by every freshman class in three Catholic schools. "My belief or disbelief is immaterial. I'm here to do my job." She masked her unexpected personality regression with a long drink of coffee. When she emerged, Sister Regina was back in her cell under a vow of silence.

"Damn. You sounded like my grade-school principal." He looked at Giulia's newly decorated cinnamon roll. "Let me buy you a new one."

Giulia smiled. "That's okay. We both have to get to work, so if you could tell me about Ms. Gil?"

"Sure. No problem." More coffee. "We got along pretty good for seven or eight months. Then she met this actor type. All about Art and The Stage. He writes these message plays that even the critics don't get, but he always convinces good actors to put them on. He plays lead when he can too. Lori latched onto him because she wanted to break from her mother and her old neighborhood." He started on the bacon and egg sandwich. "And from me."

Giulia waited, her patience with these crammed-together interviews on its last gasp. She craved action.

"Lori wanted out so I let her go. She didn't last long with the actor. I heard he got an offer from some avant-garde theater in Chicago or Detroit, someplace big enough to have an artsy crowd with money. He bailed. About a year later I saw her with Fitch and it pissed me off. I was better for her than that snake and she needed to know it." He shifted gears. "Did you ever meet Lori when she was alive?"

Giulia shook her head. "No."

"You'd understand everything if you had. Lori was gorgeous and sexy and classy. Everybody was jealous when she was mine. She said she would own her own company before her fortieth birthday and I believed her. She was unstoppable when she wanted something." He stared into his half-empty cup. "I worked in a cube farm when I got out of high school. Phone stuff. Too much pressure, too much backstabbing, and the people sucked. So I went to bartender school and never looked back. People are usually happy in a bar, and I can bust up a fight without much problem. I like what I do. But Lori, she was going places. That's why she left me."

"Tell me about the phone calls you had with Loriela and with her mother."

He stuffed another huge bite of bacon and biscuit in his mouth.

Giulia waited.

A huge swallow finished the huge bite. "You know I'm stalling, don't you? Geez, you really are like my grade-school principal. Okay, I give. I called her old number but she'd changed it. So I decided getting in touch with her was more important than my pride, and I called her mother." A shake of the head. "Have you met her mother?"

Giulia kept a straight face. "Yes."

"She's a force of nature, isn't she? That's the only way I can put it without swearing. She ripped me up one side and down the other. How dare I stalk her daughter? I must know her daughter has always been too good for me. Never call here again or I'll regret it. And then a click. I bet it really pissed her off that you can't slam down a cell phone like you could with the handset on an old-fashioned phone."

"But you didn't get Ms. Gil's number," Giulia said, softening her professional investigator manner to maintain his comfort level.

"Not from her mother. She was wrong, though, if she thought she could shut me down. I have a few connections. I called one who owed me a favor and he called a friend of a friend and a couple of days later I called Lori's new number." He crumpled up the wrappings for both sandwiches. "Ever see those cartoons where someone gets yelled at and they shrink down to about two inches high? Whoever animates those must've known Lori. She talked for five minutes straight. You might think that the worst way to attack someone is with a string of four-letter words. Hah. Lori used perfect English, never cursed once, and I'm telling you that by the time she finished, I really felt about three inches tall."

"What did you do next?"

"What could I do? I hung up." He finished his coffee. "You're fishing to see if you can catch a killer in a coffee shop. I don't blame you, it's your job, but let me tell you something. The only things I've ever killed are rats in the bar's basement. You don't strangle rats. You poison them." He plopped his hands on the table. The table quivered. "I've heard *Rocky* jokes all my life. Learned early to laugh them off. I even wear the movie costume in the bar on Halloween. Everybody jokes about it and they all like to buy drinks from 'Rocky.' But here's the thing: I can beat the crap out of most people. Had to do it a few times in the bar when morons wouldn't quit fighting. So of course I'm strong enough to throttle someone and before you ask, yeah, Roger Fitch's neck was mighty tempting. But nobody and nothing is worth jail time." He stood. "That's all you're getting from me."

He turned his back on her and walked out, flinging his trash across the parking lot.

Seventeen

When Colby Petit, Esq. arrived at the offices of Creighton, Williams, Ferenc, and Steele at the leisurely hour of 9:25 that same morning, Giulia and the fashion-plate receptionist had discovered a mutual love for Scarpulla's Deli, pumpkin spice coffee, and Denver and the Mile High Orchestra. They were in the middle of a debate on the finer points of Italian cheesecake when Giulia realized Colby was standing in the entrance way with his mouth open, staring at them.

"Good morning, Mr. Petit," the receptionist said, the fashion-plate mask back in place. "Ms. Steele would like to meet with you at ten-fifteen about the hockey parent assault case. Mr. Karloff's assistant wanted to remind you that Mr. Ferenc's stag party begins promptly at seven tonight at the Rivers Casino. Ms. Falcone-Driscoll has been waiting patiently and would like five minutes of your time."

"Uh...thank you. Certainly, Ms. Driscoll. Please come with me."

He didn't speak again 'til he closed them into his gray-and-white office.

"What magic did you work on our receptionist?" He set his briefcase on the floor next to his desk. "No one's going to believe me when I say I saw her laugh. Not just smile a genuine smile instead of her formal mouth-curve, but actually laugh."

Giulia didn't waste time trying to explain to him that lower-level staff were people too. "Mr. Petit, you neglected to give me copies of the security footage from Mr. Fitch's apartment building."

Without missing a beat, he said, "I apologize. I was focused on making copies of documents to give you and didn't think of the footage as a document." He booted his computer. "Did you bring a flash drive with you?"

"Of course." Giulia unzipped a side compartment of her bag and pulled out a plain black sixty-four gig thumb drive.

"Great. Let me open the files...here we go." He inserted the drive into a USB port and began dragging things from one window to another. "This is going to take a few minutes. Images make for huge files. Is there any progress to report?"

"I'm finishing the main interviews today. This weekend will be dedicated to collating all the data, and you know how much there is."

"Do I ever. Three minutes to go." His phone rang. "Excuse me."

Giulia opened her tablet and checked mail until he hung up the receiver.

"All set, Ms. Driscoll. This is the exact version we'll be submitting as evidence for the trial." He ejected the flash drive and handed it to her. "It's a pleasure working with someone who doesn't have to be reminded about confidentiality."

How passive-aggressive, Giulia thought, but said only, "Thank you. I'll give you a report on Monday. Mr. Fitch knows I might be calling on him any time this weekend. Please go ahead with your schedule. I know my way out."

The receptionist was fielding two different phone lines when Giulia passed her desk, so she mouthed, *I'll send you the recipe.* The receptionist gave her a manicured thumbs-up.

Giulia created yet another voice memo in the elevator ride down to the first floor: "Send Grandma's cheesecake recipe to Cathy at the lawyer's office."

Only ten a.m. and already she wanted to escape to the gym for a pounding workout and fifteen minutes in the whirlpool. Since neither were in her morning schedule, she drove to the office. No open spaces to be seen in the minuscule parking lot at this hour, so she fed a nearby meter eight quarters and set an alarm on her phone for an hour and forty-five minutes later.

Her body had burned through the six-thirty meeting coffee. But awesome coffee was never a problem for any Driscoll Investigations' employee because their offices sat above Common Grounds. Giulia pushed open the door to Heaven with a barista.

"Good morning, Ms. Falcone-Driscoll. What may I get for you?" the dweller in Paradise said.

"Good morning, Gene." She scanned the specials whiteboard. "An extra-large house blend with a shot of salted caramel syrup and two macadamia nut cookies, please."

"Coming right up."

Giulia abandoned willpower on the stairs up to DI's offices and attacked the first oversized cookie. Her stomach stopped sending her hate mail. The coffee went down smooth and rich and delectable. The day started looking up.

Sidney's coat hung on the coat rack but her desk was empty. Zane pointed to the bathroom as the printer next to him whirred to life.

"Morning, Ms. Driscoll. This," he reached for the first page coming out of the printer, "is the first draft of the retainer contract for the Diocese of Pittsburgh. Also, Mr. Fitch called twice, demanding a progress report."

Giulia rolled her eyes exactly like a sixteen-year-old girl. "We love our clients. They pay our bills. Right?"

"Right." Zane stacked the papers and handed them to her.

"Trade you." She took the papers and handed him her iPhone. "What's your schedule today?"

"Waiting for changes to the contract in your hands and bending the AtlanticEdge data to my will." He rubbed his hands together like a mad scientist.

"Excellent. Could you take a break from AtlanticEdge and sync my voice memos to iTunes? I backed them up to my tablet last night because I'm paranoid, but it would be a big help if you start transcribing them. Get through as much as you can and I'll finish the rest tonight."

Sidney came out of the bathroom. Giulia glanced from her to Zane and back again. Both of them wore green plaid Meier Farms shirts with the bright orange logo on the pocket of an alpaca knitting a sweater out of her own wool.

"Who didn't send me the email?" Giulia said. "If the store's running a promotion and needs everyone to be walking billboards, I have to do my part."

"We didn't plan it, honest," Sidney said, easing herself into her chair. "It's one of the three shirts I own that still fits me. Zane and I must be psychically linked."

Zane tried not to look worried, and failed. "Is it a problem? I need to do laundry and this was the only decent clean shirt in my drawer."

Giulia hung her head. "Zane, I swear you will drive me to beat you with a ruler. Of course it isn't a problem. Relax. But not before you transcribe my voice memos."

He snatched the spare cord from his center drawer and plugged the phone into his computer. "I'm on it."

"I look like a country-western whale," Sidney said.

"You look adorable," Giulia said. "I'm meeting the last interviewee, thank God, for lunch. The temp will be here to fill out forms at two. The only reasons anyone should knock on my door between now and eleven-thirty are fire or nuclear war."

"Ma'am, yes, ma'am," Sidney said.

Eighteen

Alone inside her lemon and ivory retreat, Giulia set the contract draft aside for later and got Roger Fitch's nerves out of the way first.

He answered on the first ring. "Driscoll? Where have you been? What's the news? Do you have any updates? Colby Petit just called to say you'd been to his office asking for the surveillance footage from my apartment complex."

Giulia schooled her voice to patient calm. "Mr. Fitch, I did tell you that it might be late today or even tomorrow before I contacted you. I'm finishing up the interviews and collating other information."

"You've got to move faster. You've got to get on the ball."

"Thorough investigation takes time. You don't need to remind me that we have very little of it. I'm aware of that." She took a deep breath. "I'll be able to work with greater efficiency without interruption. When I need to contact you, I'll do so immediately."

"All right, all right, I'm chastened. Call my cell when you're ready. I'll turn the volume up to the max because I'm going to the Penguins game with the guys tonight."

The dial tone sounded. "What a delight you are," she said to the receiver, and hung up.

She dug the flash drive with Petit's exhibit from its tiny zippered pocket and fitted it into a USB port. When that upload finished, she took the flash drive Frank had given her from a different zippered pocket and plugged it in. A few minutes later, she opened both files side by side.

The complex used motion-sensitive cameras rather than a constant video feed. Its cost-cutting maneuver might turn out to be a bad idea for Fitch. Well, she'd get what she could from the photos.

The slide show from Colby Petit's office was several megabytes smaller than the one the police received from the apartment complex manager. The first photos were identical: The landscaped ground on the balcony side of Fitch's building. The rain obscured many details, but the complex hadn't skimped on curbside appeal.

Side-by-side shots of rain. Of a human-shaped shadow. Of a lightning flash that illuminated footprints in the mulch.

The next still in the police version changed to a shot of the barberry bushes beneath the balcony. They didn't look like someone had used them for a stepstool. The fourth still in Petit's version was a shot of the balcony.

Giulia worked all the way through both sets, then reset them to the beginning and opened a spreadsheet. At the end of the second viewing, the Petit column boasted twelve photos. The unedited police column, nineteen.

The meeting alarm on her computer chirped at her.

"I'm in the middle of something."

A minute later, it chirped again.

"All right. All right. I'm going." She saved everything. Before she left her desk, she felt around for her phone to make a new voice memo. "Zane still has it. Argh." She opened the spreadsheet again and wrote her suspicions in a third column. Another save before she logged off.

She grabbed her bag and opened the door.

Sidney sat back down. "I was just going to barge in."

Zane handed back her phone as she passed his desk. "Second interview almost completely typed up."

"You guys rock," Giulia said. "See you before the temp arrives."

She ran downstairs and in three minutes was fighting lunch-hour traffic. To focus her mind for the interview, she found the local retro radio station and cranked it. The weather had turned again, so her windows were up, but she would've sung along at the top of her lungs to Journey and Van Halen no matter what. When she got to the Indian buffet restaurant, she was headbanging to Queen with an invigorated brain.

"All right, disgruntled co-worker, let's do this."

A precise, makeup-free blonde sat in the waiting area by the cash register wearing a gray peacoat, jeans, and sneakers with uneven wear patterns.

Giulia walked over to her. "Hello. I'm Giulia Falcone-Driscoll. Are you Shirley Travers?"

The woman held out her hand. "Yes. Thanks for being on time. My lunch hour is limited."

Her voice was pitched to be heard over a crowd. Giulia wondered where she worked now.

Eight minutes later, armed with full plates and bottles of water, they scored a two-person booth against the window. The other woman dug in like she hadn't eaten in a while. Giulia sampled her own. The size of the restaurant kept the ambient noise much lower than Giulia feared. She would be able to conduct this interview at standard volume.

"I coordinate the district's school busses and today I'm pitching in as driver. Breakfast happened before five a.m.," Shirley said between the saag paneer and the curried chicken.

"My first meeting today took place over coffee at six-thirty. I feel your pain." Giulia stabbed more of her saag aloo.

"Another one of Loriela's victims?" Shirley drank half her water.

"I wouldn't have put it that way."

"Hah. You haven't been digging into her past for long then. I didn't dance in the streets when she died, but I sure didn't send a sympathy card to Roger, either." She studied the eggplant pakora and chose the chicken vindaloo instead.

"I understand that Ms. Gil was focused on her career—"

Another laugh. "Is that what they call it now? Come into the ladies' room with me. I'll take off my shirt so you can see the imprint of her fancy spiked heel in my back."

"I see."

Shirley hacked a second piece of chicken in half. "Well, aren't you nice and neutral. You don't have to tiptoe around me. Loriela was a greedy, implacable bitch who wanted to be head of accounting and did anything to get there." She chewed the chicken hard enough for Giulia to hear her teeth click. "I take that back. She didn't seduce the VPs or the Big Boss. Guess that means she had some morals."

Two small children chased each other down the aisle next to them, shouting "Freeze tag! Freeze tag!" A harried older woman followed a moment later.

Giulia said, "And you know about Ms. Gil's company celibacy because?"

"Seriously? Did you ever work in an office? Anyone who doesn't pay attention to office gossip is doomed." Shirley stuffed a piece of naan in her mouth. "I love me some hot sauce. Whew. Look, I ran payroll. Started as a grunt and worked my way up the proper way. Positive employee reviews, volunteered for extra duties, peer reviews that got noticed. Then Loriela arrived. I helped her like I helped all the newbies. Showed her how AtlanticEdge did things, checked her work, stayed late when she got into a crunch. The gossip started five months later, when she became my second-in-command." She paused to finish the saag paneer. "Loriela was good. She never said anything too extreme or actionable. She never claimed I was cooking the books. All she did was imply that I wasn't working with the same exactness I used to. And that she heard I'd been keeping late nights. Oh, and my favorite one: That she, Loriela, had been putting in unpaid overtime to double-check my work because she was concerned for the company's reputation."

Giulia tore off a piece of her own naan. "To whom did she repeat this gossip? How close together did she start the rumors?"

Shirley leaned back in her chair and appraised Giulia. Finally she said, "Thank you for assuming I did nothing wrong."

Giulia smiled in a noncommittal fashion, not saying anything about the years of embezzlement.

Shirley returned to alternate mouthfuls of food and mouthfuls of information. "She targeted the company's best rumor-mongers and gave each one about a month to run with her latest tidbit. Like the smart cookie she was, she never told the boss. The whole company knew that too much stress on him could've led to a stroke, exactly like the massive one that landed him in rehab for months. That might be why she never seduced him. His daughter, the one running the company now, isn't the type that gets fooled by long legs and a big smile. It was to Loriela's advantage to keep the old guy in his executive chair as long as possible. Anyway, the rumor-mongers spread shit about me around the coffeepot timed for pre-meetings when the VPs all grabbed coffee."

"Did you try to refute any of the rumors?"

Shirley laughed. "All that would have done is give credibility to her poison. Loriela never stopped being my sweet and helpful Number Two. Anyone who didn't know what she was doing would have thought I had it made." She mopped up the rest of the curry sauce with the last bit of naan. "I had a few friends in other departments. That's how I found out what Loriela was up to. That and the talks the HR manager called me into his office for. The rumors did exactly what they were supposed to, and I got warnings in my file about the conduct expected of an AtlanticEdge employee and about maintaining focus on my job."

The table of five across the aisle from them scraped back their chairs and made a fuss with coats and last snatches of cookies.

Giulia waited until they left. "But you could prove nothing like that was happening."

Shirley inclined her head. "You got it. I wasn't accused of anything quantifiable. The more I denied it, the more Mr. HR got that look which said, 'women can't be trusted.' He's not a bad guy, but he's old-school and thinks all women should be in low-level secretarial positions where they can't do the company any real harm."

"I've dealt with many of those types as well," Giulia said.

"They piss me off and they're always the ones you have to suck up to. Fortunately or unfortunately, six weeks after the second written warning I went on an already paid-for Vegas vacation. That was the height of the rumor trifecta. Instead of going all 'What happens in Vegas stays in Vegas,' half the time I obsessed about work, the other half I gambled and went to shows—also pre-paid. Came out ninety-seven bucks ahead when I checked out of the hotel."

Giulia gave her a thumbs-up. "That's willpower."

A crooked smile. "Nah, just stubbornness. I don't like to lose. The day I got back from vacation, the HR manager's assistant called me five minutes after I logged in. Please come to his office at my earliest convenience. Corporate-speak for 'right now.' Loriela gave me her widest smile when I walked past her desk. Bitch." She laughed again. "You get points for not saying 'Don't speak ill of the dead' like my mother nags me about constantly."

Giulia shrugged.

"Similar things have happened to me."

"Ah. You've had the exit interview that requires you to immediately go out and get hammered."

Giulia thought of her last meeting with her Superior General not quite five years ago, when Rome had dispensed her from her vows. "More or less."

"What a joyous exit interview that was. I 'wasn't a positive influence in the company anymore.' 'My work had not been up to the expected standards.' All of it nice and vague and all of it damning. You can bet I talked to a lawyer that same day. Pennsylvania doesn't recognize the implied contract exemption for at-will employment. He advised me to take my severance and walk away quietly. That way when a new employer called them to check, AtlanticEdge's HR would play the game of just giving them 'name, rank, and serial number.' It's happened to a bunch of people I know."

Six college-age types took over the table across the aisle from them, laughing and talking at triple the volume of the other diners. Shirley looked at her watch.

"It's quarter after one. I've gotta wrap this up. The bitch got my job and I got four weeks' severance. Good thing my husband had landed a promotion, because it took me six months to find the job I have now. Started out bookkeeping then showed them how to coordinate the shifts better. Now I'm district coordinator. Amazing how you can get promoted without climbing a pile of your victims, isn't it?" She tossed her napkin and silverware onto her plate. "Anything else you want to know?"

Giulia debated for half a second. "Two pieces of office gossip. Did Ms. Gil do to anyone else what she did to you? And which of your co-workers liked Ms. Gil?"

Shirley chewed her lip. "Walk me to my car. I have to get moving."

Giulia followed her out. When they could walk side by side, Shirley said, "Men liked her more than women did. The one word to describe her was 'focused.' She hung out with sales a lot, because they spoke the same language."

Playing dumb, Giulia said, "What does that mean, exactly?"

"Tips and tricks to close the bigger sale. Look at everything like it's a deal to close. Listen to those motivational podcasts to up your game. She never came to a girls' night out unless there was someone in the group she could use. Same with lunch."

They stopped at the door of an old-ish Pathfinder. Giulia had her hand out to thank her when Shirley stopped with her key in the lock.

"You wanted to know who liked her. I think everyone did when they first met her. She had energy, she smiled a lot, she looked and dressed like a model but not enough to make women hate her for being perfect. After a couple of months, when you realized she only talked business and wouldn't say more than hello when you weren't in the right circles, people fell into two categories. Either they sucked up to her because she was going places or they stuck to 'Good morning' when they saw her." She held out her hand.

"Thank you," Giulia said, shaking it. "You've been a big help."

"Glad it's over." She opened the car door. "I'd appreciate it if you didn't contact me again."

Nineteen

Zane didn't flinch when Giulia handed him her phone again at one-forty.

"You're taking it like a trouper. This is the last one. I'll take care of the paperwork for the temp while you transcribe."

"Crap. I forgot. Thanks. Sorry."

"I gave you a higher-priority task. You did right. Anything happen while I was having venom poured into my ears?"

"Not a thing."

"Zane," Sidney said.

Zane blushed, for him, which meant his ghost-pale skin didn't quite match the stack of paper in the printer. "We weren't going to tell you about Sidney's water breaking because she said you'd panic."

"What?" Giulia leaped across the room to Sidney's desk. "Why are you still here? Did you call Olivier? Do you need me to drive you to—"

She stopped. Sidney lost her straight face as she pounded her desk with laughter. Behind and to Giulia's left, Zane hiccupped.

Giulia planted her hands on her hips. "Sidney, you evil woman. How dare you take advantage of..." She leaned against the desk and laughed. "All right. That was one of the best pranks ever."

"It was better than that," Sidney said. "Zane thought it up."

"Zane did?" Giulia waited a beat, then went to the bottom drawer of the file cabinet next to Sidney's desk. She took out the first aid kit, ran to Zane's desk, and slapped one of those temperature strips onto his forehead. Zane sat frozen in place, except for the occasional stifled-laughter hiccup. Ten seconds later, Giulia forced her forehead into worry lines.

"I don't understand," she said with concern. "This thing says you're not running a fever. But you have to be sick, doesn't he, Sidney?"

Behind her, Sidney choked and gasped. "S-stop it—or I'll really go into labor."

Slowly, Zane began to smile. "You liked the joke, Ms. Driscoll? You're not mad?"

Sidney groaned.

Giulia smacked the heel of her hand against her forehead. "And he ruins it. Just when he showed promise."

"I'm trying," Sidney said, switching to deep breathing exercises. "For someone so smart, he's sure slow to pick this up."

"He's young. There's still hope. Take the thermometer off, please, Zane."

The door opened and the temp walked in, minus brown wig and concealing makeup.

Giulia and Sidney, and a moment later Zane, all started laughing again.

Jane Pierce pushed jet-black bangs off her left eye and clapped her other hand over the buzzed back of her head, without obscuring the stylized sun and moon tattoo on the right side of her neck.

"Shush, everyone. Jane, welcome! Come on in. I don't have your papers ready because these two just pranked me like pros."

Jane took half a step backward. "You're not...I mean, you all started laughing when I opened the door, and I thought..."

"No, no! Of course not."

Sidney said, "You came in right after Zane made his first joke ever. And there you stood as we all looked like loons and you were probably thinking you still had a chance to run away from the crazy people."

Giulia said, "That is a beautiful tattoo. Zane, since you lost me my five extra minutes, could you print out everything for me?"

"Sure." He opened a file folder and hit the print button several times. He reached up with his free hand to scratch his forehead and felt the temperature strip. With a wry smile he peeled it off and dropped it in his trash can.

Sidney and Giulia snickered.

Giulia took the stack of papers out of the printer.

"Come on, Jane. I'll prove to you we're also professional."

Closed into Giulia's office, Jane lost a little of her wariness. "My tattoo artist took me out to dinner to celebrate me being gainfully employed for the next two months. I told him about this place. He said I lucked out."

Giulia didn't look up from filling in her parts of the forms. "Has he heard of us?"

"His aunt does piercings over at Glitz, the big multi-tasking makeup and hair and ink and piercing place over on Larch. She remembered you from a couple years back when you came in to hold someone's hand for a navel piercing." A pause. "She said you used to be a nun. Was she kidding?"

Giulia held up one finger while she filled in the last fields. A moment later she clicked the pen closed and slid it and the papers across her desk.

"No, she wasn't kidding. I remember that trip. I had to get my hair straightened for an undercover job. I told a bunch of convent stories while the chemicals cooked." She took in Jane's expression. "Is there a problem?"

Jane gripped the pen.

"Well, I'm an atheist. I didn't know this was a religious detective agency."

Giulia laughed. "It's not. I'm interested in one thing: Can you do the job? Everything else is your business."

"Of course I can do the job. I just thought, well...my experience with religious types hasn't always been positive." She stacked the forms and wrote rapidly on the top one.

"You and Zane should get along," Giulia said. "His whole

family's pagan and he's Buddhist. Thanksgiving at his mother's house is an interesting experience."

"Oh, cripes, don't talk about holidays." Jane shuffled that form to the bottom and started on the next one. "My sisters foist their spawn on me to 'encourage me to be a proper woman.' I love my nieces and nephews, but babysitting them isn't going to make my womb sabotage my brain so I'll go on a date with the dweebs they try to set me up with."

Giulia coughed.

"Go ahead and laugh," Jane said. "It's like a bad TV reality show. This past Christmas I kept checking the tree for a hidden camera feed." She unbuckled her black leather knapsack purse and took out her checkbook. "Thanks for having direct deposit. Sometimes my neighborhood isn't the safest on paydays." She voided a blank check and paper-clipped it to that form.

As she filled out the last paper, she said, "The rainforest hates US employment rules."

"Even if we could do all of this electronically, I'd still keep a paper backup," Giulia said. "There are too many ways data can be tampered with."

"Spoken like a cautious woman." Jane's pen stopped. She swallowed. Her shoulders hunched as she looked across at Giulia. "I apologize...That was inappropriate coming from the employee to the employer."

The employer studied the employee.

Giulia nodded once. "Getting used to the dynamics of an office again? Let's call this an adjustment period. Is everything complete?"

Jane exhaled. "Um, yeah. Yes. I'm all set." She handed everything back to Giulia.

"Great. Oh, look. It's only quarter to three. It ought to be midnight. Come out and meet everyone." Giulia put her hand on the doorknob. "'Everyone' being a relative term."

She opened the door on the sound of water running in the bathroom sink.

"Sidney, you are killing our water bill budget." Giulia raised her voice to carry through the closed door.

The door opened. "Mini-Sidney has no sympathy for water bills or what she's doing to my bladder." She sat in her desk chair with a sigh. "Or my feet."

Giulia tried to cover her amusement with sympathy. "Two more weeks. In the meantime, this is Jane Pierce. She will be you for the duration. Jane, this is Sidney Martin and mini-Sidney."

Sidney held up her hand. "Nice to meet you. Do you like alpacas?"

Jane's mouth opened then clicked shut. "Um...I guess."

"Great. We have a farm. I'll bring you some fertilizer. Alpaca poop is the best. It's small, it's easy to handle, and it hardly stinks at all. Seriously."

Jane was starting to appear shell-shocked. Giulia swooped in. "It really is. I use it on my indoor tomato plants. Sidney, give the poor woman a chance to get her feet under her." She turned them toward the door. "This is Zane Hall, the king of admins. Zane, Jane Pierce, Sidney's replacement while she's on maternity leave."

They shook hands. "Pleased to meet you," Zane said. "Is that tattoo for the art or the belief?"

Jane became a deer in the headlights.

"Stop interrogating the new girl," Giulia said. "We have no window to keep searching for temps. If Jane runs away I'll be forced to hire that one who told me how completely wrong I'm running my own business."

Zane put his hands together and bowed. "Sorry. Sometimes my mouth gets away from me."

"No problem," Jane said. "I chose it because it symbolizes rising from the night into the new day."

"Nice. Sorry you got my drive-by. A former girlfriend got Japanese characters down both arms that she claimed were the kanji for 'The journey of a thousand miles begins with a single step.' I don't know what ticked her off more: When I told her she'd misquoted it or when I told her the kanji actually were the names of characters in a manga series. She walked out without paying her half of the dinner check. I bet that tattoo shop got a visit from her early the next morning."

"You read manga in Japanese?" Jane said. "I have to wait for the translations. *Evangelion* or *One Piece*?"

"Both. *Death Note* or *Fruits Basket*?"

"Do I look like a *shōjo* person?"

Sidney said to Giulia, "What am I missing?"

"They're graphic novels. My nephews and nieces devour them, which is the only reason I understand this conversation." Giulia waved a hand between the manga discussion. "Zane, how's the transcribing?"

"Done. I emailed everything to you. Here's your phone."

"Excellent. Can you print them out for me by end of day?"

He handed her five paper-clipped groups of printouts. "Anticipated and achieved. Sidney reminded me that you like to spread hard copies all over the floor like a jigsaw puzzle."

"A clue collage, actually. Someday I might get the phrase trademarked." She turned to Jane. "We'll see you at nine o'clock Monday. Remember: Business casual, but jeans are okay too. Nothing raggy is the key."

The phone rang. Zane got to "Good afternoon, Dris—" before the voice on the other end shouted him down. He yanked the receiver away from his ear. Jane slipped out the door. The voice got louder.

Giulia winced. "That's Roger Fitch. I'd better take it in my office. Don't hang up 'til I pick up. I don't think he'll hear you if you try to put him on hold."

Giulia closed herself in, inhaled and exhaled slowly, and picked up the receiver. Fitch's voice assaulted her ear.

"Mr. Fitch. Mr. Fitch. I can't understand you." When that didn't make a dent in his tirade, she yelled, "Shut up!"

The voice stopped.

"This is Giulia Falcone-Driscoll, Mr. Fitch. What is the matter?"

Twenty

Roger Fitch started shouting again. "My car! They trashed my car. I just paid it off last year!" He spewed curses into the phone.

Giulia swore she could hear spittle hitting the mouthpiece at the other end.

"Mr. Fitch. Mr. Fitch." She paused. Again without raising her voice, "Mr. Fitch."

Fifteen long seconds later he ran out of steam and her steady voice repeating his name squeezed into a moment of silence.

She took the advantage. "What's happened to your car? Please don't shout at me again or I'll hang up the phone."

"What do you mean, you'll hang up on me? I'm paying you. Who do you—"

She hung up. Then she buzzed Zane. "He's going to call back in a second. I'll get it."

Half a minute later, the phone rang.

"Driscoll Investigations," Giulia said.

"It's Fitch. You really hung up on me."

"Mr. Fitch, I asked you more than once to modulate your voice. I am a professional, as are you. I expect to be treated as such. In return, I will do the same. Is that clear?"

A pause. "Are you sure you're not related to my domineering great-aunt? Okay. Sorry I lost it."

"Thank you. Now please tell me what happened to your car."

"I was out late last night. Didn't get up 'til noon and had to keep the blinds closed for an hour, if you know what I mean. It's sunny today."

"Yes. And?"

"I went down to the parking lot around two to get some groceries. No car. Walked through the lot twice. Nothing. I was sure I remembered parking at the far end of the first row when I came home, next to old lady Asher's pink VW Bug." He made a gagging noise, but sobered up right away. "This skinny broad who lives below me opened her window. She had to talk loud so I could hear her over her brat squalling inside. Said she saw two guys jimmy my lock and drive away about half an hour earlier. She called the cops but then her kid woke up and she didn't have time to come upstairs to tell me."

Giulia was typing into an open Word doc. "Did the police come around while you were still in the parking lot?"

"Yeah, two uniforms showed up. The skinny broad came out with her kid—quiet by then, thank God—and told them what she'd seen. I gave them make and model and license plate. I was mad enough to punch right through the glass entrance door of the building."

She named the document. "You said your car was vandalized?"

"Vandalized? That's too good a word for it. An hour later the cops called to pick me up. They found my car six blocks away in the back lot of some boarded-up store or other. I could kill those punks! They smashed the windows and cut through the upholstery on the seats. They slashed the tires. They stole my gym bag from the trunk. They keyed the top and sides and spray-painted insults over that. They pissed into the glove compartment!"

Giulia made a gagging face at her screen. "You said they painted insults on the car? What specifically?"

"I took photos along with the cops. Come to my place. You know where it is, right? I'll show them to you."

"I can't come over to your apartment right now. If you think this is connected to the case, please give me the information so I can attach it to the rest of the evidence."

"Fine." His tone implied offense at her unwillingness to jump on command. Or perhaps it was nothing more than Male Indulging in a Pout. "I'll put you on speaker so I can check my pics." A moment of silence. "Still there?" His voice acquired a slight echo.

"Yes."

"Just a sec…They wrote 'Die, murderer' on the hood, 'Killer' on the doors, and drew a needle with a skull and crossbones on it on the trunk."

Giulia's fingers hovered over the keyboard. "That was thorough."

"You think? Since you're too busy to come over here, when are you going to give me the report you owe me? You remember? The one on all the people you talked to who bad-mouthed me."

If Giulia hadn't spent ten years serving others in the convent, she would've told her client what she thought of his attitude. In precise, grammatical Shakespearean English. Shakespeare could insult with the best.

"Shall we say between ten and eleven tomorrow morning?"

"I might be at the car rental place then. I'll call you. You going to be around all day?"

Giulia fixed her gaze on the framed painting on the wall across from her. The twelve-by-twenty-four inch watercolor of a garden in summer—exactly the bright, sunny kind of art she preferred—eased her tension enough to answer Fitch with civility.

"I have errands to run as well. If I don't answer when you call, please leave a message and I'll call you back as soon as I can."

"Fine. No problem. I'm only one more day closer to a jury tying a noose around my neck, figuratively speaking."

"I'm aware of the timeline, Mr. Fitch. I'll expect your call tomorrow."

Giulia rested her head on the desk for a full minute after she hung up. Then she pushed herself up and went into the main office space.

"Zane, is there any chance you'd be available for about two hours of overtime tomorrow?"

Her admin stared at the ceiling, one eye half-closed.

Good Heavens, Giulia thought. He looked like Bogie in Casablanca when he did that. She kept her gaze away from Sidney, just in case they were thinking the same thing.

"I'm hosting a Final Fantasy night in my game room at seven-thirty. Beer's my contribution. I can get it tonight after work." He transferred his Bogie-look to Giulia. "Sure. Any time tomorrow up 'til seven."

"Your game room?" Giulia said.

"Don't get him started," Sidney's voice vibrated with overdone caution.

"You should see it, Ms. Driscoll." With that one sentence, Zane morphed from noir leading man to cyber-warrior. "I had the room rewired to my personal specs when I bought the house. It's got power and tables for four screens, recliners and desk chairs depending on whether you want back support or butt cushioning, surround speakers, a four-cubic-foot fridge, and a half-bath so nobody has to run all the way downstairs during important battles."

Giulia said, "Sounds...well-thought-out. I didn't realize you owned your own house."

"All thanks to PayWright. They tried to suck out my soul, but I kicked butt on commissioned sales. The house was my reward for surviving their evil maw. It's an older Cape Cod with small rooms and closets and everything, but my cats and I christened it *Veni, Vendidit, Vici.*"

"I came, I...sold? I conquered?" Giulia laughed. "I love it. Tell me you have that on a plaque above the front door."

"Well, yeah." For once he didn't look embarrassed. "What's happening tomorrow that you need me for?"

"Our client wants a report on all the interviews I've been doing. I want to scope out his apartment and get a feel for how the crime might have been committed." She dropped into Zane's client chair. "I keep having to remind myself that just because he's an arrogant, rude, entitled jerk doesn't mean he's a murderer. Anyway. I'm not foolhardy enough to walk into a possible murderer's apartment by myself. I'd like you to be silent muscle and my backup eyes and ears."

"Wait a minute," Sidney said. "Fitch is my height and weight—at least what I weigh now—and you had me begging for mercy in ten seconds at self-defense training."

"You got Sidney to yield?" Zane said. "Nice."

"I'll make the alpacas spit on you," Sidney said.

"Uncle." He raised both hands in surrender.

"Fitch has the impression I'm still the passive wallflower he met four years ago," Giulia said. "I want to use that to my advantage." She checked her phone. "I need to rewire my brain. I'm going to the gym to turn myself into quivering Jell-O in the circuit training room."

She returned to her desk, shut down her computer, gathered all the loose papers into the delivery box the lawyer had given her, and turned off her light.

"I know I'm neglecting the retainer agreement you created," she said to Zane as she put on her coat, "but we're on the clock with the Fitch case. I'll call you tomorrow as soon as His Entitledness calls me. He claims he might be busy renting a car in the morning—that's what the screaming phone call was about. I think he's power-tripping on me and fully intends to have me come to his place before noon." She opened the front door. "If the Pope himself calls within the next half-hour to hire us, you guys have permission to contact me, but otherwise I'm in gym rat mode for the rest of the daylight hours."

Twenty-One

Frank chewed and swallowed his first bite of pad thai, then took another. After the third, he said, "I like it. Did you find a new takeout place?"

Giulia threw her napkin at him. "This pad thai was created from scratch by these two hard-working hands."

Her husband laughed and tossed the napkin back at her. "I knew it all along. Let me get my phone." He stretched one arm sideways and snagged the phone from the kitchen counter. He snapped a picture of his dinner plate and sent it. A few seconds later he dialed a number.

"Sean? It's Frank. Did you get the text I just sent? Good. Tell me what it is."

"Uh...noodles and veggies and stuff." Frank's brother's voice came from the phone at full volume.

"Ignoramus. You are looking at homemade pad thai. If I could send you the aroma over the phone, I would. When do Tina and the kids get back from her mom's? And how's that frozen pizza?"

"Go n-ithe an cat thú is go n-ithe an diabhal an cat."

"I love you too, big brother. No leftovers will be coming your way." He hung up.

Giulia giggled into her noodles. "Irish curses are much cleverer than Italian curses. I have nothing to top 'May the cat eat you and may the Devil eat the cat.'"

"He deserved it. He spent years telling me what a terrific cook

Tina is, and not sharing any of it. Payback is sweet." He stopped talking and paid attention to supper.

"We have enough to bring him a bowlful."

"Are you serious?" He swallowed. "I'm not letting this out of our kitchen."

Giulia basked in Frank's oblique praise. Coming home to her own home and family after the day she'd had was something she'd never dreamed of hoping for in the bad old days. Her brother's marriage wasn't the greatest example to follow, either. He ran his house like a Catholic army barracks with him as Pope, military police, and God all in one.

Frank refilled his Coke and her iced tea. Giulia smiled.

"What?" he said.

"I'm comparing you to other husbands, and they are suffering thereby."

Frank affected an innocent expression. "Well, of course."

Half an hour later, Frank left for his Police Rec League basketball game. Giulia found a nature sounds radio station on iTunes and cranked it. She pushed the coffee table against the couch and rolled up the throw rug. From the combination office/library/den she brought six different colored highlighters and a tape dispenser.

"All right, friends, relatives, and co-workers. Let's see what you're really saying."

She started with the first interview, Geranium Asher. Yellow for her, since she was the happiest of all the people Giulia had spoken to. The marker picked out the high points. The fights. Geranium's idea that Loriela wanted power and Fitch wanted things. A lot of wanting.

Next in the pile: Len Tulley. The surprise. The stick bug, to be precise. Green for him, since envy was eating him alive.

"Brown would work too, but I can't read through it. There, where you pretend you're a dumb, beer-drinking ex-jock. There, where you reveal your capacity to hold a grudge for years. And there, where you throw three people under the bus, including Fitch's lawyer."

She sat back on her heels. "Getting information from Colby Petit, Esq. is going to take finesse. Tomorrow morning and a fresh strategy session for you." She switched to a red pen and wrote a few notes at the top of Tulley's first page.

"Mrs. Gil. Hot pink for you, only because they don't make angry red highlighters." Giulia started marking sentences halfway down the first page, continued onto pages two and three and covered half of page four.

"Ouch."

She ran back into the den for a black magic marker and revisited all the highlights, underscoring in black only the bits and pieces that appeared to have more truth than hate in the mix. She'd have to reread all of these transcripts.

Blue for Jonathan Stallone. He disappointed Giulia. She'd been all prepared to crown him Suspect Number One. He had all the markers: Jilted lover, anger issues, strength, opportunity. Yet he came across as the most well-adjusted of the five. She didn't think he was conning her either, not like Len Tulley's Jekyll and Hyde act.

"How dare you get over a failed relationship and move on with your life, Mr. Stallone?" She used hardly any highlighter on his transcript.

Shirley Travers, on the other hand...Bright orange for her and lots of it. Think of the lost income. The perceived downgrade in job status when she finally got hired by her school district. The rearranging of her entire life as her rival's status and pay grade rose higher and higher in her former company.

"Shirley ought to have SUSPECT stenciled on her forehead in fluorescent orange to match this marker. But is that too easy?" She shook her head. "Only a fool refuses a gift dropped right into her lap. I'm not a fool."

More orange on sentence after sentence. It still didn't feel quite right. She persevered anyway. When Shirley's transcript bled orange, she stretched her back and made a face at the pile of police and DNA reports. All at once she'd had enough of chirping birds and harp glissandos. Off went the radio, on went the TV. She found the Marx Brothers' *Duck Soup* in the DVD carrel and popped it into the player.

She left the papers in small piles on the floor and made herself a cup of coffee sweetened with amaretto creamer. Fetching her iPad from her bag, she stretched on the couch with a full-on view of the movie and the coffee on the table ready to hand.

As Groucho confused Margaret Dumont, Giulia booted her tablet and opened both sets of surveillance photos from Fitch's apartment building. The first "extra" photo from the police's version appeared early in the set.

"I suppose I understand why the courtroom exhibit version doesn't have this one. A photo of a skunk nosing around a barberry bush isn't clue material." She reached for her coffee with her left hand while she scrolled alternately through the photos with her right. "Number two looks like a duplicate of the first lightning photo in both sets." She enlarged it, but side by side they still looked like those drawings in the Sunday comics that wanted you to find six differences between the two pictures.

The third and fourth photos of the extra seven had caught two teenagers running through the grass. One in a hoodie, one bareheaded. The bareheaded one was laughing and her soaked hair was plastered flat.

Photo five fell chronologically between the one of the rain-soaked balcony and the one with the man-sized shadow. Or woman-sized. Shirley Travers and Len Tulley were about the same height. Tulley carried at least a hundred more pounds, but the shadow appeared to be wearing a hooded poncho. It concealed the exact shape of the person with great effectiveness.

In this photo, the shadow stood on the sidewalk with its face turned north, toward the stoplight at the nearby intersection. The poncho hood covered everything but the tip of the nose. Giulia enlarged the photo. Whoever this was, their stance indicated they were listening. The nose tip wasn't particularly distinctive. Not pointy or bulbous, not hooked or tipped up.

But if Giulia could somehow line up Shirley, Len, Roger himself, and, yes, Colby...

She stared at the photo 'til her eyes blurred. Onscreen, Chico and Harpo drove the burly lemonade stand owner to distraction. Giulia rubbed her eyes and watched the classic comedy for a few minutes.

She drank more coffee and scrolled to the sixth eliminated photo. This was also nonessential, showing possibly the same skunk crossing the footprints in the mulch.

The seventh and last appeared toward the end. The figure in the poncho was jumping the low barberry hedge onto the sidewalk. At the near end of the shot, Loriela's arm dangled over the edge of the balcony. Like the "waiting" photo, the captured movement of the running man—or woman—might be enough to pinpoint which of the four Giulia suspected.

"Wait. What about that actor Cassandra Gil and Len Tulley threw at me?"

She scooted off the end of the couch and flipped through Cassandra's transcript, then Tulley's.

"Actor and baby mama. I'm going to have to call Loriela's mother."

Onscreen, the four Marx brothers romped and sang about Freedonia going to war. Giulia had a fleeting wish that the main players in this case would somehow break into spontaneous song and dance. She hit the pause button and dialed Cassandra Gil, hoping she'd be home on a Friday night.

"Hello?"

Yes. "Mrs. Gil, this is Giulia Falcone-Driscoll. May I ask you a few more questions?"

"Of course. Please wait one minute while I check on supper in the oven."

The low-pitched creak of the door on an older oven. Giulia's last two convents had ovens that sounded exactly like that. The scrape of a baking dish sliding off the inner rack. The crinkle of foil, then footsteps.

"Your timing is very good. The chicken must rest for five minutes before George carves it. What is it you wish to know?"

Giulia plunged in. "I've heard rumors Roger Fitch got his last girlfriend before Loriela pregnant and then deserted her. Would you know anything about that?"

A Spanish profanity. "Loriela mentioned once that a woman came to their apartment to see him and he was surprised and angry. I do not know if the woman was pregnant."

"Then you wouldn't know her name?"

"No. I am sorry." Frustration edged her voice. "Is it very important?"

"Please don't worry about it. I'll ask Mr. Fitch when I see him tomorrow."

A harsh laugh. "He's willing to tell you about the evils he has done, but still claims that he did not murder my daughter?"

"He's ready to give me any information he thinks will lessen his chance of conviction."

"He is a drowning man snatching at straws."

"One more thing, and then I won't take up any more of your Friday night. Do you remember anything more about the actor Loriela dated? The one you said Roger Fitch gave a black eye to?"

A real laugh from Cassandra this time. "Oh, that one. He did not understand how funny all his words and actions appeared."

"Do you remember his name?"

"Let me think...'Henri' something. I called him 'Henry' once and he corrected me with great seriousness. Let me ask George."

The sound in Giulia's ear became muffled. She pictured Cassandra cupping her hand over the tiny phone.

"George, what is the name of that egotistical actor who stalked Loriela after she had moved on to Roger Fitch?" Her voice came through the covering hand with only a slight loss of clarity.

The rattle of cutlery underscored George's voice. "He had two first names, didn't he? Pronounced the second one weird."

"That is it." The sound cleared. "The actor's name was Henri Richard. The last name is spelled like Richard, but he pronounced it *ri-shard.*"

George's voice, saying something Giulia couldn't make out. Then Cassandra's voice again. "He performed out of a renovated church downtown. The one with the beautiful rose window."

"Next door to the open-air Farmers' Market," Giulia finished. "Yes, I know exactly where that is. Thank you so much, Mrs. Gil."

"I told you, I will give you any help I can so I may drink champagne at his execution. George is making the face that means I am getting angry again and I should come eat supper."

Giulia smiled into the phone. "I won't keep you from your supper. Good night."

She ended that call and dialed Fitch. He answered on the second ring.

"Angie?"

"It's Giulia Falcone-Driscoll, Mr. Fitch."

"Oh."

The disappointment in that one word made Giulia wonder what attributes Angie had to cause it. She braced for more shouting.

"Could you let me have the name and address—and phone number, if possible—of your former girlfriend who you're rumored to have gotten pregnant?"

To the delight of Giulia's ears, Fitch remained silent for several seconds.

"Somebody's got their knife into my back," he said at last. "The name you want is Lacy Maples." He spelled out an address. "I deleted her number from my phone two years ago. For the record: I did not tell her to have an abortion, I did not force her to have an abortion, and I did not pay for an abortion. Clear?"

"Yes." Giulia drew angry emoticons in the margin of the printout under her hand. "Then you admit it was your child."

"No, I do not admit that. Jesus Christ, what the hell have people been telling you?"

"You hired me to look into everything. That's what I'm doing."

"Great. Won't I look good to a jury now? Happy?" He hung up.

A key turned in the deadbolt on the front door. "I'm home," Frank called from the short front hall. "Sweaty, victorious, and starving."

"So of course you stopped at the Garden of Delights and brought dessert," Giulia called back.

"What? I can't hear you over the sound of my stomach growling."

Giulia laughed and dropped her phone onto the couch. "Never fear. Blueberry pie awaits. I'll make coffee. I'd make just about anything for the delight of talking with a reasonable man."

Frank came up behind her and squeezed her in his not-too-sweaty arms. "You are a model for all wives. I gather I'm being favorably compared to The Silk Tie Killer?"

"Indeed you are. Don't let it go to your head. Go away and change. Coffee will be ready in a few minutes."

When Frank entered the kitchen to carry dishes to the living room, Giulia had her questions prepared for him.

"The living room appears to have been annexed by Driscoll Investigations," he said.

"Temporarily. I'm annexing you tonight as well."

"Taskmaster." He sat at the end of the coffee table, away from the papers on the floor. After his first bite of pie, he said, "You have won me over with this dessert. Ask away."

Giulia brought up the two sets of pictures on her tablet. "The lawyer's version omits seven from the raw version you gave me. Five of them are nothing—a skunk and kids and duplicates. But look at the other two." She handed him the tablet. "See how the person in the hooded poncho is standing? Now scroll down...there. The one with the same person jumping the barberry bushes."

Frank scrolled back and forth between both photos. "What about them?"

"I'm thinking Fitch's lawyer omitted them because they have details which could identify this mysterious person. Someone with a concealed face and a body-disguising raincoat who happened to be lurking around Fitch's apartment the night Loriela was killed. The prosecution would give a lot to know who that is."

"So would we." He stopped at the photo with the bare wet arm in the foreground. After enlarging it and holding it close and at a distance, he shook his head. "It's not enough."

"What do you mean?"

"Look."

He set the tablet flat on the coffee table. Giulia pushed both coffee cups to the other end, away from the screen.

Frank started with, "I get what you're saying about the way poncho carries himself."

"Or herself," Giulia said.

"Or herself. But, to give one example, actors can imitate certain posture tics. Let's assume that the killer—we won't say who that is—hired some out-of-work actor to pose in ways that the killer knows will trip the motion-sensor camera." He reached around the tablet for his coffee. "Don't raise your eyebrows. The actor gets told it's a practical joke, because a friend watches too many slasher movies. Or that a rival security system is trying to sell the apartment building owners on a better camera. And that the trick is the actor has to imitate a certain person to make it work."

Giulia tried to see the photo with fresh eyes. "Seriously?"

"One hundred percent. A good prosecuting attorney could take those photos and twist them into whatever he wanted. Face it, the state's attorney might be doing exactly that as they prepare for the trial."

Giulia scooped the last of the vanilla ice cream from her plate.

"Better find out now than waste more time on this angle." He picked up his plate and leaned back in the chair. "That's probably why Fitch's lawyer chose his creative omission. If I had to guess, despite what I just said, the prosecution might not be wasting any time on it either. They've got a straightforward case with the DNA and other evidence."

"I'm not happy." Giulia shook her fork at Frank. "I've got a thin lead on an actor the victim dated, but it seems too easy."

"Easy? I know you know how many months it takes to put a case like this together."

"Yes, yes. That's not what I mean." She picked up her dishes. "I mean that if Fitch is willing to expose all these details to us when he has one of the best lawyers for this type of case, there must be something else to it all."

Frank followed her into the kitchen. "I applaud your determination. Because of that, I promise not to say 'I told you so' when he slips up and you realize he's a slick liar as well as a murderer."

Giulia gave him her "unimpressed teacher" look. "You, sir, have one major fault. You resist change at all costs."

He closed the dishwasher. "I prefer to think of myself as a rock to be relied upon."

"Argh. Come watch the end of the movie with me before I dive into my clue collage."

"Not the clue collage." Frank pretended to sink under a heavy weight. "I won't see you 'til midnight."

"Great art requires sacrifice."

Twenty-Two

After the movie Frank retired to the den to play Assassin's Creed online with his brothers. Giulia queued several Mozart symphonies on their multi-CD changer to drown out the brothers' running trash-talk. Through hard experience, she had a mere thirty minutes of gameplay before the multiple voices from the attached speakers became too loud for her to think. She'd checked with her fellow Driscoll spouses after the first couple of Fridays, and they shared their successful coping mechanisms with her.

Symphony number five in B-flat major burst through the living room. She flexed her fingers.

"All right, people. Fear the power of the highlighters."

She started at the left end of the TV stand with Geranium Asher's two pages detailing the police call and what she heard listening at the shared wall. Next to them she dealt Shirley Travers' naked hate. Three pieces of tape linked them. Below both of those she set Len Tulley's pages, the one in which he threw everyone possible under the bus landing off-center. Continuing the hub of a wheel pattern, she taped Jonathan's reasonable story, Cassandra's pulsing neon lust for Fitch's death, and two blank pages for Henri Richard the actor and Lacy Maples the angry ex.

The Driscoll boys' game strategy—shouting each other down— cut across the Mozart symphony. Giulia scowled at the six-inch gap caused by the door sticking to the hardwood floor. Frank kept promising to fix it before she had to hand-wax it for the twentieth time.

"Crank it down, warriors!"

"Sorry, hon!" from the den.

The almost identical male voices cut the volume by half. Giulia swapped out the highlighters for regular red, green, and blue markers. With the red, she drew arrows to the most suspicious statements. Iffy statements got blue. Positive clues, green. Then she attacked the entire collage with Post-it notes.

An hour later, pages from the police and DNA reports fanned out from the spokes of the wheel. More arrows led from information in them that connected to underlined and highlighted points from the interviews.

Muscle cramps rippled through Giulia's shoulders. Her knees hurt from extended contact with the wood floor. Only four years out of the convent and she'd gone soft. Sister Eulalia would've had plenty to say about that.

She unkinked her right shoulder enough to grope on the top of the coffee table for one of the blank pieces of paper that had been stuck in with the printouts. With the plain blue marker, she made a list for the weekend:

- Get on the internet and find the actor
- Stay on the internet and find the baby mama
- Try to contact both and have an in-person meeting Sat. or Sun.
- Fitch's apartment (block out two hours)
- Groceries
- Sleep?
- Food?

She focused her eyes on the DVD player's clock. Eleven forty-five. Enough for one day. She capped all the markers and paper-clipped all the un-collaged documents in separate piles. Slowly, with attention to her left foot returning to life with a thousand phantom bee stings, she stood up for the first time in two hours.

The CD remote cut off Mozart's symphony number twelve in the middle of the second movement. Frank's voice rushed into the gap. She bent in half and picked up the clue collage at the bottom, folding it more or less in half, then in quarters. The loose edges flapped, but she tamed them into a semblance of neatness and set the rhombus on the coffee table underneath the semi-empty delivery box.

Off with all the lights except the front hall and the stairs. Check the locks. Trudge upstairs and into the bathroom. Strip and fall into bed. She was so whipped she postponed her nightly Bible reading, something Frank had taken a while to get used to, especially on their honeymoon.

She had no idea when Frank came to bed. She only noticed his presence when he whispered in her ear, "Told you it'd be after midnight."

She slept the sleep of the righteous and weary until her phone rang at nine a.m.

"I thought you said you'd be ready for me?" Roger Fitch said. "It rang so many times I thought I'd get dumped into voicemail. You can come over now."

Twenty-Three

Giulia stuffed the phone under her pillow. But only for a moment.

"I'll be over soon, Mr. Fitch. Thank you for calling so early."

She returned the phone to her nightstand and pulled the blanket over her head.

Her husband said from the pillow next to her, "I love it when strange men call my wife while we're in bed together."

"It's all part of my nefarious plan to keep you on your toes."

He peered under the blanket. "Ruh-roh, Shaggy! We've got a recret ragent in our red!"

Giulia giggled. "You are the only person who can make me giggle like Sidney."

Frank kissed her ear. "One of the many reasons I love you is that you are nothing like Sidney." He kissed her neck. "Where are you going at this hour on a Saturday?"

She moved her hair away from her neck so he could get to more of it. "Roger Fitch's apartment."

Frank jerked up onto one elbow. "What?"

"I want to walk through the crime scene. He wants a report on what everyone said about him."

"He's a killer. Okay, alleged killer."

Giulia knew how to interpret his words and body language. "I'm taking Zane with me as my personal muscle. You should know I'm not naïve enough to go to an alleged murderer's apartment by myself."

He fell back onto his pillow. "Sometimes I worry. Tell Zane to wear a tight t-shirt and a leather jacket, if he has one. He's got good muscle under those button-downs he usually wears."

"Spoken like a cop used to sizing people up." Giulia draped one leg over his. "I promise," she kissed his shoulder, "that I won't take," his collarbone, "any foolhardy risks." Her lips found his.

She tapped his shoulders a few minutes later. "I really have to show up for this appointment," she said with her mouth still against his.

He pulled her on top and kissed her harder.

A few more minutes later, she tapped his shoulders again. "I mean it."

A pitiful sigh. "I'm losing my touch."

She pecked his nose. "No, I'm obsessive about doing my job."

He let his arms drop to his sides. "One hundred percent true. Fine. Go. Leave me here cold and alone and unloved."

Giulia's feet touched the carpet. "You are the farthest thing from unloved. There must be UK soccer on live at this hour. I plan to be back by noon, unless I can get hold of a French actor or a jilted lover. I'll call you if that happens."

"I don't want to know, do I?"

"You will when I tell you thrilling stories of the Jerry Springer kind." She dialed her admin's number. "Zane? It's Ms. Driscoll. Can you be ready in twenty minutes or so? I'll pick you up."

"No prob, Ms. Driscoll." His voice sounded alert and prepared. "Should I wear menacing clothes?"

Giulia smothered a laugh. "Actually, yes, if you possess them."

"Awesome. The thug life for me. See you in twenty."

She set down the phone and said to Frank's attentive face, "Why do men automatically think alike?"

"It's programmed into our DNA. Seriously, be careful. Don't trust that guy."

"I don't. That still doesn't mean—"

"That you're not going to do your best to find the truth, regardless," he finished for her.

"I need a new line," she said, and headed for the shower.

*   *   *

Twenty-five minutes later she pulled into Zane's driveway. March had performed another about-face and the clouds threatened snow. Giulia refused to turn on the heat in the car on principle, but she had chosen jeans and her violet wool coat.

Zane opened his door and Giulia almost didn't recognize him. Her fashionable admin wore cowboy boots, thick jeans, a black t-shirt, and a leather bomber jacket. His white-blond hair, wet and combed straight, should have made him look like he was playing dress-up. Instead, it combined with the clothes that emphasized his kickboxer's physique to make him look exactly like the label she'd given him earlier: Understated muscle.

He blew it by jumping into her car with a, "Hey, Ms. Driscoll. What do you think? My girlfriend says I look like Trunks from *Dragonball Z*, except my hair's not purple."

"From what?"

"Anime. Never mind. Trunks is badass. I'm channeling him today to be your backup."

"I—good. You look great." She backed out of the driveway and headed east. "Your presence will maintain Fitch's illusion that I'm a wuss in body and spirit."

"PayWright was never like this." He leaned forward in the seat, the seat belt keeping him anchored. "What are we looking for?"

The light ahead of them turned green. Giulia drove straight for a few blocks. "Three things. One, I want to get a feel for the apartment, the balcony, the landscaping. That's right. You haven't seen the photos. Open my tablet. They're in the Fitch folder on the desktop."

While Zane scrolled through the photos, Giulia continued, "Two, Fitch wants a summary of all the interviews I've done. Three, I'm going to ask him more about his ex-girlfriend who got an abortion."

Zane whistled. "He's going to blow a gasket."

"Probably. That's another reason you're here. He's more likely to behave with another DI employee in the room." She turned left, then made a quick right. "Only a couple miles to go."

"These surveillance photos sure make it look like he didn't kill her."

"I know, but the obvious inference is that the man or woman in the poncho was casing the apartment building for future burglaries. Then when he or she saw Fitch strangle Loriela, he—or she—hightailed it out of there." She signaled and turned left into the apartment building's parking lot.

Zane repacked her tablet. "I almost forgot. Yesterday afternoon I found it. I finally found something on the AtlanticEdge documents that might be the essential clue to the problems I'm having with the financial records."

"You just made my day. Tell me that Fitch is the one who's been skimming off the books for the past two years and you'll make my month." She parked and shut off the car.

His eager posture wilted, but only for a moment. "I can't say that for certain yet. And honestly, he may not be involved at all. Here's what we saw—"

"Later. Right now we have to focus on the Silk Tie part of Fitch's life." She turned in her seat to face him. "What I'm going to do is make Fitch walk me through the night of the murder. I'll get the summary of interviews over with first so he'll be more willing to do what I want." She unbuckled her seat belt but didn't get out of the car. "You've never done anything like this, which makes you twice as useful. Watch Fitch's body language. Assess the logistics of the apartment and the balcony in relation to those footprints and the landscaping as they looked on the night of the murder. Don't write anything down, because that will put Fitch on his guard. I know you have an excellent memory. This is your chance to test it."

Her phone alarm rang.

"What?" She unlocked the phone. "Oh, crap. I forgot about confession."

"Huh?"

She cancelled the alarm. "Confession. It's a Catholic thing. I set an alarm for it this week because I've been lying for the sake of the job more than usual. Without confession, I shouldn't really take Communion at Mass tomorrow."

She put away her phone. Zane's face could've been the poster image for bewilderment. Giulia smiled and waved it away. "It'd take too long to explain. Sidney would file it under 'Catholics sure have a lot of rules.' Come on. Time to beard Fitch in his den."

Zane jumped out of the car. Giulia followed and locked it. "Please stop looking like a puppy waiting to catch its first Frisbee."

He sobered up. "Sorry. I'm your silent muscle. I'll remember."

In the foyer, Giulia pressed the button next to Fitch's name. He buzzed them in without asking who they were. She pushed open the stairwell door and they walked up two flights of scuffed steel-tread stairs. When she rang Fitch's doorbell, she wondered if Geranium had her ear to the wall between the two apartments.

Fitch opened his door. "Come in. I'm all yours 'til lunch." He caught sight of Zane. "I didn't know you were bringing someone else."

"You remember my assistant, Zane Hall."

"Oh. Yeah."

They shook hands, and Giulia caught Fitch's startle at Zane's strength. Perfect.

He led them into the deep-carpeted living room. Giulia's feet sighed with envy even as she assessed the art on the walls and the cologne wafting from Fitch. It smelled like something new from a *Sports Illustrated* tip-in.

"You want coffee?"

"Thank you, no," Giulia said. "Let's get right to what we came here to report."

She gave Fitch an edited version of Geranium's interview. A good thing, too, since his only comment was "Nosy old fart."

"Can you tell me any more about the night the neighbors called the police because of the argument between you and Ms. Gil?"

He waved it away. "We fought. We got loud. So what? Lori

wasn't a timid little flower. She had fire in her. That's what I like in a woman. Not our fault the neighbors eat dinner at four o'clock and want to go to bed at seven. If landlords wouldn't cheap out on the sound baffling in the walls everybody'd be happier."

Giulia let that slide and proceeded to Len Tulley. Fitch stopped her two sentences in.

"I'm the one who told you Len found the video. I know that makes Len look bad, but it doesn't mean his hand is sticking the knife into my back."

"Mr. Fitch, you hired me to look into everything that could save you from the death penalty."

"Jeez, you're using that patient voice again." He gave Zane a grin that attempted to exclude Giulia. "Does she use that on you too?"

"Mr. Fitch." Giulia wrested the steering away from Fitch's hijack attempt. "Len Tulley also mentioned you and Mr. Petit have a history."

Fitch blinked at her. Giulia waited.

"Yeah," Fitch said. "Yeah, we went to the same high school. So what?"

"I understand there was some rivalry between you and the possibility exists that it may still be ongoing." This roundabout way of coming at vital questions made Giulia itch.

"Are you kidding? That was sixteen years ago. Nobody cares what happened in high school once you get a real job and a life."

Tendrils of red inched up his neck. Giulia could've kissed them.

"That may be true for certain people, but Leonard Tulley's condo is a shrine to his teenage football triumphs."

Fitch barked a laugh. "He gave you that old sob story, eh? You should hear him at the bar. He ought to have a warning label for new customers coming into Long Neck. Poor Len, could've been somebody, would've made the NFL Hall of Fame if only his rivals hadn't tackled his knees in the State Championship game his senior year. Blew 'em both out." He leaned back in his chair. "Truth is, Len was the big fish in a small pond at his D-2 college, but he would've been outclassed in any Division I school."

"That's somewhat harsh."

Fitch shrugged. "A short stint in the pros would only have delayed Len's permanent career as a bloated has-been. He's a good brewmaster, though. Long Neck's profits have increased at a slow but steady rate since he signed on."

Giulia said with no change in her voice, "Do you work at the bar with him?"

"With him?" The sneer in his voice matched the one on his face. "I'm part owner of Long Neck. He works for me, in the strict sense of the word. Want to know the best part of being on top? Minions."

Still without a change in inflection, Giulia said, "But we were talking about history between you and Colby Petit. This was in basketball, not football. Am I correct?"

Fitch looked like he'd just thought better of giving Giulia another insult disguised as a grudging compliment. His charming sales smile reappeared. "It was so long ago, but—hey, just a second."

He jumped up and went to the artistic glass-and-chrome shelves on either side of the TV. From one at waist level, he took out an oversized crimson book and flipped through it.

"Here you go. This is our varsity team picture. I'm holding up the right side of the trophy. That's Colby in the back row, behind me."

Giulia studied the faces in the photo. The face of the future Colby Petit, Esq. peeked out from behind Roger Fitch's shoulder. His "Say Cheese!" smile foreshadowed the smile that appeared at exactly the moment to win a reluctant jury. His eyes looked at Fitch holding the trophy, not at the camera.

"I see." She handed the book back to him. "Thank you." She segued into a quick summary of Jonathan Stallone's early-morning interview and a longer one of Shirley Travers' vitriol and lunch meetup.

Roger whistled. "Whoa. I forgot about her. Lori sure proved she had what upper management wanted with that deal."

Next to Giulia, Zane shifted on his couch cushion, but kept quiet.

"That's an interesting way to describe it," she said.

"Oh, come on. You've been in business. It's like rugby. Trample the weak and leap over the dead. Travers was weak."

"Shirley Travers welcomed Ms. Gil as a new employee and trained her to do the job she was hired for."

"Yeah, and Lori outstripped Travers in less than a year. Lori would've been an idiot not to turn that to her advantage, and Madre Cassandra sure didn't raise an idiot." He pointed to Zane. "You. You're younger than your boss here. By default you should have a better grasp on current methods and practices. In the proper order of things, if she doesn't scramble to keep ahead of you, you're going to replace her within a year or two. That's business. Travers didn't keep her ears open. Never rest, you—Zane, right? Stay hungry. That's why Lori was a success."

Giulia chose her next words with care. "The police reports contain no evidence of a motive for Ms. Gil's death. They posit some theories, but that's all we have after a year: Theories." She crossed her arms over her knees, the gesture bringing her closer to Fitch. "What do you believe was the motive for Ms. Gil's murder?"

Fitch didn't miss a beat. "Revenge. What else could it be? Sure, her killer took our credit cards, but that was opportunity at hand. If the killer'd been serious about cleaning us out, he—or she—wouldn't have stopped at Lori. He'd have taken care of me while I was sleeping it off ten feet from Lori's body."

Taking the cue, Giulia stood. "I know we haven't yet discussed Cassandra Gil's interview, but I'd like to walk through the murder scene."

Fitch stared up at her for a moment, then shrugged and stood. "Why not? Come on, Zane. I'll give both of you the Hollywood Horrors tour of Apartment 212."

Twenty-Four

He led them through an open door into a bedroom that still showed traces of a feminine decorating scheme. The bedspread, a forest green shadow-stripe, layered a seafoam dust ruffle under an actual ruffle. The duvets matched the dust ruffle, and that was it for anything feminine. Sales and software books filled the headboard book niches. The room was just narrow enough with the king-sized bed to allow no space for nightstands. A 36-inch TV took up the top of the chest of drawers on the left side of the bed. If there had ever been a dresser for Loriela on the outside wall, a gas fireplace now filled a third of that space, with seascape watercolors on both sides. Good ones, too—Giulia's friend Sister Bart had taught Giulia what a talented painter's work should look like.

On the other side of the TV, the glass balcony door offered a view of the solid brick wall of a refurbished 1940s cinema across thirty feet of bushes and grass studded with patches of old snow.

"Lori slept on the side near the balcony. Her dresser used to be against that wall. I put in the fireplace last September. That night, when we got home from the bar, we finished celebrating my birthday and passed out more than fell asleep. You know how it is when you've had a few too many."

"Once or twice," Giulia said, figuring he'd accept this even from the prude he'd said she was. She was also prepared to step on Zane's foot, but Zane picked up her cue.

"I don't know why she woke up. The way I pieced it together

when I was sitting in jail for the two days after, the guy—or girl—made some kind of noise that got through to Lori right about the time she woke up to pee. Something like that, where she'd be coming out of how heavy we were both sleeping."

Giulia walked over to what had been Loriela's side of the bed. "The balcony door has a deadbolt? Yes, I see it does."

"We used it because we both grew up in crime-filled neighborhoods, but we never expected somebody to climb up that way. Everyplace nowadays is covered by security cameras." He opened the door and pointed to the left of the balcony. "The one that took all the pictures in Colby's trial exhibit is up there, a foot above my head."

Giulia passed him and stepped out onto the pressure-treated wood, weathered to a natural gray. Beads of melted snow lurked in the shaded corner, so it had at least been waterproofed. But Loriela had been strangled, not stabbed, so there'd been no reason to retreat for bloodstains.

She eyeballed the eight-by-six space fenced in by wrought-iron railings in a simple twist pattern. "Mr. Fitch, did you have to step over Ms. Gil's body to see if she was still breathing?"

"Yeah. When the phone woke me up and I saw the rain coming in the open door, I sobered up fast. Didn't see that my tie was missing, but I'd yanked them off her wrists and she untied her ankles after we finished, like always." He glanced at Giulia, then at Zane. "Well, not always. I don't want you to think we indulged on a regular basis. We'd made up after a big fight and she wanted to—"

"Mr. Fitch," Giulia turned her back to him and leaned over the railing to study the landscaping, "I'm interested only in that evening as it pertains to Ms. Gil's murder. The tie was on the footboard and available to the killer. Your intimate relationship details are not my concern."

"Yeah. Okay. So there was a little round hole in the door and wet shoe prints on the rug leading out to the kitchen. Lots of rain had soaked into the room from the open door. That's when I called 9-1-1. Then I found Lori. He'd left her right where you're standing. I dragged her inside and untied the tie from her neck and tried CPR. I don't know CPR, but you see it all the time on cop shows, and I wasn't thinking straight."

"I see." She came into the bedroom again. "Where exactly did the wet prints lead?"

"Out here, to the kitchen." He led them, walking in a shorter stride than usual. "The guy—yeah, I know, or woman—sneaked past me. Grabbed my wallet from the top of my dresser and Lori's from her purse on the kitchen counter." He pointed to it. "We didn't use our computers in the kitchen, so he kept going into the den."

He stopped at the doorway. "Then he—she—grabbed the laptops as the lightest things to carry, I guess, and went out the same way." He shook his head. "Bastard jumped poor Lori's body like a hurdle and took off."

Giulia walked the killer's path again, opening the closet door, reaching for a phantom wallet in a nonexistent purse, placing each foot in measured steps along the bed's footboard and back onto the balcony. The floor plan of the apartment could have been made for thieves as much as for tenants who wanted the illusion of as much space as possible.

"Thank you," she said to Fitch as she came inside, closing the glass door behind her. "This has been quite helpful."

"Anything for my cause." Fitch glanced at Zane again.

Giulia braced herself. "Now, about my interview with Cassandra Gil."

Twenty-Five

The entrance buzzer sounded.

Fitch glanced at the clock-radio on the headboard. "Damn. Time flies when you're being interrogated." He loped into the hall and pressed his own buzzer to unlock the main door.

"Sorry," he said to Giulia and Zane when they came into the kitchen. "Thought we had more time before lunch. Got a friend coming over."

Giulia gave him her best customer-service smile. "We only have one last interview to discuss."

He looked at the door, then back at her. "Yeah, but the company won't be right for it."

"Mr, Fitch, you requested this meeting. As you pointed out to me earlier, your trial for murder is ten days away."

"I know, I know. Who knows it better than me?"

The doorbell rang.

Fitch cursed under his breath and opened the door. A spectacular blonde stood on the threshold: Clingy sweater, pencil skirt, four-inch heels, bright red lipstick, dark blue mascara. Her sparkling blue nails curled around two Styrofoam takeout containers.

"Come on in, Angie." Fitch took the containers.

"Hey, baby," Angie said. "I thought it was going to be just the two of us."

"It is. They were my morning appointment. We're just

finishing up." He beckoned to Giulia and Zane. "Come into the den. Angie, give me five minutes. You want to grab a couple of beers from the fridge?"

"I'll expect repayment for my services." She winked at Fitch.

"You know you'll get it, baby." Fitch closed Giulia and Zane into the den with him. "Summarize, okay? Angie isn't long on patience."

Giulia drew on her own deep reserves of patience and began with Cassandra's version of the Christmas week fights that led to the botched restraining order.

"Come on, you didn't swallow all that after all this time?" Fitch knocked the back of his head against the door. "Everything she says means only one thing: 'I hate Roger Fitch.'"

A delicate knock at the door. "Roger, the buzzer went off. I pressed it because I know you never bother to ask who it is."

"I wasn't expecting anyone else," he said in a low voice. Then louder, "Thanks, Angie. Be out in a second."

Giulia said, "It goes without saying that I weigh each interview against the others and against the official documentation."

"Good. Good." Fitch shook himself. "We'd better finish this tomorrow. Wait, tomorrow's Sunday. You go to church or anything like that? What time is good for you?"

The doorbell rang. Fitch opened the door to the den.

"Hey, Roger," a different female voice said.

"Who are you?" Angie's voice.

"Oh, shit," Roger muttered.

"Who are you?" The new voice.

Giulia and Zane slipped into the hall behind Roger.

"Tammy. Hey, doll, what's up?" Roger's charm was all but visible in the restaurant-like air. A tall redhead in skintight jeans, spike-heeled boots, and a leather top with the center zipper open to her cleavage stood in the doorway. The aroma of orange-spiced beef rose from the casserole dish in her hands. The spicy scent of General Tso's chicken wafted from Angie's unpacked takeout containers on the table.

"Who's the Barbie doll?" the redhead said.

"Uh, Angie, this is Tammy. Tammy, meet Angie." Fitch's smile faltered. "You said you'd be in Philadelphia 'til Monday, Tams."

"The client canceled. I thought I'd surprise you with homemade Chinese for lunch." She walked around Fitch and used her casserole to push aside the takeout containers on the table.

The front door buzzer sounded a third time.

The redhead stalked over to the small, square speaker and held the "open door" button down with her thumb. Then she turned to glare at Giulia. "How many more women are you entertaining today?"

"It's not like that. This is Giulia Driscoll and her assistant, from Driscoll Investigations. They're working to prove my innocence before the trial starts."

The redhead defrosted a few degrees. "Nice to meet you. Hope you're doing a better job than the cops did. I'd like to keep this guy around for several years."

"Wait a minute, honey." Angie slipped her arm through Fitch's. "Where do you get off thinking you have rights to Roger?"

Tammy planted herself in front of Fitch. "Roger, you want to tell blondie here who can't cook to take a hike?"

Angie blew a kiss at Tammy. "I feel for anyone who has to buy affection with food."

Tammy inspected her manicure. "Guess you have to buy affection with some other talent."

Angie's smile gave her a feral air. "Roger, if you don't tell this bottled redhead to take a hike, I'll make her leave minus a few chunks of that henna'd hair."

The redhead laughed in the blonde's face. "Please. What are you good for besides hanging on a guy's arm? Roger appreciates multi-talented women."

Roger sent one pleading glace at Giulia. Giulia pretended to be in a conversation with Zane.

Roger made a conciliatory gesture.

"Tammy, it's like this..."

The redhead dropped her superior pose. The blonde clung tighter to Fitch's arm.

"Tammy, the reason I asked Angie over here when you were going to be out of town is because I wanted to break it to her easy."

The blonde un-clung. "What?"

The redhead, all superiority again, picked the blonde's fingers off Fitch's arm. As though that small physical contact was a starter's pistol, the blonde shoved the redhead backwards.

The redhead backpedaled one step, pivoted, and slapped the blonde's face. "Cow."

"Tams, Angie, come on." Fitch's plea lacked sincerity.

"Pig!" The blonde grabbed the redhead's shoulder and yanked her away from Fitch.

The redhead's shirt zipper popped a few teeth. The redhead got a handful of the blonde's sweater. It stretched off her shoulders, revealing black lace bra straps.

"Bitch!" The blonde stepped into the hold and aimed her pointed blue nails at the redhead's face.

The redhead ducked. The blonde stumbled past her and caught herself on the table edge. They both blistered the paint with their next set of insults.

Giulia stepped away from the wall. "Mr. Fitch," she raised her voice over the screeching women, "since you're otherwise entertained, I'll call you when I'm ready to give you my next update. Let's go, Zane."

"Giulia—Ms. Driscoll—wait, please." Fitch threw out a hand toward her.

The doorbell rang.

The redhead swatted Fitch's hand down. "How many women are you stringing along, Roger?"

"I'm not—Tammy, listen to me—"

The blonde hip-checked Roger into the table. "You bastard!"

Giulia opened the door. A spotlight blinded her. An unseen hand shoved a microphone in her face.

"Ken Kanning here with *The Scoop* at The Silk Tie Killer's

apartment. Miss, are you Roger Fitch's new girlfriend? Don't you worry that one of his ties will end up around your neck?"

Every syllable of that theatrical voice grated on Giulia's nerves.

"Please move and let me by." She didn't trust herself to say anything else.

Behind her, one of the women screeched something unintelligible. The spotlight swerved to Giulia's left. Giulia glanced over her shoulder.

The blonde picked up the redhead's casserole and heaved it. The redhead ducked. The casserole dish shattered against the wall. Beef, broccoli, rice, and sticky orange sauce splashed the wall, the rug, and Fitch. A shard of milky glass bounced off a picture frame and impaled Giulia's purse.

Ken Kanning shoved Giulia out of his way and ran into the apartment, the cameraman a step behind him.

"More violence, Scoopers! Accused murderer Roger Fitch has two women tearing up his apartment. What kind of man revels in this behavior? What kind of woman—"

Giulia shoved open the stairwell door and cut off that voice. She didn't stop or look around until she and Zane were safe in the Nunmobile.

"Holy crap," Zane said in an awed voice.

Giulia managed a weak laugh. "Still prefer working for a private investigator to a nice, safe desk job with sales commissions?"

"You bet. The only exciting stuff in my life used to be beating my gang on gaming night." He whistled. "Wait 'til I tell the guys about this."

Giulia rested her forehead on the steering wheel. "Tell them to watch *The Scoop* Monday at three-thirty. We might be on it."

"Holy crap."

Giulia raised her head. "It's not exactly the TV debut I'd have picked."

"Oh, no, Ms. Driscoll. This is awesome. I'll tell my girlfriend to DVR it but I won't tell her why."

"We'll watch it Monday at work. I might need to do damage control with the Diocese." She started to toss her purse in the backseat. A glint of light stopped her mid-throw. "At least the sliver of casserole impaled my purse instead of me." She pinched it out with her fingernails. "Zane, could you grab a tissue from the pocket on the door?"

Zane held one out and she set the piece of milky glass in its center.

"Ash tray, please." This time her purse made it into the backseat. She started the car and pulled into Saturday afternoon traffic.

"Ms. Driscoll, did you want me to write up a report about that visit?"

Giulia hit the brakes at the next intersection as a black pickup ran a stop sign. "Learn how to drive!" She looked twice in each direction before turning left. "Sorry. I don't usually lose my temper on the roads. I blame the Roger Fitch circus." After another block, she said, "Did you ask me a question?"

"Um, I wanted to know if I should write a report about today."

"Yes, please. All your impressions of the apartment, all your thoughts about Fitch's story, everything." She caught three green lights in a row. "That man will give me an ulcer."

"I meant to tell you. You know when he was telling us about using his neckties as part of sex with his girlfriend? When you weren't looking, he winked at me. Twice." Zane shivered. "It creeped me out that he thinks I'm one of the guys who are into that."

"That's good." She squeaked through a yellow light. "Sorry. Not that he thinks you're like him. If he's manufactured camaraderie between you then he'll be more willing to trust us." She stopped at the next yellow because of heavier traffic. "His starring episode of *The Scoop* today truncated my report before he got everything he wanted to know. That gives us the advantage. I'd like to see him suck up to us for a change."

"I've never seen you this angry, Ms. Driscoll."

Giulia turned left again onto Zane's street and laughed a little. "It takes a lot to make me angry. Everything about Roger Fitch falls under that heading." She pulled into Zane's driveway. "Thank you for backing me up in there. I've got a mental note to add two hours' overtime to your next paycheck."

"Anytime, Ms. Driscoll. I have to say I'm better with gaming violence than real-life crazies." He opened the car door.

"Wait," Giulia said. "I seem to remember you were going to tell me about the embezzlement case."

"Oh, yeah. Man, that seems like forever ago." He stared out the windshield. "It'll keep 'til Monday. I want to write down what happened today before I lose it."

"So do I. Monday morning, then."

Giulia drove straight home, found Frank in the garage building storage shelves, took the hammer and nails out of his hands, and kissed him.

"What did I do?" he asked when she allowed him a breath.

"You are not a possible murderer and embezzler who doesn't know the proper use for a silk tie and who's stringing along two women at once, both of whom choose to scream and throw things."

"Well, when you put it that way, I'm awesome."

Twenty-Six

Sunday morning after ten o'clock Mass, Frank headed to the car while Giulia talked with Father Carlos, the pastor of Saint Thomas'. The parishioners exited the parking lot like NASCAR contenders or headed down the street like marathon runners.

"Your husband is impatient," the tall, bearded priest said.

"I made cinnamon rolls this morning and he says they've taken hold of his mind. He won't be free 'til he eats one more."

Father Carlos laughed. A withered old woman jerked her head toward them, shock freezing her wrinkles. Father Carlos nodded at her and she walked away, shaking her head.

"She's new here," Giulia said.

"Depending on what their last parish was like, it takes the new ones time to get used to a priest who isn't grim."

"You radical. See you next Saturday for confession. Make sure you don't watch *The Scoop* show tomorrow."

"I never do...wait a minute. Why shouldn't I watch it tomorrow? Are you telling me I should schedule a special extended confession slot for you?"

Giulia laughed and walked down the steps. When she rounded the corner of the church, a spotlight snapped on right in front of her face.

"Scoopers, this is Giulia Falcone-Driscoll, investigating the Silk Tie Murder. Tell us how a former nun can sleep at night knowing you're helping a cold-blooded killer get off scot-free?"

Giulia's vision adjusted to the glare. Now she could see Ken Kanning shoving his foam-covered microphone so close to her face she smelled someone else's chili dog on it.

Every cell in Giulia's body wanted to grab that microphone and bash it into the camera's spotlight. But she hadn't survived ten years in the convent and eight years teaching high school in the inner city by losing her cool under pressure.

She pushed the microphone aside with the back of her hand and kept walking.

"Come on, Mrs. Falcone-Driscoll." Kanning's movie star voice followed her. "The Silk Tie Murder Case is number one with our viewers. What do you know about Roger Fitch's two girlfriends trashing his apartment? What about..."

Giulia walked faster than usual, but Kanning and his cameraman glued themselves to her. She could see her head and shoulders outlined faintly on the asphalt by the camera light. Fifteen steps to the car. Ten. Five. Frank's hand opened the passenger door. Three. Two. Giulia slid onto the seat and closed herself in. Frank locked all four doors and hit the gas. Too fast for the small parking lot, but their Camry was the only car remaining.

"Good job," Frank said when they made it through the nearest green light without *The Scoop's* white creeper van following them. "I knew you'd have the self-control not to respond to their trolling."

"It took them less time to track me down than I thought. They must have a roomful of minimum-wage researchers scouring the Net for information about their latest targets." Giulia stared at her hands. "I'm still shaking. You don't know how hard it was not to smash that microphone into their camera."

"Yes I do. They showed up at a crime scene a few months back."

Frank turned left, then left again.

"Why are you taking a different way home? Do you think they'll follow us?"

"Not really, but why take chances? This route cuts off three or four minutes on a slow traffic day, like today. If they're planning to stake out the house, we'll be safe inside while they're still four blocks away."

Seven minutes later, Giulia locked their front door and pulled the curtains closed, even though their street was free of traffic.

"Those miserable bloodsucking parasites." Giulia paced the living room, kitchen, and laundry room and back again. "Those disgusting stalker leeches. And I guarantee Roger Fitch told them who I was."

Frank stopped her with a bear hug around her shoulders. "I'm sure he did. We'll have to set up strategies for getting to work and ditching them when they tail you."

Giulia grabbed her hair and yanked. "If he didn't kill Loriela Gil, I'm going to be tempted to execute him myself."

"You need cinnamon roll therapy."

The tension drained out of Giulia. "What you mean, Mr. Driscoll, is *you* need cinnamon roll therapy. Come on. I'll make fresh coffee."

"It's a scientific fact that homemade baked goods increase brain power as much as one of those little bottles of B-12 plus caffeine." When Giulia gave a disbelieving snort, he threw his hands out in a protestation of innocence. "Go ahead. Look it up."

While the coffee brewed, Frank tore off a piece of paper from the pad on the fridge. "Strategy time. Since *The Scoop* knows where and when you go to church, they know where you work and live. Which reminds me—"

He returned to the front hall, keeping away from the diamond-patterned frosted glass inset on the front door. Giulia stayed in the kitchen doorway. Frank sidled up to the front window and moved the edge of the curtain the barest half-inch.

"Yep. They're parked four houses down."

"*Luridi codardi.*"

"What?" Frank said.

Giulia's ears heated up. "I called them filthy cowards."

"Tsk, tsk, tsk." Frank shook his head. "Marriage to me is cracking the pedestal I put you on way back when."

"Frank, I—"

He kissed her. "Don't be a goose. Hearing even a mild insult from you is a red-letter day. So fear not, Mrs. Driscoll. Their choice of vehicle is about to work against them." He retraced his surreptitious path and unlocked his phone. "Gordon? Frank. Need a favor. *The Scoop* is parked on our street...Yeah, aren't we lucky? They're after my wife...I know. Ever see their van? Plain white, windows painted white too, and a beat-up license plate that's hard to read...Exactly. A predator van...That's what I was thinking. A concerned citizen would call the police to report the presence of such a vehicle lurking in a neighborhood with kids...Thanks. I owe you one."

He ended the call and turned a pleased face to Giulia. "Come get a front-row seat to watch the results."

A police siren neared their street two minutes later. It got louder and louder, finally blaring past their closed windows and cutting off close by. Frank opened the curtains. All the other curtains across the street were already open. A black-and-white, lights whirling, blocked the front of *The Scoop's* van.

A voice through a loudspeaker from the police car: "Step out of the vehicle with your hands where we can see them."

Silence for five...ten...fifteen seconds. Then both doors opened. Ken Kanning's raised arms preceded him out of the passenger side. Someone Giulia didn't recognize appeared from the driver's side.

"That must be the cameraman," Giulia said.

"Yeah. I met him once, when VanHorne offered to take him outside and beat the crap out of him. You don't know how much we wanted to pound both of them into jelly."

"I do. They make me wish I could practice the small bone-breaking techniques we learned in self-defense class."

Frank stared down at her. "That is the second time today I've heard you speak positively of violence."

"This case is making me not recognize the person I see in the mirror," Giulia said.

On the street, one police officer was talking to the two men who comprised *The Scoop* while the other inspected the van. Kanning's theatric hand gestures proclaimed his righteous innocence. The cameraman stood next to Kanning, saying nothing. The second policeman closed the van's back doors and took his time walking around to his partner. After another short dialogue, *The Scoop* got into their van and drove away.

"It's all about who you know," Frank said.

"They're going to be seriously ticked off."

Frank let the curtain fall. "I have no sympathy. Let's work on the various tactics you're going to use for the next several days to ditch them."

Twenty-Seven

No white van lurked on the street at six-thirty Monday morning when Giulia looked out her bedroom window. At seven she came downstairs and peered through the front curtains. The neighbor two doors down pulled out of his garage and a certain white panel van inched along the street in his wake.

"Blast and drat," she muttered on her way to the kitchen. The timed coffee maker faithfully filled the first floor with the scent of dark roast. "They've only had their radar on me for a day and a half and they already know my schedule. Did they ask the neighbors what time I leave for work?" She took the travel mugs from the cupboard. "We might have to rethink who we invite over for driveway basketball this summer."

"They're in front of the Anderson's," Frank called from upstairs.

"I know. Implementing Plan A as soon as I pour coffee."

"I'll be down in two minutes."

"Please put on some clothes. They have a video camera." Giulia split the coffee between her Godzilla mug and Frank's Manchester United mug. Nothing added to Frank's, cinnamon-sugar creamer in hers.

She chose her red quilted jacket more for the brightness of it than for the weather. The days were steadily warming, so while the current temperature hovered near freezing, the weather forecast promised sun and fifty degrees later. Besides, if she was going to make an involuntary TV appearance, Frank always complimented her when she wore this coat with this particular snug pair of jeans.

Frank's bare feet clomped down the carpeted stairs and slapped onto the wood floor of the front hall. "You're wearing that coat and those jeans. Woman, you are a tease."

Giulia kissed him. "Ready to be my door warden?"

He followed her into the kitchen. "My muscles are ever at your service. Keep your windows rolled up so they can't stick that mike in your face or grab onto the sill."

"Of course." She opened the door to the garage and navigated the step using the light from the kitchen. "Give me ten seconds to start the car."

Frank passed her and placed his hands on the metal garage door handle. "Don't get arrested."

"Yes, dear."

She buckled herself in and turned the key. Frank raised the garage door. She backed out the Nunmobile at a prudent speed and Frank closed the door behind her. The white Scoop van hit the gas and screeched to a stop halfway across her driveway. Its doors opened. Light from the rising sun bounced off the TV camera lens.

Ken Kanning's voice penetrated her closed windows: "Driscoll Investigations is out before sunrise in its quest to help a murderer escape justice."

Giulia gunned her Ion onto the narrow strip of grass between the sidewalk and the street, bumped over the curb, and drove in reverse past the next five houses. While Kanning and his minion got themselves back into their van, she whipped through a three-point turn and drove forty miles per hour in a thirty zone for two blocks. The light turned green a few seconds before she reached it and she turned right.

The van turned right seven or eight seconds later. Giulia turned left at the next street. Left again, then right. At last she came up to a light as it turned yellow. She ran it. In her rearview mirror she saw the white van brake hard with its nose in the intersection. Early morning cross traffic had no intention of giving anything the right of way, which gave her the precise advantage she and Frank had planned.

Grinning, Giulia began a winding route to the office. Leaving before seven-thirty got her downtown fifteen minutes earlier than usual. For practical purposes, that meant the best parking spot in her building's minuscule lot.

It also meant a fresh out of the oven raspberry streusel muffin from Common Grounds. Giulia climbed the stairs and unlocked Driscoll Investigations' main door surrounded by the aromas of raspberry jam and cinnamon.

She turned on the lights and the printer and booted her desk computer. The muffin tasted as good as her nose promised.

"Since I never did my planned research this weekend, let's put my Google-fu to the test." She typed in a search string for local theaters.

"The Glass Arts. Of course. I've driven past their sign a dozen times. Managing director...not Henri Richard." She clicked on the Past Performances tab. "There you are. Director Emeritus as of last year. Current productions...great. Chicago. When did you leave town?"

She opened a new browser tab and brought up the Arts Weekly archives. Typing his name in the search window brought up a couple of dozen hits, mostly reviews of his plays. But the article title from the month before his Emeritus date on the theater site showed promise. She clicked it and a collage of photos popped up of a man on the order of pro basketball player Dirk Nowitzki: Scruffy blond hair, sculpted muscles, so tall other actors on stage with him looked out of proportion.

"What a puff piece." Giulia skimmed to the end of the article. "Come on, where is it...he moved to Chicago...blast. Two and a half months before Loriela's murder. Maybe I'll have better luck with the woman Fitch seduced and abandoned."

She opened her tablet and scrolled through the interview notes. "Thursday's...Friday's...There. Lacy Maples."

A new tab and a new Google search. "How nice of you to have a

Facebook page, Twitter account, and LinkedIn profile, Ms. Maples."

Giulia started with the Facebook page. "And especially nice of you to keep so much information public without needing a friend request. Attending the International Culinary Center in New York City. Not enough. What's on your Twitter feed?"

Ten minutes of clicking through tweets and attached comments gave Giulia the answer. "You didn't move out of Cottonwood 'til this past August. All right, Ms. Maples, what's your revenge quota?" She clicked through more tweets.

The end of March:

@HOWARDGEEK THX FOR DRIVING ME TO THE ER. LOOKS LIKE SURGERY. #NOTFUN

Nothing for two days, then:

@BFFJULIE @HOWARDGEEK @BLUEEYEDDOLL I WANT PIZZA! #HOSPITALSTAY #NOTFUN

A few more tweets complaining about food and making a food wish list for her discharge date, then on April second:

@BFFJULIE NEWS! ROGER-THE-SCUMBAG IS IN JAIL! SEEMS HE STRANGLED THE SNOTTY BITCH. #POETICJUSTICE

Giulia read through a four-way conversation between Maples, BFFJulie, HowardGeek, and BlueEyedDoll. Schadenfreude and rejoicing dominated the tweets for the first few days, followed by accusations of bribes and police inefficiency at Roger's release. This culminated in great excitement from Maples: The police visited her. She bragged about her calm replies, made fun of the haircut on one of the police officers, accepted praise from her friends, and ended with:

@BFFJULIE NEVER THOUGHT I'D BE HAPPY TO BE IN THE HOSP. CAN'T KILL YR RIVAL IF YR GETTING YR APPENDIX OUT THE DAY BEFORE. #SUX2BROGER

Giulia scowled at the monitor. "I had hopes for you. Fine. I'll stick with Tulley, Travers, Fitch himself, and I'll keep an open mind about Petit 'til I can talk to him about basketball and school rivalries."

She opened Sidney's and Zane's files on the AtlanticEdge

embezzlement case and started to read through them. Columns of numbers and paragraphs of her assistants' analysis actually relaxed her.

Zane arrived at eight-fifteen. "Ms. Driscoll?"

"In here," Giulia said. "I had to dodge *The Scoop*. They staked out my house."

Zane's white-blond head popped into her doorway. "No way."

"They showed up last night too. Fortunately, their white van looks exactly like a creeper-mobile. We called the cops, who kicked them out of the neighborhood. They returned this morning half an hour before I usually leave for work. I wrecked part of our front lawn escaping them."

The rest of Zane followed his head. "Can they do that? Isn't there a law or something?"

"Not really. They didn't attack me. Technically they're reporters going after a story."

Zane snorted. "If they're reporters, I'm Bill Gates."

Giulia laughed. "When you get settled, come tell me what you discovered about AtlanticEdge. You know, whatever you were going to tell me on Saturday before the Great Roger Catfight."

Sidney came in at twenty to nine and announced, "I'm not in labor and I'm ready to train my replacement."

Giulia applauded from her desk.

"Mini-Sidney kept me up all weekend, so I am one cranky preggo lady."

Giulia called, "You couldn't be cranky if someone paid you to do it."

Sidney waddled into Giulia's doorway. "That's what Olivier says."

"That's what everyone who's known you for more than a week says."

Sidney considered the idea. "If I had to stay pregnant for eleven months like Jingle and Belle, I might be inspired to crankiness."

"You would be entitled."

Zane said in a pleading voice, "You're giving me the gross-outs with this pregnancy talk."

Sidney mouthed something unintelligible at Giulia, but Giulia knew they were thinking the same thing because their grins were identical. Giulia pulled out her tablet and logged onto The Before and After Shop's website. When she had the image she wanted, she brought the tablet out to Zane.

"Let me introduce you to placenta art."

Twenty-Eight

Zane's face shifted from incredulous to horrified to nauseated.

Giulia and Sidney laughed.

"I'm totally making a print from mini-Sidney's placenta," Sidney said. "Giulia gave me the kit at my baby shower."

The door opened and Jane Pierce came in, dressed in black trousers and a bright red sweater.

"Someone normal," Zane said. "Thank the gods. Come here, please, and prove I'm not alone in the world. Have you ever heard of...this?"

"Of what?" Jane walked up to Giulia and Sidney.

Giulia turned her tablet to face Jane, without explaining the image.

"Oh, yeah. Placenta art. My tattoo artist transfers them onto mothers in whatever size they want."

Zane escaped to his desk, placing his monitor between himself and the three women. "I am scarred for life."

Giulia tried to stop grinning and failed. "I love my job. Jane, I'm extremely relieved you showed up. Zane—good Heavens, you two rhyme. I promise not to start giving instructions in iambic pentameter. Zane, I forgot to ask you to make up a timesheet for Jane."

"Did it Friday before I left."

"Anticipating my needs again. And yet you still question my hiring acumen. Sidney, I leave Jane in your hands."

"No prob. Pull up my client chair, Jane. There's a lot to learn, but I promise it's all organized."

Giulia turned a wide-eyed, incredulous gaze on her.

Sidney made a repentant face. "Mostly organized."

Zane stood. "I can tell you the discovery now, Ms. Driscoll."

"Excellent. Come into my sanctum."

Zane dragged Giulia's client chair around next to Giulia's own desk chair. "You're already reading it?"

"It's a sanity break from The Roger Fitch Show."

"Okay. Close those files and bring up the surveillance videos."

"Which ones?" Giulia clicked several windows closed.

"Start with the week of November fifth, two years ago."

She double-clicked on the requested video file. Sharp black-and-white digital footage showed her the tops of several heads in the bookkeeping department, plus their desks and computer monitors. The screens pixilated, but otherwise all the elements were crisp and identifiable.

Zane pointed to a shaved brown head. "That's Leonard Tulley. He'll get up and go over to Loriela Gil's desk...now."

Tulley stood and walked to a larger desk in front of a wide window. Loriela Gil looked up and appeared to listen to and answer a question. She smiled without sincerity, the careful expression of an impersonal manager dealing with a subordinate.

"She doesn't like him," Giulia said. "When I spoke with him on Thursday, I got the impression he was jealous of losing his chance at her to Fitch."

Zane brought his face closer to the screen. "I don't see that."

"That's okay. What next?"

"Week of December fifteenth, same year."

In this video, Loriela bent over a redhead's desk. Giulia leaned away from the screen and narrowed her eyes. "Is that...yes, it is. Autumn Tate." Tate's fingers whitened on the pen she held. Loriela's index finger poked at the printouts on Tate's desk. She poked again and again, while Tate nodded and her fingers gripped tighter and tighter.

"She's one of my original five embezzlement suspects...If Loriela rode her like that, she may have stolen to prove she was smarter than her boss thinks."

"That's why I pulled this week," Zane said. "She wasn't on my list originally, but look at this progression."

For the next half-hour, Zane piled video on top of video. Len Tulley spent an inordinate part of each week hovering at Loriela's desk. Her smiles never got warmer. As the surveillance dates closed in on the last week of March before her murder, she stopped bothering to hide her impatience with Tulley.

Giulia opened the accounting files that corresponded with the last three months before Loriela's death.

"Zane, have you worked some analysis magic that connects Loriela's emasculation of Tulley to the embezzlement? Please say yes."

In reply, Zane got out of the chair and went to the connecting doorway. "Sidney, can you explain what you think you found with the surveillance videos and the purchase orders?"

"If I can heave myself out of this chair...Thanks, Jane." The sound of casters and a chair thumping against the wall. "You come too."

Both women lined up behind Giulia.

"Oh, you've already got the ledgers up." Sidney read the dates. "Not those. Go back to two summers earlier. We saw something that coincided with a Fourth of July sale of their retail stock."

Giulia minimized all the open files and found the ones for the end of the July Sidney wanted.

"Whoever designed their bookkeeping system is either clueless or devious," Sidney said. "We went for clueless first, because they still do business transactions with paper checks. But Zane came up with two companies a little bigger than AtlanticEdge who are still into paper too. So we voted for devious because, well, they had to hire us. See the multiple entries for software purchases the last week of June? Now go to the scanned purchase orders for that same week. Good. Now open the check images from the bank deposit."

Giulia manipulated all three windows until they crowded side by side on her monitor. "What am I looking for? No, don't tell me. Let me see if I can spot it."

She stared at one after the other. The ledger entries added up, at least in her head. When she enlarged the check images she compared the numerical dollar amounts versus the handwritten amounts.

"I didn't realize AtlanticEdge sold to this many smaller local businesses, but it makes sense. They're big on keeping money in the community."

She turned her scrutiny on the purchase orders. "The numbers match. The delivery dates match the entries in the ledger. The dollar amounts match." She pushed the heels of her hands into her eyes. "Too much staring at computer screens. Give me a second. Sidney, do you need to sit down?"

"Kinda. My ankles keep puffing up like water balloons."

Zane gave up the client chair to her. Jane dragged over Giulia's empty trash can and placed it upside down under Sidney's feet.

"Ohhhh, yes. That's what they needed." Sidney eased herself into a slouch. "This'll calm my back for about fifteen minutes."

"I promise not to take that long," Giulia said. "You've challenged me. Nobody say anything until I either spot something or give up."

She enlarged the first purchase order by date and its companion check. They looked identical to her. The next ones. Same result. She got through ten when the phone rang.

Zane picked it up at Giulia's desk. "Good morning, Driscoll Investigations."

A familiar voice spoke on the other end.

"I'll see if Ms. Driscoll is available, Mr. Fitch. One moment, please." He hit the hold button.

Giulia sighed and held out her hand. Zane took the call off hold.

"Giulia Falcone-Driscoll speaking. How may I help you, Mr. Fitch?"

"I want to apologize for that mess on Saturday." He actually did sound apologetic. "Can you meet me someplace? I'd like to explain things."

Giulia couldn't come up with an excuse. "It's almost ten o'clock. I have a brief window in half an hour. Where would you like to meet?"

"Colby's office is too far, huh? What about we take advantage of the weather and talk under that spiky abstract thing they call art in front of the library?"

"Fine. I'll meet you there at ten-thirty." She hung up.

"You know," she said to her three employees, "I never thought the relatively minor sins I've committed would merit this kind of punishment."

Sidney giggled.

"I can quote the Buddha on karmic balance," Zane said. "My sisters and brother would lecture you about the Rule of Three."

Jane kept quiet until Giulia twisted around in her chair. Then Jane said, "Don't look at me. Best I can come up with is 'it pays the bills.' My ex would blame it on Mercury Retrograde. He was famous for never taking responsibility." She gulped. "Uh—not that I mean you're not owning your own actions—er—sins, or whatever. I mean, um, what I was trying to say..."

Giulia dropped her face in her hand and laughed. "Jane, stop worrying. But try not to answer the phone 'til you're used to working under pressure, even the light pressure of this place." She straightened up. "Okay, everyone quiet again 'til I nail this."

She enlarged a purchase order with an attached order for a refund on unsold stock. Nothing there. She closed them at the same moment her brain said that it had seen something "off." She reopened the two scans.

"Son of a gun. The handwritten amount was one-zero-three-zero and it's been changed to one-zero-eight-zero. I can see the place where the other half of the eight doesn't quite match up." She shrank the document to its original size. "But when I look at it like this, it's seamless." She opened the ledger page. "The wholesale amounts would have less than," she scrolled down to an actual order for one thousand thirty units, "two hundred dollars' difference."

She tapped her nails in a syncopated rhythm on her desk.

"If I were going to rip off my prosperous employer, two hundred bucks is nothing," she said, mostly to herself. "But similar amounts skimmed often enough over the course of two-plus years, invested in a high-yield...no, no, that's traceable. Gambled with? Played the stock market with? Never enough to trigger an alarm during a cursory check of the books, so they could keep stealing until they decided they had enough. Do thieves ever feel they have enough?"

She swiveled to face Zane. "This is the first mistake you caught?"

"Yeah. Once I figured out what it was, I dragged Sidney onto it and we split June, July, and August of that year. Then we had to close up for the night because you said not to pull overtime unless we cleared it with you."

"No, no, you did the right thing..." Giulia stared at the documents on the screen. "When did old Mr. Howard have the stroke that forced his daughter to take over the company?"

Zane ran out to his computer and his fingers tapped his keyboard. "May twenty-third, last year."

"She was defending her thesis for her MBA then, right? Right. Dad was in the hospital, worry over that. Yanked from the intensive thesis process to wrangle nearly one thousand employees and a company worth half a million. She's twenty-five years old. Most, probably all, of the employees are older than her. She'd let them do their thing because it worked for Dad all these years. Zane, when does their fiscal year close?"

Zane reappeared in the doorway. "January thirty-first."

"Did someone complain about their bill or did she finally have time to look at the books? One after the other? Or did our embezzlers play with the numbers to shut the customer up? Both, I bet."

She closed the documents. "Zane, Sidney, you guys are fantastic. Sidney's training, so Zane, can you keep digging into the scans, now that you know what to look for? I've got to listen to Roger Fitch spread himself. Again."

"Already blocked out the day for it."

"Perfect. I'm going to bury myself in all things Silk Tie Murder until 3:30."

"What's happening at 3:30?" Sidney said.

"We might be unwilling TV stars."

Twenty-Nine

Giulia walked as fast as she could through the crowded sidewalks. She could see the roof of the art museum now across the stupidest, most dangerous intersection in the city. She'd perch beneath the sculpture's variegated spikes and try again to see it as a chrysanthemum, like the artist's plaque claimed.

"Hey, thanks for meeting me." Roger Fitch's boisterous voice appeared without warning out of the crowd.

"Good morning. Let's get out of this crush before we discuss Saturday."

They formed a two-person wall, pushing to the edge of the sidewalk as buses and delivery vans whooshed past. The light opposite turned yellow. A taxi sped up, the light turned red, and with a shout Fitch stumbled into the street. Giulia grabbed his arm and yanked him out of danger back onto the sidewalk. The taxi leaned on its horn and kept going. Giulia sat down hard. Fitch landed next to her.

The other people on the curb crowded tighter around them.

"Are you okay?"

"Idiot cab driver!"

"Somebody call 9-1-1."

"Nah, they're not hurt. You're not hurt, are you, lady?"

"Back off, people. Give them some air."

Traffic zoomed past. Giulia pulled her trembling feet farther in from the curb. Her hands shook from the adrenaline rush too.

"Are you all right?" she asked Fitch. "What happened?"

Fitch looked up at the faces all around them. "Somebody pushed me. Who pushed me, you sons of bitches? Let go of me, Driscoll." He jerked himself free of Giulia's quick cautionary grip.

At the word "pushed" Giulia's brain rattled back into its professional gears. "Are you sure?"

"Of course I'm sure. Somebody shoved me right between my shoulders. How the hell else would I fall off a three-inch curb?"

He got to his knees, then his feet. The half-dozen concerned bystanders gave him more space.

"Now you recognize me? Yeah, I'm supposed to be the Silk Tie Killer. So what? Ever hear of innocent until proven guilty? Ever hear of the justice system?"

Giulia reached up and put her hands on his arm again. "Mr. Fitch, this isn't a good idea."

He shook her off. "Which one of you tried to commit murder by taxi? Huh? Got the guts to look me in the face?"

Two women at the outer edge of the circle faded away, their steps lost in the traffic noises. The light turned green for the second time since the near-accident. A mother picked up her preschool-age son and crossed the street. Two men in suits followed, then an older woman with a purse big enough for an overnight trip. By the time the light shone red again, a new group of people surrounded Fitch and Giulia, still giving them breathing space.

"You okay, lady? Need a hand?"

Giulia smiled up at the teenager in a hoodie and ripped jeans who probably should have been in school. "Thanks, no. I'm okay." She clambered up, checked her purse, and rubbed her tailbone.

"Mr. Fitch, this serves no purpose. Let's get over to the museum's lawn."

She waited a four-second gap in traffic to cross the street and made for the gray steel chrysanthemum without checking for Fitch. When she sat on one of the green benches beneath the sculpture, Fitch sat beside her a moment later.

"Don't start," he said. "Somebody shoved me. I can't prove it.

That doesn't make me a liar. It's no secret I've got a lot of haters in this town. Any one of them would love to hurry me down to hell and save the taxpayers the cost of the trial." He rubbed his left shoulder. "Feels like somebody tried to pull my arm out of the socket."

Giulia gave him a tight smile. "You're welcome."

"Huh? What are you talking about?" He stopped rubbing. "Wait a minute...I'm not a speed bump right about now because somebody dragged me back onto the sidewalk. You?"

"Yes, me."

"Sheesh. Thanks. Didn't mean to be an asshole. Got caught up in the moment."

"You're welcome," Giulia said with less ice this time. "I agree that you won't be able to prove someone pushed you into traffic. My advice is not to waste time in speculation. Let's concentrate on the reason you hired us in the first place."

"Good girl—woman. First, though, I want to apologize for what happened with Tammy and Angie on Saturday."

"I might suggest you not string two women along simultaneously, but that's your business."

He looked rueful for the first time since the initial meeting in Colby Petit's office. "Things got away from me after the indictment. Lousy day for *The Scoop* to track me down. Perfect timing for them. Kanning and his stooge hugged the walls while I tried to pull my girls off each other, then the mike and the camera swooped in. I kicked those bloodsuckers out as soon as I could, but Angie ran after them, talking a mile a minute."

"So it wasn't you who gave my name to *The Scoop*?"

"Oh, uh, no. I wouldn't sic them on anybody, including Madre Cassandra, and that's saying a lot."

"Well, they're stalking me at home and at church. I'm not looking forward to five o'clock today."

"Why? Oh. You think they'll be outside your door."

Giulia would've sworn on her mother's grave that Fitch was thinking, *That means they won't be outside mine.*

A taco truck pulled up to the curb in front of them and started to set up for the lunch crowd. Beef marinated in cumin and chili powder saturated the air. Giulia wondered if they had enchilada fixings in the freezer for supper.

She brought herself back to Fitch on the bench next to her. "You'll be pleased—or not—to hear that both Henri Richard and Lacy Maples are no longer on our informal list of suspects in Ms. Gil's murder."

"Shit. How come?"

"He moved to Chicago long before last April and she was in the hospital with appendicitis for the week surrounding the murder."

He didn't bother to hide his annoyance. "Who does that leave, then?"

"Leonard Tulley, Shirley Travers, Colby Petit, and you."

He blustered. "But I told you—"

"Mr. Fitch, I'm in charge of this case. No possibility is excluded until I obtain definitive evidence to the contrary. If this is unacceptable to you, we can terminate the contract and I'll bill you through the court for time spent."

He flinched. Giulia patted herself on the back.

"No, no, of course I don't want to fire you. Who else can pull my ass out of the death chamber?" His charming smile flashed out. "I need a beer to celebrate my escape from death. Want to join me so I can toast my life-saver?"

"Thank you, no. I have a busy morning still." She stood. "Hopefully I won't be watching myself get ambushed by *The Scoop* this afternoon on TV."

He chuckled. "There's no such thing as bad publicity, Ms. Driscoll." His head swiveled in the direction of the food truck. "I want a taco."

"Good morning, Mr. Fitch."

"See you later." He walked toward the open side of the truck.

Giulia started back to her office, thinking that if the death penalty loomed over *her*, she'd hit Common Grounds twice a day for a new flavor of coffee.

Thirty

"Giulia Falcone-Driscoll for Mr. Petit, please."

She stared at the phone keypad, willing Fitch's lawyer to pick up before *The Scoop's* TV show started. Fifteen minutes should be plenty of time for him to dredge up his high school memories for her.

Click. A different voice than Cathy's, the receptionist Giulia shared recipes with. "Ms. Driscoll? Mr. Petit is on another call, but he should be no more than five minutes. Are you able to wait?"

"Yes."

"Thank you." *Click.*

Giulia put the call on speaker and took a red Sharpie over to the clue collage pinned to the wall next to her door. She drew fat red Xs over bartender Jonathan Stallone's pages and a line through Lacy Maples' name on the extra page she'd added yesterday. The one she'd headed "People Thrown Under the Bus."

Click. "Ms. Driscoll? Colby Petit. What can I do for you?"

"A few questions for you, Mr. Petit." Tact. A bucketful of tact. "I understand you and Roger Fitch went to the same high school."

A sound as though the lawyer swallowed a bite of very late lunch. "Pardon me. Crazy day. Yes, Roger and I graduated from the same school."

"Specifically, in the same class. And you were both on the basketball team."

Wariness and puzzlement came through the speaker with the next drawn-out word: "Yes."

"Also that Roger bested you at the sport, relegating you to the bench while the five starters, Roger among them, achieved glory." Not tactful enough. Blast.

A longer silence. "I see. It's been implied that a sixteen-year-old grudge drove me to murder Roger's girlfriend and pin the blame on him." Papers rattling. A metallic *clunk*. A curse. "I just spilled my soda. Let me put you on hold."

Giulia stared at the phone through the peculiar dead silence of hold-limbo. A lawyer known for his glib tongue had to resort to a fake spill to buy time. She flipped over to a new page on her current legal pad and wrote "Colby Petit" on it with the red Sharpie.

Click. "Ms. Driscoll, the idea that anyone would orchestrate a convoluted murder as much-belated revenge must sound as ludicrous to you as it does to me. If it were presented to me as part of a case, my first action would be to explore the motives of the accuser."

"Mr. Petit, neither of us needs to teach the other how to do their job. Thanks for confirming the information. I'll let you get back to your lunch."

She ended the call while she had the upper hand. Five minutes to the show. She swapped a ballpoint pen for the Sharpie and wrote several questions and notes to look things up. If nothing panned out fast enough, she'd try pumping Tulley for information this time instead of bile. Fitch's natural fear of the death penalty made him an unreliable source.

Her speaker buzzed. "Three minutes, Ms. Driscoll."

Giulia capped the pen and ran out to the main office. Everyone was crowded around Sidney's monitor.

"So I don't have to stand up," she said to Giulia.

"Smart." Giulia swapped places with Zane, who positioned his taller self between Giulia's shoulder and Sidney's head.

Sidney clicked on the streaming window and it filled the screen. As soon as a commercial faded to black, she un-muted the sound. A drumroll began, soft at first but reaching a dramatic crescendo within five seconds. The screen softened from black to gray and a dramatic clash of cymbals, trumpets, and French horns followed. The screen changed one final time, to pure white, and a deep voice imitated James Earl Jones' classic CNN introduction, "This...is *The Scoop*."

Sidney giggled. "Are they for real?"

Ken Kanning's face with its gleaming smile and sculpted cheekbones appeared in the middle of the screen.

"*The Scoop* exists to bring you the news the other outlets don't dare report. We give you, our loyal Scoopers, news you didn't know you needed to hear." A grim yet sincere expression replaced the smile. "In today's edition, Cottonwood's story of the year: The Silk Tie Murder. A callous killer, his new women, and the amoral private eye working to set a killer loose among our unsuspecting citizens. This footage may not be appropriate for younger viewers, so please send the kids into another room."

The camera pulled back until Kanning's entire torso came into view. The background changed to the pattern of the tie used to strangle Loriela Gil.

"And now, *The Scoop* presents: The Silk Tie Murder."

"Heaven help us," Giulia murmured.

Kanning's voice-over gave the high points of the story starting with Fitch's 9-1-1 call the morning of April second last year to his indictment for Loriela's murder thirteen weeks ago. Video clips of Fitch's initial arrest and his release two days later. A replay of the bar fight video with *The Scoop*'s lurid commentary. Kanning depicted Cassandra as the world's worst mother-in-law. Loriela got the sainthood treatment. Jonathan Stallone and Henri Richard blipped into and out of Loriela's life as failed suitors. *The Scoop* had access to none of the AtlanticEdge information, which meant no mention of Shirley Travers and a lot of vague praise about Loriela's rise to Head of Accounting and her bright future prospects, cut short by Fitch's silk tie. As the show went to commercial Roger Fitch's mug shot filled the screen.

"What creative journalism, and I use the latter word loosely," Giulia said.

"It's half over and they haven't reached last Saturday's catfight," Zane said. "Maybe they'll run out of time and concentrate on the fight more than us."

Giulia shook her head. "We can only hope."

The show returned from commercials with a reprise of its opening music.

"*The Scoop* is always looking under the rocks people are afraid to turn over," Kanning said, his Serious Face onscreen again. "But you know our motto, Scoopers: The juiciest stories lurk in the darkest places."

Zane laughed. Sidney shushed him.

Kanning dissolved into an exterior shot of Fitch's apartment building.

"Evil still inhabits one of these luxury apartments. Our clairvoyant, Madame Aurore, will perform a spiritual cleansing live on next week's show."

"Aurore?" Zane said. "She's the biggest charlatan in Pittsburgh. The Pagan community cringes whenever her name comes up."

"Shush!" Sidney said.

Kanning, on tape now, spoke to the camera in the apartment building's parking lot. "...got a tip that things were happening in the apartment Roger Fitch uses for his trysts. The apartment he and Loriela Gil purchased together, decorated together, and shared together until last April first."

The camera cut to a new shot of Kanning in the hall outside Fitch's door.

"I don't know if you can hear what we hear, Scoopers, but someone behind this door isn't very happy. Let's find out together what's going on."

The camera swung around as Kanning rang the bell.

In her office, Giulia watched herself open Fitch's door.

Kanning's microphone obscured the lower half of Giulia's face. "Ken Kanning here with *The Scoop* at The Silk Tie Killer's apartment. Miss, are you Roger Fitch's new girlfriend? Don't you worry that one of his ties will end up around your neck?"

On-screen Giulia's face replaced its startled expression with one that resembled a shuttered window. "Please move and let me by." Her voice was as expressionless as her face.

One of the girlfriends screeched behind Giulia. The camera's spotlight picked out Angie's blonde hair. At the same instant, she picked up Tammy's blue-flowered casserole and heaved it. Tammy ducked.

The camera jiggled for a second, then righted. The casserole dish shattered, splattering meat, rice, and sauce around the hallway, in Fitch's hair, and on the camera lens.

Ken Kanning's arm pushed Giulia aside. The camera followed his bouncing hair as his head swiveled back to the camera and forward to watch the show.

"We're at Ground Zero, Scoopers! Two furious women are tearing up accused murderer Roger Fitch's apartment. What kind of man revels in this behavior? What kind of women fight over a man who might already be measuring their lovely necks for one of his silk ties?"

Angie tripped Tammy and they both crashed to the floor. More censoring *bleeps* than actual language came from Sidney's computer speakers. Tammy clawed up a handful of her ruined sticky beef and smeared it on the blonde's face.

Angie hooked two fingers into the redhead's left chandelier earring and yanked. The camera zoomed closer in time to get a few drops of blood on the lens on top of the drying food.

Both women screamed. Blood streamed from Tammy's ripped earlobe. Angie brought her hand to her face and it came away brown with sauce and red with her own blood.

Fitch knelt on the floor next to the two women, napkins in both hands. The screams' volume dimmed and Kanning took over.

"Violence and bloodshed continues to surround The Silk Tie Killer. How can anyone with reasoning powers doubt he deserves death for Loriela Gil's savage murder?"

The women and Fitch engaged in more bleeped-out

conversation. Fitch left the camera's line of sight and returned jingling his car keys.

"Come on, Tams, Angie. You've got a date with Urgent Care."

More bleeps directed at Fitch.

Kanning stuck his face and microphone in the middle of the Roger/Tammy/Angie sandwich. "Roger Fitch, how can you pretend to care about these women when you left Loriela Gil's still-warm body in the rain on that very balcony?" He pointed to his left.

Fitch stood and said directly into the bloody camera lens, "Get that piece of *bleep* out of my face or I'll shove that light so far down your throat you'll be able to use your *bleep* for a nightlight."

Zane choked with laughter. Sidney and Jane snickered. Giulia facepalmed.

The scene switched to the exterior of Saint Thomas' church in late morning light.

"Oh, no," Giulia murmured.

All three of her employees turned to look at her.

Kanning's voice again: "It's Sunday morning, Scoopers. We're outside Saint Thomas' Catholic Church on Garrett Street. Inside is the head of Driscoll Investigations, the private investigators Roger Fitch hired to cherry-pick evidence and bully the prosecution's witnesses. If they succeed, a murderer will walk the streets of Cottonwood, a free man. The streets where your daughters and sisters walk. Will any of them be safe again?"

The camera zoomed in on Kanning's face. "The head of Driscoll Investigations claims to be God-fearing. She attends church on a regular basis. She used to be a nun—yes, Scoopers, she was once a real, live nun. Why would someone like that take money from a cold-blooded murderer to save him from the ignominious death he so richly deserves?"

"This isn't good." Sidney adjusted herself and mini-Sidney in her chair.

The camera refocused on Saint Thomas' as the church's double doors opened. A jump cut framed Giulia and Father Carlos talking and laughing on the top of the front steps.

"There she is, Scoopers," Kanning stage whispered. "Never fear, in a few minutes we'll get her to give us her excuses from her own hypocritical lips."

Giulia descended to the sidewalk and walked around the side of the church toward the parking lot. Kanning ran toward her, his image bouncing as the cameraman followed him. They angled to the left and cut her off. She stopped when Kanning planted himself and his microphone directly in front of her.

"Scoopers, this is Giulia Falcone-Driscoll, investigating the Silk Tie Murder! Mrs. Falcone-Driscoll, tell us how a former nun can sleep at night knowing you're helping a cold-blooded killer get off scot-free?"

"The camera makes my hair look like I've been fighting high winds." Giulia reached up and tried to smooth it. Sidney pulled her arm down.

Onscreen, Kanning's microphone hovered half an inch from her nose. Once again, Giulia's face became an expressionless mask. She pushed aside the microphone and walked toward Frank's Camry quickly, but not running.

"Come on, Mrs. Falcone-Driscoll." Kanning and the camera followed her. "The Silk Tie Murder Case is number one with our viewers and you have the inside track. What do you know about Roger Fitch's two girlfriends trashing his apartment?"

Giulia kept walking, her back ruler-straight. The camera kept the same two-foot gap between them. Its spotlight threw her shadow on the faded asphalt.

"Mrs. Falcone-Driscoll, does your conscience keep you awake at night? Don't Catholics have to go to confession when they sin? Is that what you were talking to the priest about?"

Giulia slipped into the Camry and Frank drove away. Kanning turned to the camera, using the Camry's exit as his backdrop.

"Her silence speaks for itself, Scoopers. Just goes to show you can't trust anyone, not even the kindly nuns who teach our children their prayers. Tune in next Monday at three-thirty when we'll be broadcasting live from the Silk Tie Murder trial. For *The Scoop*, this is Ken Kanning reminding you: The juiciest stories lurk in the darkest places. And we bring them to you every week."

The dramatic fanfare played over the closing credits. Sidney stopped the feed.

"Scum buckets," Jane said.

"Agreed," Giulia said.

Sidney said, "What do we do?"

"Nothing. We have to take the high road on this. We don't respond to anybody. If they call here, we hang up without replying. If they come to the door, we lock it. We don't give them the tiniest opening."

The phone rang. Giulia cringed.

Zane answered at Sidney's desk. "Good afternoon, Driscoll Investigations...One moment, please."

He held the receiver out to her. "It's Mr. Driscoll."

She took it. "Go ahead. I'm ready."

"You left that food fight before the good part," Frank said, laughter in his voice. "Jimmy's forcing me to tell you that since you can handle two crazed females and *The Scoop*, you can certainly handle working here. I already refused the offer for you."

"Don't tell me everyone in the building saw the show."

"Of course. I have a famous wife now."

Giulia groaned. "Infamous is the word you want."

The second line rang. Zane ran over to his own desk.

"I'll let you go," Frank said. "I can hear your public calling."

"Thank you, dear. You're so supportive."

Frank laughed again and hung up.

Zane put this call on hold. "It's the producer for *The Scoop*."

Giulia pinched the bridge of her nose. "I definitely need to remember what sins I'm being punished for. They must have been spectacular."

She nodded at Zane and he transferred the call to Sidney's phone.

"This is Giulia Falcone-Driscoll."

A forceful voice with a polite overlay. "This is Nina Steele for

The Scoop. Ken Kanning would like to schedule a one-on-one interview with you for the Silk Tie Murder special airing next Sunday night."

"Thank you for the offer, but we're not interested."

"But Ms. Falcone-Driscoll..."

Giulia hung up. "I've cut off more phone calls this week than I have in the past fifteen years."

"Which means one, right?" Sidney said.

"Two."

"I never expected it of you. What will Jane think?"

Giulia stuck out the tip of her tongue at Sidney. Sidney reciprocated. Jane got that startled look again.

The phone rang.

"Aargghh." Giulia waited for Zane to give her the bad news.

He pressed hold. "It's Roger Fitch."

"Saint Monica, give me patience."

All three of her employees got the same confused expression.

"It's a Catholic thing. Sidney, you should know that. I'll tell Father Pat on you." She nodded at Zane and he transferred this call too. "Yes, Mr. Fitch?"

"Awesome show, wasn't it?" Delight filled Fitch's voice.

"I wouldn't put it that way."

"What do you mean? Kanning is biased against us so bad we should get sympathy votes from everybody who's been on the fence." Fitch chuckled. "I can't wait for Kanning to eat his hat when you prove I didn't kill Lori."

"I'll get back to working your case now, Mr. Fitch. Thank you for calling." She depressed the switch hook, listened to the beautiful silence for a second, and hung up.

She looked at the clock over the door. "It's 4:20. I hereby declare this workday over."

Giulia's phone rang at 1:17 the next morning. She wriggled one arm out from under Frank's and groped on the nightstand.

"Mmrgh...h'lo?"

"Wake up, Driscoll!" Roger Fitch's voice.

"Mmm...Fitch?"

"Of course it is. Must be nice to sleep all cozy and worry free."

Giulia moved the rest of her body out from under Frank's leg and slipped out of bed. When she was in the spare bedroom, she said in a quiet voice, "Mr. Fitch, has something happened?"

"Why the hell else would I call you in the middle of the night? Tulley and I spent a few hours at Long Neck letting the regulars buy me drinks for the full story of Angie and Tammy's fight."

Giulia yawned. "Did you call at this hour to tell me bar stories?"

"God da—Of course not. I got back to my place and somebody'd broken in and trashed everything. Busted my TV, threw paint on the rugs and the walls, stole my Xbox—"

"Call the police, Mr. Fitch."

"Are you kidding? You have to help me. The local cops all hate me."

The whining anger in his voice penetrated her sleep-muddled brain. "Too bad. This is a crime. Report it."

She ended the call, turned off her phone, and crawled back into bed.

Frank pulled her against his body and she shivered as she absorbed his warmth.

"Tell me in the morning," he muttered.

Thirty-One

Zane held out four slips of paper as soon as Giulia opened the office door.

"Monsignor Harris, Mingmei Burd, Laurel Drury from Stage Door Soup Kitchen, and Colby Petit."

Giulia set down her Godzilla mug and took the messages. "A senior official of the local church has no business watching slimy daytime TV."

"He sounded annoyed but not angry. The soup kitchen lady wants to make sure you're okay. Mingmei said to tell you that an eyebrow piercing will make TV audiences remember you better."

Giulia huffed. "She only says that to get a rise out of me. Thanks, Zane. I'm locking myself into my office to deal with these."

"Right. Only interrupt you for fire or nuclear war."

"Good man."

Giulia left a message on Mingmei's voicemail that amounted to a long, enthusiastic raspberry. She caught Laurel as she chased her two-year old daughter who once again was running naked through their condo giggling in delight as mama chased her.

"Laurel, tell Katie that Aunt Giulia says no more tickle fights unless she gets dressed."

When Laurel relayed the message, Katie let loose a high-pitched squeal.

"You're a life saver," Laurel said. "I'm subbing at the soup kitchen for one of our early shift regulars who fell and fractured his hip. Of course that means Katie's having one of her ball of energy mornings."

"I'd much rather be back working at your soup kitchen. *The Scoop* hadn't heard of me then."

"Katie, bring mama your socks." A scuffle and more giggles. "I need to bottle her energy and sell it."

Giulia laughed. "I'm sure you're only the millionth mother to wish for that."

A *clunk* as the phone hit the floor. A second later Laurel's voice returned. "Just wait 'til you and Frank have kids. I will sit on your couch and eat popcorn and—Katie!"

"I'll talk to you on the weekend. Go wrangle your sweet little princess."

"Hah. Don't give *The Scoop* any ammunition."

Fortified with Katie giggles, Giulia dialed the number on Colby Petit's message. When he answered, Giulia heard traffic and the BBC news report.

"Hello?" Petit's voice echoed.

"It's Giulia Falcone-Driscoll, Mr. Petit."

"Oh, good. Let me mute the radio." The cultured female voice disappeared. "Thanks for calling back. I'm stuck on 376 fifty cars behind a jackknifed semi. I gather you watched *The Scoop* yesterday."

"Unfortunately, yes."

"They're calling my office, but—" a barrage of car horns interrupted him—"our receptionist is adept at stonewalling unwanted reporters. Have they harassed you since the Sunday morning church episode?"

"Did you doubt it? I've avoided them so far. We worked up several strategies to keep out of their searchlight." She paused for a siren.

"Another police car has joined the party." Petit's smooth voice showed only a hint of annoyance. "Unless he's a tow truck in disguise, there's no point in him adding to the chaos."

Giulia fished a cranberry granola bar out of her bottom

drawer. "Mr. Petit, did you need anything in particular?"

"Sorry. Yes. Roger told you his place was broken into and vandalized."

"He called after one a.m. to whine. I told him to report it to the police."

Petit chuckled, the sound barely registering against the horns and distant sirens. "He called me right afterward. I gave him the same advice. He's not pleased with either of us."

Giulia unwrapped the granola. "I'm not concerned with whether or not he likes me. My job is to search through the evidence and see if someone else might be the Silk Tie Killer."

"Yes, of course. I really called you to put the high school rivalry story in its grave."

"I see." Giulia scrabbled for her legal pad and a pen. "Yesterday you belittled the idea."

"There. That skeptical tone in your voice is why I called. Athletes have rivalries. It's one of the ways we keep up a healthy level of competition." A pause, even though the noise on his end hadn't increased. "Roger was known for his charm and cleverness, but 'devious' would have been a more exact term. He bested me on the basketball team with his technique."

"Mr. Petit..."

"Ms. Driscoll, I'm not talking about his jump shot or his defense. I'm talking about his ability to skirt the edge of foul territory without getting caught." More sirens. "Thank God, they're clearing a lane for us to get out of this mess. Roger won that starting position because he cheated."

"A surprising comment from Fitch's defense attorney." She wrote it all down in a makeshift shorthand.

"That's not—I mean, you're misinterpreting me."

"If I am, please explain."

"Ms. Driscoll, you've heard of my record in the courtroom."

"Of course."

"Then you'll have realized I have a reputation for championing the underdog, much like Driscoll Investigations. The concept of a person's ability to change is at the heart of it. That's why I'm representing Roger. He's still a jerk and a blowhard and a womanizer, but I don't allow those qualities to prejudice me in this matter."

Giulia heard the implied, "And neither should you."

"Point taken, Mr. Petit. Is there anything else?"

"Not from me. Good luck avoiding *The Scoop*."

"And to you."

Giulia ate her granola bar as she reread her notes. "He must realize every word of that conversation makes him more of a suspect." She buzzed Sidney. "Is there any chance Colby Petit is in humongous debt and using Fitch to skim money from AtlanticEdge?"

Through the intercom, Sidney whistled. "Does 'slim to none' count? His name doesn't come up in any connection or on any document."

Giulia sighed. "I didn't think so. I've got to return one more call, then I'm going to immerse myself in the AtlanticEdge shenanigans."

Zane's voice added, "If Loriela Gil hadn't died, I would've bet money she and Fitch were the masterminds."

"I agree," Giulia said, "but it's gone on too long after her death. Zane, you and I are working this together, right?"

"Yes. Can we afford the time wasted with two people going over the same round?"

"Absolutely, and it's the opposite of wasted time. In a perfect world we both come out with identical lists of altered documents."

"Oh. Got it."

Giulia called the diocese. Monsignor Harris—the one who didn't belong in the fourteenth century—expressed sympathy and commended her force of will on camera.

"Before you ask, Ms. Driscoll, one of our cleaning staff watches TV on her phone while working. She thinks we don't know. She came running into the kitchen when she saw your face onscreen. We're all pretending that she didn't see it while on the job."

"Thank you for spinning it for the Bishop."

"Frankly, he's so pleased with your results that you'd have to commit a mortal sin live on the six o'clock news to shake his confidence in you."

"I can state with confidence that no such plans are in my future."

After she hung up, she stared at her shadowy reflection in her monitor and shelved for the moment any homicidal thoughts relating to Roger Fitch. "Falcone, you've turned mercenary."

For the next two hours, she pulled up scans of checks and purchase orders and cross-checked them with AtlanticEdge accounting ledgers. Now that she knew what to look for, it was much like buying a green hatchback and suddenly seeing green hatchbacks on the roads everywhere.

Threes became eights several more times. Ones became sevens and fours became nines, but never as the leading digit. Most of the alterations occurred on the small business orders and the majority of those on special pricing promotions. A few daring changes appeared on yearly and half-yearly consulting and setup contracts for the larger clients.

And there was no distinct pattern. No wonder it had taken her, Zane, and Sidney this long to break through. Giulia muttered several words her Sicilian grandmother had taught her and then forbidden her to repeat. She refused to give Fitch points for cleverness. An ingenious thief was still a thief.

At the end of the scans and ledger sheets, she stretched her back and stuck the heels of her hands into her dried-out eyes. Her handwritten list of ninety-two altered documents spanned two and a third years. Roger Fitch had written or signed off on all the purchase orders. Not surprising for the head of the two-person sales department.

The ledgers were all computerized, so there were no handwriting samples to compare them with. Not that it needed comparing. Len Tulley was the only employee in accounting whose employment spanned the entire period. Loriela Gil worked there for the first fifteen months of the thefts, so there was a definite possibility she'd known what Fitch and Tulley were up to.

Which made her a good target for murder if she'd threatened to blow them in.

Giulia stood, got her balance, and opened her door.

"Fitch and Tulley," she said to Zane.

"Ninety-seven instances," he said.

"Blast. I only found ninety-two."

"What about Gil or Tate?"

"The videos don't support Tate. Gil might have suspected them, but she died a year ago and the embezzlement continued."

Zane frowned. "I suppose so. Why not Miles Park?"

"A gut feeling. I can't see Roger Fitch bringing his sales subordinate in on such an elaborate scheme. If Fitch and Tulley trust each other, why split their loot three ways?"

Jane said from Sidney's desk, "You came up with all those answers from two hours of research?"

"More like eight solid days of research," Zane said.

"Nothing comes easy," Giulia added.

"No argument there," Jane said.

"I need food," Giulia said. "Is anyone going out?"

"We could order in," Sidney said, and the door opened.

Thirty-Two

A middle-aged man wearing the jacket of a local courier service stood in the doorway.

"Uh, Giulia Driscoll?" he read from the nine-by-twelve envelope in his hand.

"That's me." She came forward.

"Sign here, please." He offered her a pen and she wrote her name on the carbonless delivery slip attached to the back of the envelope. He tore off the top sheet and traded her the envelope for the pen. "Have a nice day." He closed the door when he left.

"At least I know this isn't from the Diocese officially severing our business relationship." Giulia eased a finger under the flap and ripped open the envelope. She pulled out a single sheet of printer paper and read its message out loud.

"Be at the Maple Road Park shelter number two at 9:00 tonight if you want to be certain about Roger Fitch."

She turned over the paper. Nothing else. Zane, Sidney, and Jane watched her, the latter with both eyebrows raised. Giulia acknowledged the skepticism.

"This is straight out of a *Scooby-Doo* episode. Maybe one of the women in his apartment on Saturday is still angry."

"Maybe it's from Leonard Tulley," Zane said. "You know, to throw us off the trail."

Giulia considered. "It's possible. He didn't remove his easygoing ex-jock mask by accident during our interview. Sidney?"

Sidney finished readjusting herself and mini-Sidney. "My vote goes for one of the girlfriends. Olivier used to date this drama major and when they split up...oh, man. For something like two months she called him every day and night, screaming and crying. When she threatened to kill his next girlfriend—which'd be me—he called in the campus police and her department advisor."

"How did it end?" Giulia said.

"She started sleeping with the campus cop they sent to talk to her."

Giulia laughed. "You can't make up a story like that."

"I know, right? At least she stopped bothering me and Olivier."

"Two votes for one of the girlfriends, one for the accountant." Giulia reread the plain black type centered on the page. "What if Fitch wrote this?"

"He's that devious?" Zane said.

"After three years of skillful embezzlement? What do you think?"

"Good point. I volunteer to get Chinese takeout."

"Excellent. Shrimp mei fun for me, please. Jane, did you brown-bag or do you want to get in on Chinese?"

A shy smile altered Jane's tough persona. "Thanks. Now that I'm working I can afford lunch."

Giulia didn't embarrass her by pointing out that she should have known Giulia wasn't the type of boss to exclude Jane from their company rituals because she was both new and a temp.

Giulia returned to her desk and called Frank.

He answered from a suspiciously quiet office. "Anything wrong?"

"This isn't a basketball night, so are you free between eight and ten?"

"Yeah. Our next sting is still in its infancy. Why?"

"I received a plain brown envelope with a plain white anonymous letter—typed, of course—telling me to be at Maple Road Park at nine tonight where All Will Be Revealed."

He choked. "It actually said that?"

"No, silly man. It said I'll learn important information. To get this information, I will require a strong, handsome detective to protect me. Are you up for the challenge?"

"You know it. Think Fitch has gone off the deep end?"

"Not him. We're divided over here. Two for one of the food-fight girlfriends, one for Fitch's ex-jock co-worker."

"If it's one of his girlfriends, make sure you don't wear big earrings."

Giulia laughed. "You either. Pork chops for supper."

"Oh, yeah. I'll do anything for a pork chop."

"I'll make a note of that."

Giulia and Frank waited in the Nunmobile for the car clock to reach nine p.m. The half-moon illuminated the area less than Giulia liked, but at least it wasn't cloudy or raining.

Frank wore all black, including the knit hat covering his ginger buzz cut. He would blend in nicely with the darkness to maintain the illusion she'd kept the appointment alone. Giulia wore a bright white jacket paired with the neon-green pants all the Driscolls wore for a family photo last St. Patrick's Day.

"They can see you from space in that outfit," Frank said.

"All the better to give a potential attacker pause. There. Nine o'clock."

She opened her door and stood by it to let Frank squirm across the seats and crouch around the back. When he was clear, she closed it and crossed the grass to the picnic shelter. She couldn't hear Frank following her, but she didn't have to. He'd be close enough to help her restrain a crazed girlfriend or accountant before any damage could occur. She loved him for wanting to protect her, but sometimes she wondered if he'd forgotten she'd passed three different self-defense courses and had a gun license.

"Hello?" She peered into the shelter.

"Are you alone?" The whisper from the dark sounded neither male nor female.

"Yes." A lie of course.

"Are you prepared for the truth about Roger Fitch?"

"Yes. What do you have to tell me?"

A thin figure in all black stepped out of the darkest corner of the shelter. A hoodie concealed the face, but it wasn't baggy enough to conceal its feminine shape.

Score one for Giulia and Sidney. "Are you Angie or Tammy or somebody else Fitch tossed aside?"

A sound of wordless rage sounded from beneath the hood. A hand emerged from the pocket and yanked the hood backward. Angie. Giulia was glad there was nothing for her to throw.

"That piece of shit thinks he can humiliate me and get away with it." When she spoke, the cuts on her face from the shards of glass her rival had attacked her with moved like bloodworms.

"What do you have to tell me?" Giulia kept her voice steady.

"I don't know if Roger strangled that Loriela Gil, but you need to check out where he's getting all his money." She pointed a long fingernail at Giulia. "He says it's because the bar's doing good business. You know he's part-owner of Long Neck, right?"

"Yes."

"Of course you do. You're a detective. You don't look like one. You look like a schoolteacher. That's pretty good camouflage."

Giulia sighed inwardly at one more nail in the coffin of her hopes to look like a *Cosmo* woman.

"Roger took me on a pricey weekend to New York City last Christmas," Angie said. "Penthouse suite with room service—in the City! Then he gave me real diamond earrings on Christmas morning. That was before he got tired of me." That incoherent anger returned to her face. "I'm telling you he isn't making that kind of cash at his day job."

Giulia said after a beat, "You think he might be laundering money through the bar."

Angie's smile was feral. "I want you to nail him for it."

A spotlight flooded the shelter.

"You heard it here first, Scoopers! Roger Fitch is a murderer *and* a thief! His ex-girlfriend, Angie Rossler, agreed to work with us to put the Silk Tie Killer in the Death Chamber where he belongs."

Giulia stiffened at that predatory voice. With an effort she achieved the expressionless mask she'd started to refer to as her Scoop Face. The camera turned on her.

"Ken Kanning with *The Scoop*, here in the dead of night with the head of Driscoll Investigations. Well, Mrs. Falcone-Driscoll, are you prepared to admit you've been working for a murderer?"

Giulia kept her voice even. "Nine p.m. is hardly the dead of night. Thank you for your information, Angie."

She turned and walked back to her car, thinking that her butt looked huge in the screaming-green pants, and would probably be all over *The Scoop*'s show tomorrow.

She didn't dare look around for Frank. He wouldn't come near the car with that camera trained on her, but it wasn't a cold night. She could come back for him later. *The Scoop* probably wouldn't stay more than half an hour getting location shots and finishing up with Angie. Maybe.

When she latched her seat belt, Frank's voice whispered from the backseat, "It's me. Drive."

Giulia drove straight home, fitting puzzle pieces from Long Neck's bank balance into the AtlanticEdge jigsaw. As soon as the garage door closed them inside, Frank unfolded himself and sat up.

"I'm not built for the fetal position anymore."

"Some backup you are." Giulia let herself out.

He followed. "I knew you were safe the minute they turned on the camera light. They used night vision for your meeting with the ex-girlfriend. I heard most of your conversation before I snuck back to the car when the spotlight made it too risky for me to hang around. You didn't give anything away that'll hurt you on TV." He patted her butt. "Those pants, on the other hand..."

"Don't remind me. They were all I thought of as I walked back to the car. Won't they make me look great on TV?" She tossed her purse on the kitchen counter. "There's no legitimate reason for DI to talk the judge into issuing a subpoena for the Long Neck's books, is there?"

Thirty-Three

Giulia walked into work on Wednesday, said a general "good morning," and hung up her jacket. When she turned toward the room again, all three DI employees formed a blockade across the narrow space between Zane's desk and the opposite wall.

"Well? Did you go? Who was it? What happened?"

Giulia struck a pose with her coffee mug. "You see before you a budding TV star."

"What?" Sidney stepped out of line, supporting mini-Sidney above and beneath with hands and forearms. "Not *The Scoop* again."

The pose drooped. "Yes, *The Scoop* again. Fitch shouldn't have dumped Angie."

Zane moved over to his desk. "She's the blond, right? The one who threw the casserole on Saturday."

"Yes. She sent the message and Kanning and his minion hid in the shelter. They filmed the meeting with a handy-dandy night vision attachment on the camera."

Zane raised his fingers from his keyboard. "Oh, crap." He clicked the mouse and turned the monitor to face the room.

The first few notes of *The Scoop's* trumpet fanfare played over a black screen. Then a brief shot of Angie, her skin and hair an eerie green. "Today on *The Scoop*," Kanning's voiceover began, "a jilted lover and a conscience-stricken private eye." Angie dissolved into Giulia, her white coat glowing like it came direct from the Emerald

City. "Film of their clandestine meeting at three-thirty today. No dark deeds can hide from *The Scoop*!"

The video ended with the TV station logo.

"Oh, crap," Sidney said.

Giulia took a long drink of coffee. "I've never wanted so badly to duct-tape someone and lock them in a damp, mold-infested cellar."

"Fitch?" Zane said.

"And Kanning. If I could only find a cellar that had mold and rats."

"I can recommend my first apartment out of high school," Jane said.

"Don't tempt me." Giulia sank into Zane's client chair. "Angie the Jilted joined the 'Throw Fitch Under the Bus' group. I keep expecting it to show up in my Facebook feed. According to her, Fitch is cooking the books at the bar he's part-owner of, Long Neck."

"Really." Zane typed on a few keys and stopped. "We don't have access to their records."

"That was my first thought, too. I checked with Frank, who agrees with me that we don't have a snowball's chance of getting a look at them."

Sidney said, "We couldn't use it in the AtlanticEdge case anyway. But maybe when *The Scoop* puts it on TV, the other owner of the bar will get suspicious."

"And what?" Giulia said. "It won't help us. As much as the thought of Fitch in jail warms my heart, to help make that happen we have to prove either we're right about the AtlanticEdge embezzlement or that he really did kill Loriela Gil. And if we can't find glaringly obvious proof of either embezzlement or murder, Fitch walks."

Silence.

"I sucked the air out of the room, didn't I?" Giulia smiled at them all. "Sorry." She stood. "I have to dig into a sixteen-year-old sports rivalry to see if Petit thinks it's still worth murdering for.

Zane, after that you and I need to cross-check our lists of altered purchase orders and ledger entries. Sidney, I see that face. If you complain about being left out and neglect Jane's training, I will be at your house after every two a.m. feeding, keeping you up with work."

Sidney hit the keys on her keyboard as though it had reverted to a manual typewriter. Jane hid a smile behind her hand.

Giulia closed herself in and hit the Net. Yearbooks, sports articles, school district archives. The glut of information in searchable online formats worked to her advantage.

She brought up the yearbook photo of Fitch and Petit's senior year basketball team. "Weren't they cute in those little shorts?"

Fitch's smile hadn't altered in the intervening decades. Petit's smile looked a little sour.

She searched for prom pictures. According to the photographic evidence, the basketball team stuck together in sports and recreation. Fitch posed with a blonde similar to Angie. Three other players had their arms around two blondes and a brunette. Petit and a tall kid with unfortunate acne bookended the photo, without girls to hold on to. Both of their smiles left something to be desired.

She switched to college archives. Fitch received a Bachelor's in Marketing and Petit passed the bar exam his first try. Fitch's smiling photo appeared in the business section of the paper several times as he achieved promotion after promotion. Petit joined Creighton, Williams, Ferenc, and Steele straight out of law school but five years later still hadn't been made partner.

Petit coached summer basketball camps for inner-city kids. Fitch's name appeared only in the business section.

"Yeah, but Petit can be the best sports mentor around and still be a murderer. Wait."

She ran a search for "Colby Petit + Loriela Gil." Nothing. "Colby Petit + Leonard Tulley." Still nothing. Then she thought, *Why not?* and typed "Colby Petit + AtlanticEdge." Zilch. "Colby Petit + Cassandra Gil."

"Well, well, well."

The five-year-old newspaper article read:

LEGAL EAGLE SAVES SINGLE MOM

Colby, Petit, Esq., the latest acquisition of the prestigious local firm of Creighton, Williams, Ferenc, and Steele, proved he's more than a jury favorite yesterday. Petit was returning from a late deposition when he heard the sound of breaking glass and a scream. He ran toward the sound and saw a figure in a ski mask jump through the broken window of the ground-floor apartment of Cassandra Gil, 55. Petit, 29, followed the attacker through the window and subdued him with the help of a decorative stone cat statue.

The alleged thief, whose name has been withheld because he is a minor, is connected to several recent break-ins using the same pattern. He is in the Cottonwood Holding Center awaiting arraignment. Ms. Gil is the mother of Loriela Gil who was recently seen in the company of Henri Richard, Cottonwood's rising star of experimental theater. Mr. Petit is already known for his skill in winning a jury's sympathy for an underdog defendant. When asked what prompted him to interfere in a potentially deadly situation, he replied that anyone would have done the same.

Giulia rubbed her hands over her face. "Okay, Dudley Do-Right, why didn't Cassandra mention any of this, since she's one hundred percent certain her rescuer is working for the man she's one hundred percent certain killed her daughter?"

An answer came to her straight out of her years of teaching Catholicism: If he didn't kill Loriela himself, he's defending Fitch to expiate all the years of hate and jealousy. If he did kill Loriela, he's covered his tracks like a master. Which he is if he's absorbed lessons from any murderers he's defended.

Giulia leaned away from the screen. She tried to picture Petit tracking Fitch and Loriela's movements, desperate enough to climb her balcony like a perverted Romeo and watch his old rival and the unattainable woman make love in that king-sized bed.

Was he the type to stalk their drunken arrival home on April first and the sex that followed? To hate Loriela enough to kill her for—what? Destroying some angelic image of her he created in his own mind? Wanting to be the one tying her to the bed?

Giulia shivered. "I'm going to need an extra-large jug of brain bleach when this is over."

If Petit had lured Loriela out to the balcony and pleaded with her to give him a chance...with the rain soaking both of them and making that thin blouse cling to her naked skin...or if he lost it and kissed her? Groped her? And she swatted him away? Those silk ties were so easy to reach, only five feet away, so easy...

Giulia grabbed a pen and the legal pad and wrote.

Fitch:
Motives: Boredom. Jealousy. Money?
Opportunity: Unlimited.
Gain: Freedom. Both from a committed relationship and from jail because all evidence so far is circumstantial.

Petit:
Motive: Jealousy? Hate. Lust/Love?
Opportunity: If he stalked her, why didn't he choose a night when Loriela was home alone?

Giulia made an exasperated sound and scratched out those last lines.

Opportunity: If he stalked them, he would choose a night when Fitch at least was falling-down drunk so he wouldn't be able to fight Petit off—or remember? Maybe. Also, to let Fitch take the blame. If Petit planned that, he has succeeded brilliantly—so far.

Gain: Negative. Nobody gets to "have" Loriela now that she's dead.

Gain Part Two: If Petit planned Loriela's murder with the same meticulousness he crafts a defense, he would have known he could spring Fitch within forty-eight hours because of lack of evidence. He'd also know that, barring any counter-evidence surfacing and everything modern DNA testing can discover, there'd be a strong possibility Fitch would be indicted for the murder sooner or later.

She reread the lists. "Then what? He had a whole year to get an attack of conscience? Who's the real Colby Petit? Dudley Do-Right or the Boston Strangler?"

She started a third page.

Tulley:
Motive:

Giulia recalled all the AtlanticEdge surveillance videos in which he sucked up to Loriela. But was it sucking up? What if they were his awkward attempts at wooing her?

All the men in the case loved or yearned after Loriela. All of them except for Petit, and Giulia admitted her Motive-Opportunity-Gain list for him was nothing more than theory.

"Any one of the three could've strangled Loriela with that tie." Giulia pulled her emergency sweater from the extra-deep bottom desk drawer. She wrapped one sleeve around her coffee mug and pulled the ends tight. Her arm muscles hardened. "I have enough strength to strangle someone with a tie if they're too drunk to fight back. Fitch, Petit, and Tulley could certainly do it even if Loriela retained enough of her senses to fight back."

She continued Tulley's sheet:

Motive: Lust/love. Fear of jail re: embezzling.
Opportunity: Less than Fitch, more than Petit. Did Fitch take Loriela to Long Neck to get hammered for his birthday? Tulley would've seen them and snatched his chance.

Gain: Peace of mind. Continued money. Knowledge that Fitch couldn't turn him in without exposing the embezzlement scheme, because Tulley would then have nothing to lose.

She pushed away the legal pad. "Not only could any of them be the killer, my lists make all three look like prize scumbags. These kinds of cases almost make me miss the Sister Mary Regina Coelis years. The world was simpler. Evil wore fewer masks."

She could recite Frank's lecture on that idea word for word: The world isn't the warm and fuzzy place you want it to be. You want to be a private investigator? Be prepared to fight the evil in the world. That means facing facts.

"All right, Frank." She printed out Petit's heroic rescue article, his prom photo, and basketball team photo.

A minute later, Zane knocked on her door and handed her the pages. "Ready when you are to compare bogus purchase orders."

Giulia stared at the clue collage on the wall. "Thanks. Give me a few minutes."

She taped the photos and article next to Petit's page and spaced the three Motive-Opportunity-Gain lists across the top of the collage. Then she stepped back and looked over the multicolored chaos.

"Tulley and Fitch and the bar. Petit and the rescue and the edited security photos. Fitch and Tulley and the altered documents. Fitch and his expensive New York City weekend. I wonder..."

Her left hand groped behind her for the desk phone. After half a dozen empty clutches, she succeeded and pulled it toward the edge. Turning from the collage, she dialed Petit's office.

The sound of a phone ringing obscured his voice. "Yes, Ms. Driscoll—not again. Sorry, that wasn't directed at you. Hold on for a second, please." The silence lasted for less than ten seconds. "Sorry. The prosecutor's been crawling up my butt all morning. What can I do for you?"

"Mr. Petit, I want to convince you to let me look at Roger Fitch's bank statements."

Thirty-Four

Giulia blessed the state prosecutor in her heart when she hung up the phone. Petit's "frazzled" level had reached new heights. Giulia made use of her calmest voice, the one that had successfully defused three student fights and one knife threat. She hadn't scrupled to imply that she'd added Petit to her list of suspects. She'd let the lawyer talk, paused in strategic spots when he asked questions, and listened to him sweat.

While she was still on the line, he buzzed his secretary and asked her to call a courier.

"I've got all Roger's financial information as part of the pre-trial disclosures," he said to Giulia. "Send them back tomorrow morning, please. We're getting everything in order for the trial next Wednesday, which will happen in some form even when you find evidence pointing to the real killer."

"Of course. Thank you."

She opened her door. "Zane, I'm all yours. Petit is letting us look at Fitch's bank statements. I've got an idea."

Zane whistled. "How'd you convince him to give us access to those?"

"I let him convince himself. The prosecutor is making Petit's life miserable this morning and Petit is still spooked over me digging into his past with Fitch." She dragged Zane's client chair behind his desk. "Let's do this."

Sidney and Jane lowered their voices as Sidney demonstrated

forms on her screen and Jane made notes on all the how-tos Sidney had created.

Zane brought up scans of the five alterations Giulia had missed.

"Those are not my fault," she said after the fifth. "They're even more scattershot than the other ninety-two. Like this one at the end of January, after the post-Christmas returns. The next year they chose an invoice from five days later, at the beginning of February. There's no logic to it."

Zane opened his mouth at the same time Giulia said, "Wait. That is their logic. Look how many months it took the new CEO to spot something. If only we had that kind of time."

She squinted at a number nine which started out life as a four. "Can you pull the dates of all ninety-seven into a spreadsheet for me?"

"Just a sec." Zane copied and pasted and sorted.

Sidney headed for the bathroom. Jane flipped over a stapled page and wrote more notes on the back.

"Got it," Zane said.

They studied the column of dates.

"The frequency increased starting last July," Giulia said.

"But did the amounts?" Zane clicked over to the purchase orders. "Two hundred fifteen. Three hundred one. Two hundred twenty-four. Here's one for three hundred sixty-three."

"That's an outlier."

"Yes, the larger, risky numbers stopped in..." he moused over the entire list, "the third week of April."

"One month before the emergency CEO switch and three weeks after Loriela Gil was murdered," Giulia said. "Was Loriela part of the scheme after all? Did she make sure the altered documents went through without question?"

"I didn't consider her," Zane said. "Possibly."

"And without her, they didn't want to take a chance on larger numbers. Come on, Petit, where are Fitch's bank statements? If Angie the Jilted is right about money laundering at the bar...and if an angel is sitting on my shoulder whispering these ideas to me, Fitch's bar thefts started after Loriela's death made document scrutiny too risky. He got greedy."

Zane frowned. "If she was part of it and her death spooked them, why did it take them 'til the middle of last summer before they ramped up the frequency?"

Giulia sat very still as another idea lit up her brain. "I don't have that answer yet. I'm still elbow-deep in murder. Did Tulley kill her because she caught him? Did Tulley or Fitch kill her because she was in on it and became too scared of getting caught? Did she demand a bigger share of the loot? Did Petit kill her...no, those two don't connect here."

Sidney said, again behind her desk, "Fitch is a nasty piece of work, but does this Tulley person have the guts to commit murder?"

"If properly provoked. He's stuck in the glory days of his past and is looking, I think, for a way to prove to himself he's still a macho star chick magnet. He doesn't have enough money to counterbalance his post-football self."

Sidney made a face. "When I'm on maternity leave I'm going to expose mini-Sidney to every Disney movie ever made to get the taste of real life out of my mouth."

Giulia smiled. "That is the most cynical sentence I've ever heard from you."

"Olivier says the third trimester is filing off my super-sweetness. Poor guy. Between me and Jingle spitting at him, he needs a vacation."

Jane said, "Olivier? Jingle?"

"My husband. Olivier, not Jingle. Oh, poop!" Sidney dived into her backpack and brought out a doubled zipper baggie stamped with a bright orange Meier Farms logo. "Here you go. The best fertilizer ever. Tell all your friends."

Jane held the gift by the zipper.

"This is manure?"

"No, no, it's alpaca poop. Hardly any stink from the time you scatter it under your plants to the time it disintegrates. Go ahead, smell it!"

Giulia coughed to cover her laughter at Jane's expression of helpless fear. "Really, it's safe to smell. I've been using it for years."

Jane brought the plastic bags near her nose and took a delicate sniff.

The door opened and the same courier who delivered Angie's letter walked in. Giulia and Zane burst into laughter at the look on his face.

"You have something for me." Giulia stepped in front of him, blocking his view of the office.

"Uh, yeah. Sign here, please." He held out a pen.

Giulia signed the carbonless slip on the back of a much thicker envelope than the last one. The courier tore off the top copy, handed her the envelope with a "thanks," and left a little too quickly.

"I think we've scarred him for life," she said.

"He'll be talking to *The Scoop* next," Zane said with a frown. "My girlfriend liked my bodyguard appearance in Monday's show, but she'll get creeped out if those vultures create a DI-is-a-freakshow episode."

Jane stared at the bag of fertilizer in her hand.

Giulia said to her, "Are you wondering what you got yourself into?"

The temp shook her head, her stylized bangs flipping back and forth. "No. Really I'm not. You people are like a kooky family. The good kind. That's a compliment, since my last experience with family was my ex and his harpy mother." She set the bag on the floor next to her black backpack. "Work now?"

Giulia covered Jane's assimilation awkwardness by ripping open the envelope.

"Oh, this is lovely. Zane, come over by the window."

She got on her knees on the wood floor and fanned out the folded papers. "Five years of savings, checking, and credit card. Oh, look: Two years of another checking account with cash-only deposits. Can you say Long Neck money? Mr. Petit, I like you when you're cooperative."

"I'll take savings and credit card," Zane said.

He sat cross-legged at Giulia's left and dealt the statements like a solitaire layout. Giulia did the same with both sets of checking statements. A minute later, Zane unfolded himself and headed for his computer. He returned with pens and two copies of the just-created list of altered purchase order dates.

"You're going to find more than I am," he said.

"Don't bet on it. He's smart enough to spread the AtlanticEdge money between both accounts to deflect suspicion."

They worked on their separate tasks, muttering and scribbling and checking off dates. Sidney and Jane talked in low voices. Half an hour later, Giulia sat back on her heels. Zane followed a minute after.

"He's smarter than I gave him credit for," Giulia said.

"If you mean that his deposit dates don't connect to the purchase order dates, I agree."

"They don't connect directly, but I see a sideways type of pattern. Look here." She knelt again and placed the written-on page of dates against one of the July savings statements. "His checking account is pretty dull. Paychecks and bonuses from AtlanticEdge go in and rent, gas, and utilities come out."

"He's the type who pays for his groceries by credit card," Zane said.

"Indeed. His credit card shows a cycle of food, entertainment, hotels, and restaurants. Here's the PO for the Fourth of July sale at one of the smaller stores, dated June second. Fitch tacked a measly one hundred bucks onto it by changing a five into a six. He split the deposit in two: Thirty-five on June twentieth and sixty-five on July seventh."

"His savings shows transfers from checking in late May and early August. One hundred twenty-two in May and one hundred ninety-three in August."

"It's not enough," Giulia said. She found the cash-only

checking statements for those periods. "This one has regular deposits logged in every Monday and Friday morning. Thursday and Saturday happy hours? For the first time in my life I regret not being the type that drinks in bars."

"Yes," Jane said from her seat at Sidney's desk. "Long Neck advertises in the arts weekly. They have Happy Hour on Thursdays and a microbrew tasting every third Saturday. My ex was hugely into microbrews. Long Neck's tastings are always packed."

"And you thought I decided too quickly to hire you," Giulia said. "When I die, I'm going to have them carve 'No one appreciated her genius' on my tombstone."

"My little brother is taking violin lessons," Sidney said. "I'll have him come by after school tomorrow and play you a sad song."

"I will come teach mini-Sidney to grow up as sweet as you used to be."

Sidney tried to keep a faux-sympathetic face, but failed.

Giulia looked from her to the clock above the door. "Hey, gang, it's after twelve. Go to lunch. I'm staying here, so I'll get the phone."

Zane was the last to leave. Giulia locked the door behind him. She needed silence to put this puzzle together. Only her overdeveloped work ethic prevented her from turning off her cell and the desk phones.

"First things first." She removed the clue collage from her office wall and pinned it to the wall next to the front window of the main office. It was too wide for this space and she had to wrap it around the corner. It cleared her own doorframe by half an inch.

"Now. Roger Fitch savings account at ten o'clock. Credit card at eight o'clock. Checking account at twelve o'clock. Long Neck checking account at two o'clock. List of altered PO dates dead center. Tablet." She returned to her office and retrieved it from her messenger bag. "Surveillance footage at my fingertips." She stared at the blank screen for a moment. "Surveillance..." She opened Google Earth and zoomed in on the Long Neck bar. "I thought so."

She called Frank. "Hello, darling husband who is also a detective with access to citywide cameras."

Frank groaned. "I know that opening gambit."

"I could hang up and call your boss."

"No." Frank's voice snapped to attention. "You will not get into debt with Jimmy. You know he'll use it to hound me day and night to get you to work for him."

She laughed. "The idea never crossed my mind. To prevent that situation, I would like a favor."

"You are devious."

"I prefer thorough. Can you get me the traffic cam footage for the intersection of North and Seventh streets?"

"Traffic cams? Why?"

"Because the front door of a bar called Long Neck sits on that corner in full view of the traffic camera. Long Neck happens to be owned in part by Roger Fitch."

"Is that so?"

"If I remember correctly, Detective, you're also working on the Fitch case."

A long-suffering sigh. "I know. Helping you out might help me out too. I'll do what I can."

She blew him a kiss. "I knew I could count on you."

"As a reward I request homemade enchiladas for supper."

She performed a quick mental inventory of the refrigerator. "Chicken or beef?"

"Cook's choice."

"Good, because we have chicken in the freezer but not beef. Why are you keeping me on the phone? I'm on deadline."

"Are you kidding?"

She laughed harder. "Thank you, sir. I expect to hear from you this afternoon."

"Abuse of power. That's what this is." He hung up.

Thirty-Five

Sidney returned from lunch first. "This place looks like you detonated a bomb in a paper factory."

Giulia climbed up from the floor using the corner of Sidney's desk. "Ow. My back popped. I know where every single paper belongs, thank you. Now that we're alone: I know it's only been three days, but is Jane getting the hang of how we work?"

"Yeah, she's great. She's kinda unsure of herself and thinks we're weird, but she's smart." Sidney lowered herself into her chair. "Should I be doing magical things to make myself irreplaceable?"

"That's your hormones talking. Perish the thought. Jane is a temp. When you return full-time, she goes." Giulia froze in place. "If Jimmy isn't merely sweet-talking me and really needs an assistant..." She unlocked her phone and pressed the voice message icon. "If Jane works out, recommend her to Jimmy when Sidney comes back from maternity leave."

"That's why you make the big bucks," Sidney said. "I wouldn't have made that connection."

"You're not under continual bombardment from a persistent police captain."

Zane and Jane returned one right after the other.

Giulia groaned. "If you two keep doing this, I really am going to end up giving instructions in rhyme."

"I will take every step possible to prevent that happening," Zane said. "It'd make this place like a kids' video game."

"Too cute for me," Giulia said. "Okay, here's what I've come up with in the past hour."

The phone rang.

"Sometimes I think it knows the moment I get back from lunch," Zane said. He picked up the receiver. "Good afternoon, Driscoll Investigations." His eyes widened. "One moment, please." He hit the hold button. "It's Colby Petit and he's freaking out."

"Wonderful." She took the handset and Zane took Petit off hold. "It's Giulia Falcone-Driscoll, Mr. Petit."

"Damn him. Damn that prosecutor. Damn that judge." His voice snapped off the ends of the words.

"Mr. Petit, what's going on?"

"The prosecutor's been on my back all day, demanding results from the two-week stay the judge granted us. When I couldn't give him much, he went to the judge and claimed we were delaying the trial without cause."

"But that's not true—"

"I know that. You know that. But that son of a bitch convinced the judge. I just got off the phone with her. She moved the trial start to Friday morning at nine. I need Roger's financials back. Send it all by courier now, please. And please, please, whatever leads you have, pry some instant results out of them." His phone rang. "Dammit. I'll call you back."

Giulia hung up. "Did you guys hear that?"

"Yes," Sidney said. "His voice carries."

"What's the plan?" Zane said.

"Give me a few minutes. If the phone rings, let the machine get it."

Silence filled the office. Giulia stared in the direction of the paper-covered floor, but her eyes didn't see it. She let her mind unfocus at the same time. Images of the people she'd interviewed, the documents she'd studied, and the videos she'd analyzed advanced and receded, swapped places and slipped into the background as she studied everything without studying anything specific.

A few minutes later she blinked the room back into focus and turned around.

"Can you two stay late with me tonight? Jane, not you. Sidney and Zane."

Sidney opened her phone calendar. "I'm good."

Zane was already nodding. "I've got nothing."

"You are both awesome. This means shifting gears from the embezzlement to the murder. I've been thinking they're connected, but it's the germ of an idea only. That's got to change with all three of us working on it."

Sidney said into her phone, "Hey, sweetie, it's me. Everything's fine. We're all staying late for an emergency deadline." She put a hand over the phone. "Any idea how late?" she said to Giulia.

"No. But I'm not chaining you to your desk. Leave when you have to."

"No idea," Sidney said into the phone. "There's leftover baba gnoush in the fridge. Expect me when you see me. Love you."

"Olivier is a prince," Giulia said as she dialed Frank. "Hey, long-suffering husband. I'm pulling an all-nighter...No, not literally, but I don't know how long it'll take...The judge moved Fitch's trial up to Friday morning and we're getting trickle-down panic...Okay. Don't wait up. Love you."

She pocketed the phone and turned to Zane. "First, copies. I'll hand them to you in bunches so my diagram doesn't get messed up."

"But they're confidential."

Giulia lost her patience for an instant, but didn't answer 'til she regained it. "DI is confidential. Everything goes in the shredder at the end of tonight's session. Petit can't expect us to come up with answers if he takes away our tools. Here. Credit card statements first."

Zane shut up and made the copies.

Twenty minutes later he replaced the originals in the same envelope and called their usual courier.

"That little print/copy/fax machine has never seemed so slow,"

Giulia said. "I'll call Petit's office and let them know the courier's on their way here."

Zane said, "That's my job. Let me—"

Giulia had already lifted the receiver and pressed the first digit in the courier service's phone number when Roger Fitch's voice from the earpiece said, "Hello? Is this Driscoll Investigations?"

Give me strength. Giulia inhaled deeply and said in an imitation of Sidney's voice, "Yes it is. May I help you?"

"Give me that Driscoll woman now, dammit."

In the same imitation-Sidney voice, Giulia said, "One moment, please." She pressed hold and swiveled to face first Zane and then the other two, a finger over her lips to signal silence. Then she took Fitch off hold.

"This is Giulia Falcone-Driscoll," she said in her normal voice.

"This is your client, the one who's paying you good money for doing nothing!"

About that infusion of strength..."Mr. Fitch, I've already spoken to Mr. Petit."

"Yeah, and he's just as useless as you. Both of you are siphoning money off me and giving me nothing in return."

"Mr. Fitch, I understand that the judge's decision came as a surprise. However—"

"Don't give me customer service speeches. I hear them every day at work. Listen, you spineless do-gooder, I'm paying you to keep me off of Death Row. You're no detective. You're a thief and a con artist and I'm going to—"

Giulia hung up on him. Heat radiated from her face. Her ears throbbed.

"Are you okay?" Sidney said. "Want me to get your spare coffee mug for you to smash?"

A short laugh burst out of her mouth. "Do I look that bad?"

Zane said, "You look like my sister when her kids have pushed her to the edge."

"I gather that's bad."

"She needs a warning siren. What did he say to you?"

Giulia exhaled a long, slow breath. "First he accused me of stealing his money, then he called me a spineless do-gooder. Then he called me a thief and a con artist. That's when I hung up."

"Whoa," Sidney said.

Jane said, "He packs a lot of insult into a few words."

Giulia said, "He would've used more words if I'd let him."

The phone rang again. Zane grabbed it before Giulia could. Everyone in the room heard Fitch shout: "Tell that bitch I'll sue her for taking money under false pretenses! I'll take her for every cent she's got!"

Zane hung up. "Ms. Driscoll, speaking as your admin, I think we should place a service call with the phone company. They've obviously crossed our lines with someone's anger management therapy session."

Giulia leaned both arms on his desk and laughed. It was a thin laugh, but with it the heat drained from her face and ears.

"Someone host a séance and call up Alexander Graham Bell," she said. "This complaint should go right to the top."

Sidney and Zane replied with thin laughs of their own.

Giulia straightened up. "All right, team, let's get this boil off our butts as soon as possible. Zane, please call Petit's office to tell them the records will be there shortly. Sidney, here's my iPad. Please queue up any surveillance videos which correspond to the dates of the altered POs. Jane, please go through Long Neck's checking account and make a list of the Friday and Monday morning deposits starting with April of the year before last."

"Why April?" Sidney said.

"I have an idea that Roger Fitch's ego is the kind to make him start important plans on dates that mean a lot to him. April first is his birthday."

Giulia returned to the corner by the window and studied her collage. The courier arrived a few minutes later. Frank called right after that.

"Remember that Italian cheesecake I asked you to make for DeWitt's stag party?"

"Yes. So?"

"So, lovely bride, that cheesecake got you a flash drive with six months' worth of traffic cam footage from the corner of Seventh and Larch."

"Yes." Giulia fist-pumped. "Can you send a courier over with it?"

"Will do."

She hung up and said to the others, "We have photos from the traffic camera that faces Long Neck's front door."

Sidney stopped searching files on Giulia's tablet. "I'm missing something. Why do we need to see what happens outside of Long Neck?"

"There's a connection between Fitch, Tulley, and Long Neck that goes beyond the obvious. Long Neck sells Tulley's microbrews. That makes Tulley a vendor for Long Neck. Sort of. I don't know if Tulley tends bar too, which would make the connection a bigger knot. I have an idea about those microbrew nights." Giulia massaged her temples. "Roger Fitch thinks I'm not giving him his money's worth. Hah."

Thirty-Six

A different courier brought the flash drive. Giulia took charge of it and plugged it into a USB port on her computer.

"Dear God, there are thousands."

She pulled up the previous year's calendar in a different window and scrolled to the camera images from the first Thursday in January.

"Early morning rush hour...more rush hour..." She hit the down arrow until the time stamp read 4:30 p.m. A considerate red Buick ran the light as an employee of Long Neck set out a chalkboard sidewalk sign. Which Giulia couldn't read, because the sidewalk was covered with snow and the sign was set up in the doorway to protect it.

"You are being uncooperative," she said to the back of the unknown employee. More arrow keystrokes until the timestamp read 5:15 the following Saturday. The sidewalks were wet but clear and the chalkboard had been moved out from the doorway. She enlarged the photo and slid it down and to the left then enlarged it some more.

The sign read:

Microbrew Tasting Tonight
7-9 p.m.
Touchdown Ale
Play Action Lager
Small cover charge

"Those would be Tulley's creations, all right." She wrote the date on a clean sheet of her legal pad.

She checked week after week of camera stills from every Thursday and every third Saturday nights. The camera caught a large group of regulars every Thursday. Sometimes the Saturday tasting featured three beers, but the regulars—a fancier set judging by their clothes—didn't increase proportionately.

That intersection featured a quick yellow light which meant a lot of red light runners. Enough that Giulia went through the Thursday and Saturday photos a second time and came out with a ballpark estimate of how many people took advantage of Happy Hour and Microbrew Tasting nights.

A lot.

She'd tuned out any sounds from the outer office. When she entered that room again she saw there wasn't a lot to tune out. Jane had left and Sidney and Zane were hunched over their monitors.

Sidney pointed at the clock with her right index finger while keeping place on her screen with her left. "Jane left a list of all the deposits you asked for and said she'll see you tomorrow."

Giulia blinked at the clock. "It's quarter to six? Good Heavens. Shall I make a caffeine run downstairs before they close?"

"Yes, please, if you don't mind," Zane said.

"You're awesome," Sidney said. "Chamomile smoothie, please? They make it for me even though it's not on the menu."

"Large regular, three sugars, please," Zane said.

"Be right back."

Giulia took the steep wooden stairs two at a time, something only accomplished without injury after much practice. The afternoon barista at Common Grounds was just starting to straighten chairs and wipe tables.

Ten minutes later, Giulia returned triumphant. "He locked the door behind me. Sidney, he says you should name the baby 'Chamomile.' I didn't tell him what I thought of that."

Sidney sucked a mouthful of the smoothie. "Men. No offense,

Zane. Oh—" She massaged her belly with slow circular motions. "Mini-Sidney always jumps when I drink these. Olivier's going to be disappointed if she's a vegetarian like me."

"He'll sneak her bits of steak behind your back. It'll be their bonding ritual."

Sidney sucked another mouthful. "That's actually kind of cute."

Giulia sipped her coffee. "Hmm. Cherry-lime syrup is not a winner. Sidney, you're mellowing. I vividly remember a certain wedding with carnivore and vegetarian food stations at opposite sides of the room."

Sidney blushed. "I'm not saying I'd eat steak. It's only fair to give Olivier's viewpoint equal time. It's like church. We're going to raise mini-Sidney Catholic, but she should be able to choose when she grows up."

Zane muttered, "I'm so going to tell my mother that the next time she calls to nag me about deserting the family religion."

"What do you usually say to her?" Giulia said.

"I usually hang up."

"Been there. Are you guys ready for a brainstorming session?" Giulia grabbed her legal pad from her desk.

They gathered at Sidney's desk.

"All I can say is that Long Neck must put something addictive in the beer," Sidney said. "The deposits on the days after their tastings and happy hour are a little less than huge but a lot more than respectable."

"I like it when I'm right." Giulia set her list of cover charges and estimates of bodies passing through the door on each targeted evening. "Here. Third week of April, two years ago. Based on the traffic cam photos, about sixty people paid the cover charge. Let's figure I missed another forty because of inconsiderate drivers who didn't run the red light. If we make it an even hundred, there should be, what? An extra five hundred in the Monday deposit from the cover charge, maybe. That is, compared to a Monday deposit on any other week of the month."

Sidney poked at Jane's handwritten numbers. "Four hundred ten the first week, four hundred thirty-four the second week, eight hundred six for Microbrew week, three hundred sixty-one the fourth week. Whoa."

"Those numbers make too much sense. Let's try the next month."

The deposits followed the same pattern for May through July.

"Wow." Sidney circled August's third Monday deposit. "Twelve hundred and change."

Giulia checked her own list. "No way. They had fewer people than usual for that tasting."

Zane said, "Are you sure you got the numbers straight? My eyes are starting to cross and I've had to triple-check a few things. Um, no offense."

"None taken. Let me check." Giulia returned to her computer and found the relevant dates in the photo index. "Nope," she called. "It poured that Saturday and only about half the usual number showed up." She was smiling as she came back to Sidney's desk. "Thank you for being greedy, Roger."

"Yes, but how can we use it?" Sidney said.

"This was my idea: Fitch is using the bar account to launder the money he's embezzling from AtlanticEdge. What we need now is Frank. I only know the basics of money laundering. He knows a lot more." She glanced at the clock. "He's probably on the way home from basketball. I'll try him in a little bit."

A single knock sounded on the door and it opened at the same moment.

"Olivier!" Sidney stood as fast as a woman with a baby ready to pop could stand.

"I bring food for the hard-working detectives," Sidney's husband said, plastic bags with smiley faces on them hanging from his hands.

"You are awesome."

"I agree," Giulia said. "Let me take those." She set the bags on Zane's desk.

"You brought Buddhist Delight. I love you." Sidney unpacked the bag nearest to her.

"I know you do," he answered in his calm, deep voice. "I also brought hot and sour soup and eggrolls for Giulia, General Tso's for Zane, barbecue ribs for me and water for everyone."

Giulia pecked him on the cheek. "You are a life saver. Our deductive skills were circling the drain."

They shoved everything on Zane's desk to one end and used the other end as a table. No one spoke for a good five minutes.

Another knock and the door opened again.

"Pizza delivery! Hey..." Frank stopped in the doorway. "Who stole my idea?"

Thirty-Seven

Everyone laughed. Giulia set down her eggroll and pushed back her chair.

"Sidney and I have the most thoughtful husbands in town." She stacked all the papers on Sidney's desk and laid them over her keyboard. "Do I smell black olives?"

Frank set one small and one large pizza box on the cleared space. "Of course you do. I brought water since I didn't remember what Sidney couldn't drink. Hi, Olivier. Do I say great minds think alike and do you say we tapped into the collective unconscious?"

Olivier winced. "I'll book several sessions for you in which I will open your eyes to the true nature of the collective unconscious."

"Only if you ride shotgun on my next drug bust."

Giulia cut this short. "Gentlemen, all of the wonderful food is getting cold. Frank, grab my client chair and join us. Want an egg roll?"

They alternated between their Chinese takeout, a pepper and mushroom pizza for Sidney, and a pizza with everything for the rest of the group.

When the eating slowed from ravenous to human, Giulia said, "Now that you're both here, may I pick your brains?"

"Of course," Olivier said.

"We have two cases that are jumbled together. First, AtlanticEdge wants us to see if certain employees are embezzling.

They gave us certain employee files, two years' worth of accounting ledgers, and their internal security camera footage. Second, Roger Fitch, the accused Silk Tie Killer, hired us to prove he's innocent."

Olivier tried to stop a smile. He was unsuccessful. "I saw a replay of Monday's Scoop episode."

Giulia took a bite of pizza and chomped it like it was Ken Kanning's head. "The mere thought of *The Scoop* raises my blood pressure. So does Fitch, since his trial judge and prosecutor are the reason we're pulling this late-night session. The prosecutor convinced the judge the two-week delay Fitch's attorney wrangled is nothing but a stalling tactic. Since we didn't have anything concrete as of this morning, the trial's been moved up to Friday at nine."

Olivier whistled.

"Exactly," Giulia said. "On top of that, we've narrowed down the list of embezzlement suspects to Fitch and one of his buddies who also works at the bar Fitch is part owner of."

"Technically," Zane said, "we think Fitch and his bar buddy are both embezzling."

"And stealing from the bar," Sidney said. "Maybe."

"You meet the nicest people in this business," Frank said. He pushed back his chair and walked over to the clue collage. "Give me specifics."

Sidney and Zane described the altered purchase orders and the surveillance footage involving Tulley and Loriela. Zane took over for the ledger entries. Giulia tied it into the bar deposits.

"Frank," Giulia finished, "come look at these bank statements. I don't know enough about money laundering, but you do. Isn't there a way Fitch and Tulley could verbally claim one price as the cover charge for Happy Hour and Tastings but on the books list it as a higher charge? Please say yes."

"Yes," Frank said. "If there aren't any written records of their cover charge, they can deposit what they want and label it how they want."

Giulia and Sidney fist-bumped.

"Don't get excited yet," Frank said. "How are Fitch and Tulley getting this embezzled money? You'll notice I'm going with your assumptions for the sake of this analysis."

"I saw it on the surveillance videos tonight," Sidney said. "Tulley makes the AtlanticEdge deposits once or twice a week, depending. If they ran a retail sale, then he goes twice."

"Wait," Olivier said. "Don't they bank electronically?"

"No." Giulia pulled a page of Loriela's employee file off the Collage. "It says here one of the reasons Loriela got promoted to head of accounting was her, quote, forward thinking, unquote."

"Corporate babble," Frank said. "What's that really mean?"

"She pitched a cost-effective way to switch from physical checks. Right now, because of their current bank's procedures and their own systems, AtlanticEdge pays vendors with paper checks, and vice-versa. Employees get paper checks too."

"Seriously?" Frank said. "I thought every company with more than twenty-five employees went paperless years ago."

"A surprising number have not," Zane said. "I researched cost-benefit analyses of paper versus electronic. The break-even point isn't as—"

"Zane," Giulia said. "Later."

"Who cuts the checks?" Frank said.

Giulia and Sidney glanced at each other.

"Good question," Giulia said. "Just a second."

She ran into her office and opened the AtlanticEdge files on her computer. "Eat something, you guys. This may take a minute." She moused down the list of Human Resources files. "Research and Development, Testing, Quality Control, Marketing, Sales, Accounting, thank you...Somebody not on any of our lists is in charge of timesheets, somebody else cuts the checks, but...just a sec...oh, look at that. Tulley totals the purchase orders and gives the amounts to the check-cutter."

"Did they do any employee screening before they hired us?" Sidney said.

Giulia came through the doorway and nabbed a skinny slice of pizza. "Tully comes across as the right kind of employee. He's good with numbers, has a hobby that keeps him in town, and if we can believe the surveillance videos, sucked up in a big way to Loriela when she was his boss."

Olivier said, "That is all surface polish."

Giulia sat. "Tell me more."

"May I read what you know about him already?"

Giulia pointed. "It's on the wall. Start with the third row left, then read across the top row."

Olivier stood and read as he finished a rib. "He's in a bitter time loop of his own making, and he refuses to recognize his other qualities. I went to one of his microbrew tastings last year. He has definite talent, but he squanders it as minion to Roger Fitch while he focuses on the great football player he once was." He took the interview pages off the wall. "Here, where he shifts from lazy former jock to crafty traitor. Here, where he pretends he isn't interested in marriage, yet he deliberately searched for Loriela Gil's online presence."

"You mean he threw Roger under the bus because they were rivals for Loriela?" Giulia pointed at her interview pages. "No way. She chose men based on how high they'd climbed the success ladder. Always higher than the last one. Tulley was going nowhere."

Sidney came out of the bathroom. "If Tulley wasn't Fitch's rival, then he's got the biggest case of 'I hate my job' ever."

"That's too easy," Giulia said. "Besides, how would he know for sure Fitch killed Loriela?"

"Fitch admitted it one night at the bar when they were both hammered?" Zane said, yawning.

"Do any of us think Fitch ever gets that hammered?" Giulia said.

"If he doesn't, then his story of his alcohol coma the night of the murder falls apart," Frank said. "Speaking in a purely helpful brainstorming fashion, that is."

Giulia stood very still facing her clue collage. "Nobody say anything for a minute, okay?"

Her gaze stopped on the empty space where Tulley's interview pages had been. Then on Fitch's pages. Cassandra Gil's pages. The DNA evidence. The crime scene photos.

There's something here. Think.

She rubbed her hands over her face. All she really wanted was silence and her own bed.

Bed. Footprints. Rain and an open door and a body on a narrow balcony and a man too stupefied-drunk to hear any of it happening a mere five feet away.

"Zane," she said, "if you compare the crime scene photos to everything you saw when you and I went to Fitch's apartment, would you say an intruder killed Loriela?"

She didn't worry about the silence that followed. Silence meant Zane in super-think mode.

"Yeah. Yeah, I would, even though I still think Fitch did it."

"Me too. It's not just his work background and the history of the case. The more I talk to him and get exposed to his body language and inflections—shush, Frank, you know what I mean— the more I'm convinced he's the killer." She grabbed the air in front of the Collage like she was choking it. "But he didn't kill her. So who did, and why are we hung up on him as perpetrator?"

No one replied.

"He said something to me last Saturday. Something along the lines of 'It's good to be the king.' Zane, do you remember—no, wait. Minions. He was talking about Tulley working for him at the bar."

"I remember," Zane said. "He said he liked being the owner because people had to do what he said. He didn't use those words, but he was talking about having power over people."

Giulia turned to face the room. Her right hand drew bullet points in the air as she spoke.

"Fitch likes power. Women. Money. The arguments with Loriela escalated up 'til the night of her death. We only have his word on the drunken birthday party and happy reconciliation. Okay, let's assume the reconciliation because of their bedroom escapades afterward."

She stared at the air in front of her, cataloguing the points.

"Fitch and Tulley are stealing from AtlanticEdge. Fitch and Tulley are stealing from Long Neck. Zane and Sidney, what's the probability of both?"

Sidney said, "Ninety-five percent from AtlanticEdge, eighty percent from the bar. We don't have enough data for that yet."

"Point taken. Zane?"

"One hundred percent from AtlanticEdge, eighty from the bar, for Sidney's reason."

"Agreed." Giulia didn't shift her focus from her invisible bullet points. "What if I said Loriela was also embezzling?"

From the edges of her vision, Giulia saw Zane and Sidney both sit back in their chairs.

"Interesting," Zane said. "It blows her image of the beautiful, hardworking, wronged woman."

"She never had that image, except in her mother's mind," Sidney said. "What about that woman who said Loriela left heel prints in her back when she walked over her to get her job? Something like that."

"The higher you climb, the more expensive and frantic life gets," Zane said. "I saw the damage at PayWright when somebody clawed up to assistant manager level, then manager, then floor supervisor."

"Loriela was smart," Giulia said. "She had power and brains to work out an embezzlement scheme. Or to improve Fitch's, if the idea was his."

"But not Tulley's?" Frank said.

"No. Embezzlement wasn't Tulley's idea. He's a follower now, not a leader." Giulia unfocused her eyes on the clock above the door. She didn't really want to know how long this workday was lasting. "He wants to turn back the clock to his high school most popular athlete days. Because he can't do that, he's nursing a spectacular load of hate and bitterness. Maybe he decided sticking it to his employer was the best he could manage, since women don't seem to want him. Loriela sure didn't." She focused at last on the people in the room. "Tell me this doesn't sound crazy: Tulley killed Loriela."

"Why?" Sidney said.

"He finally realized she'd never dump Fitch for him?" Giulia said.

"Fitch told him to?" Zane said, then made a disgusted noise. "Forget that. Tulley isn't stupid, either. This isn't *Of Mice and Men*."

"He wanted more money?" Giulia said.

"From who?" Sidney said. "If the three of them were already stealing, and the two who worked at the bar were stealing more, why get extra greedy?"

"He was fed up with being the minion?" Olivier said.

"Fitch is a top salesman," Giulia said. "His bonuses prove it. He's been trying to sell me on the idea that despite his current tomcatting, he truly loved Loriela. I think it was mutual exploitation, not love. I think he and Loriela were using each other first to further their careers and then to get rich quick."

"More than two years of embezzling is hardly quick," Frank said.

"It's smarter than robbing a bank." Giulia locked eyes with Frank. "They're both smart. They're both charming when they want to be. Loriela had a reputation for turning on the charm to the right people and using the rest for stepping stones." She took a step toward him. "Fitch is using Tulley. Loriela might have used Tulley. Tulley might have interpreted that as something more. Picture this: Loriela leading Tulley on to keep the embezzlement going, with Fitch laughing at Tulley all the while."

Frank gave her that challenging smile he always used when they were nearing a solution together. "So what then? Fitch got tired of Loriela and wanted her share of the money so he killed her?"

Giulia shook her head hard enough to whip her curls against her face. "Yes, he wanted her money. No, he didn't kill her. The whole murder scene is set up like a locked-room mystery. It's been bugging me for days, when Fitch himself wasn't the biggest annoyance in my life. You and your team must've seen it."

Frank raised his eyebrows. "All the evidence, including DNA, points only to Fitch."

"I know. I know."

Olivier said, "Jealousy."

Giulia's head snapped toward him. "Tulley jealous of Fitch? Of course. What if he wanted to one-up Fitch by stealing more and doing it better?"

Zane's fingers pounded his keyboard. Sidney moused through documents.

"Last July," they said almost in unison.

"The bar thefts started in April, after Loriela's murder," Sidney added.

"That's Fitch celebrating his freedom," Giulia said.

"From?" Frank said.

"Jail and Loriela." Giulia paced the distance from wall to wall. "If the July escalation is Tulley's doing, what triggered it? Don't answer that." She stopped and stabbed a finger at different sheets of the collage. "Fitch forced Tulley to steal from the bar. Tulley rebelled by taking more risks at AtlanticEdge."

"So they're playing 'mine are bigger than yours'?" Zane said. "What are they, five?"

"No," Giulia said. "They're in high school. That's why I got distracted by Petit."

"The lawyer?" Frank said. "You have him on the suspect list?"

"Tulley told me how Fitch and Petit were high school basketball rivals. Petit spent too much time coming up with wordy, plausible refutations of my suspicions."

Olivier snagged the last piece of carnivore pizza. "I am already looking forward to the relative simplicity of my more convoluted patients tomorrow."

"Hah," Sidney said. "And you thought all we did was chase deadbeat dads and screen wannabe priests."

Zane said, "If this is real life imitating a soap opera, Tulley wanted Loriela. Fitch didn't want Loriela anymore. Tulley tried for her and she rejected him."

Giulia stood very still, looking at all the elements as one giant pattern. "Fitch pushes and twists and goads Tulley until Tulley's ready to do anything to revenge himself on Loriela's rejection. Fitch plants the idea—revenge or greed, it doesn't matter, maybe both—and sets everything up. On April first he gets Lori falling-down drunk, pretends to everyone he's just as drunk, and gives himself the perfect alibi—because he really is innocent. In fact, if not in spirit."

"Ye-es," Sidney said. "It makes more sense than Fitch doing it himself."

"Because Fitch likes to get his minions to do things for him," Zane said.

"Yes." Giulia slapped the photo of the footprints in the muddy landscaping below Fitch's balcony. "Fitch got Tulley to kill Loriela. And it's festered in him with all his other festering wrongs until he told me to look at Petit and Fitch, the other rivals. Misdirection." She turned to Frank with a grin. "Fitch didn't kill Loriela."

Frank grinned back. "You sure?"

"I am, but we have something better than being sure: We don't have to prove it. Proof is Colby Petit's problem. Providing him with ammunition to create reasonable doubt is ours. Sidney, do you agree?"

Sidney was studying her screen. "It makes sense...I could put a summary document together to double-check." She looked up. "Tomorrow?"

"Zane?"

"I can see it. Do we have anything concrete? Anything at all?"

"No." Giulia leaned on Sidney's desk. "We never had anything concrete against Fitch, either. Neither did the police. Right, Frank?"

Frank opened both hands. "Technically correct. You will admit, however, that the circumstantial evidence is damning enough to justify murder charges."

"Well, tomorrow I'll give Petit enough to plant doubt in a jury's mind. Then I bet you'll get a call to start digging through some old evidence." Giulia would have danced if she wasn't so dead tired. She squinted at the clock as though seeing the time through the smallest opening would soften the blow.

"It's nine thirty-three, hardworking investigators. You are hereby kicked out of this office for the night. Go to sleep thinking of how fat your next paycheck will be." She held up a hand. "But be here on time tomorrow, because we have a lot to write up. I'll call Petit tonight with the good news and the bad news."

"Bad news?" Sidney said. "Oh, right. He's not a killer, but he is a thief."

"He's not technically a killer, we think."

Zane gathered all the food boxes and empty water bottles and stuffed them in the plastic bags. "I vote we take out an ad in the paper exposing him. It'd sure make me feel better."

Frank winked at Olivier. "I think we should call *The Scoop*."

Giulia threw her crumpled napkin at him.

Thirty-Eight

Giulia awoke at five a.m. and slipped out of bed without jostling Frank.

She threw on lounge pants and a sweatshirt and tiptoed downstairs to start coffee. While it brewed, she opted for pen and paper to outline the final report. Her eyes threatened to mutiny at the mere thought of an LED screen at this hour.

AtlanticEdge Findings
Based on Driscoll Investigations' analysis of video surveillance footage, bookkeeping ledgers, purchase orders, and check scans for the three-year period in question, we have reached the following conclusions.

Giulia added several bullet points about Tulley and Fitch. Loriela too, with a footnote to be written explaining that her involvement up to her death was a deduction without actual proof.

"I'll need to scan in the lists we made and add them to the PO scans, plus the corresponding pages from the books. This PowerPoint is going to be huge."

The coffee finished brewing. She chose a Monet water lilies teacup from the cupboard and the caramel creamer from the fridge. With the practiced hand of the desperate, she poured the fragrant, life-giving fluid into the narrow china cup.

The first hot, delicious mouthful warmed her inside and out.

With renewed purpose, she flipped over those pages and started her report for Colby Petit.

No PowerPoint for this one. Using the same reporting format, she began:

Based on the evidence and Driscoll Investigations' analysis, it is our conclusion that Leonard Tully is the murderer of Loriela Gil. However, it is also our conclusion that Roger Fitch was the driving force behind the murder. In addition, we have compiled evidence that this murder was part of ongoing embezzlement at AtlanticEdge by Fitch, Tulley, and possibly Loriela Gil herself. There is also evidence of ancillary money laundering at the Long Neck bar by Fitch and Tulley.

Following are the facts on which we base these conclusions, beginning with the AtlanticEdge embezzlement.

She filled three more pages, drawing in big boxes labeled CHECKING ACCOUNT and LONG NECK DEPOSITS and TULLEY SCREENCAPS FROM MURDER NIGHT PHOTOS.

Corroborating information from AtlanticEdge would have buttressed their case, but there was only so far Giulia could walk the tightrope of Fitch as Killer vs. Fitch as Thief. Sharing confidential AtlanticEdge information wasn't one of them. As it was, she could barely stand on the narrow ledge she'd created for herself by taking on these two cases.

The first cup of coffee was long gone by the time she had the summary in a format Zane could work with. She poured another cup and added creamer.

Now the phone. She'd turned it off at eleven o'clock after she left the message for Petit, thereby achieving six whole hours of sleep. Sure enough, when the phone powered on, a red number four appeared over the little telephone icon. A red twelve covered the top corner of the missed calls icon. She took a long drink of coffee. There was no way she could take an incensed Fitch without assistance, even a recorded Fitch.

She dialed voicemail. It was Petit, not Fitch. Weariness and strain thinned the lawyer's voice.

"Ms. Driscoll, I've called several times and you're not picking up. It's after midnight. I need details. The message you left earlier was so sparse as to be nonexistent. Please return my call as soon as possible. Thank you."

"Mr. Petit," she said to the screen, "you should try yoga. It helps relieve stress."

Another few sips of coffee and she pressed the next message button. The expected voice hit her ear. He didn't bother with a salutation.

"I'm going to tell everyone that Driscoll Investigations is nothing but a front for thieves and con artists."

Somehow Fitch too angry to scream was nowhere near as cartoonish as Fitch at full volume and spitting mad.

The message continued. "Colby called and said you had news for us. Said you didn't leave any details in your message. He thinks there's hope. I think you're full of it."

That message ended and she pressed the next one.

"Pick up your phone, you bitch!"

Ah, the real Roger Fitch is back. She moved the phone away from her ear.

"I called you six times in the last hour! Don't you stonewall me or I'll come to your cozy little house and show you what happens to women who don't behave!"

Frank's hand came over her shoulder and hit the end button. Giulia jumped and gasped and dropped the phone.

"I believe that's an actionable threat," her husband said. "I do like it when the scumbags take care of our work for us."

"If you give me a heart attack you can't blame it on Fitch." Giulia kissed him. "Want some coffee? What time is it now?"

"Yes, please, and it's ten after six."

"I need a mental health day. Preferably at a girly spa with aromatherapy and pedicures." She poured coffee for Frank.

"I can think of a better way to relax."

Frank put his hands on her hips and kissed her neck.

"There's men's ways to relax and there's women's ways to relax." Giulia leaned against him and moved her hair out of the way of Frank's lips.

Frank kissed more of her neck. "Right now they look the same to me."

Her skin muffled his voice. Right now she agreed with him...

Giulia channeled her inner workaholic and extracted herself.

"Here. Coffee. I have another voicemail to endure before I shower and get to the office. We get to wrap up two cases today."

"Cruel woman. Put this one on speaker."

The timestamp on this last message read 1:15 a.m.

"You're sound asleep, aren't you?" Fitch's voice slurred a little. "Think you're safe in your bed with your big, bad cop hus-sband next to you, huh? Lori thought she was safe in bed next to me 'til s-somebody opened the balcony door." He laughed, belched, and hung up.

Giulia flicked the phone across the kitchen table. "Everything that man does and says is slimy."

Frank was smiling. "You don't appreciate the little gifts he just left us. If you're right—and I think you are—concluding he finagled his co-embezzler into killing Gil, a good lawyer can use those two messages to bolster that part of the case. The prosecuting attorney for Fitch's trial is a very good lawyer."

Giulia considered that. "Then why did he allow Fitch to delay the trial for us to chase this wild goose?"

Frank shrugged. "Strategy. He wanted the extra time to refine his case. Also, hiring you gave Fitch more rope to hang himself. Win-win for the other side."

"But he didn't win. Fitch didn't kill Loriela. I'm even more sure this morning now that I've got it down in order on paper. Petit will be able to get an acquittal on reasonable doubt. You know he will. He's that good."

"Doesn't matter to me. The state will find enough to indict the other guy and will find ways to work around the fact that all this new evidence is circumstantial like the Fitch evidence. From what you've said about the other guy, he'll stab Fitch in the back to get a reduced sentence, and that will be that. I'm not even counting the embezzlement issue, which will put both of them in jail anyway." Frank downed the rest of his coffee and grinned. "I hope they get assigned to the same cell."

Giulia stood and brought her cup to the sink. "When I asked Fitch about his pregnant ex-girlfriend he talked about backstabbing. Tulley was the one who told me about her. I should've picked up on their rivalry earlier." She rinsed the cup and put it in the dishwasher. "Today might be another long day. We have to get everything to Fitch's lawyer before noon and I want to complete the AtlanticEdge report by five."

"I will revitalize your day by opening the door for you tonight wearing only a kilt and a smile."

Giulia splurted a laugh. "I dare you."

Thirty-Nine

Giulia left identical voicemails for Sidney and Zane: "I'm bringing breakfast." That meant the Garden of Delights, which was worth every extra minute in rush-hour traffic. She positioned the logo side of the box so it preceded her into the office.

Sidney squealed. "You are the best boss ever."

"Whoa," Zane said. "Thanks."

"It was the obvious choice." Giulia searched for a place to set down the box. "Sidney, you're right. We need a table in here."

A cough from behind Sidney's monitor sounded a lot like "I told you so."

"Set it on this corner." Zane dumped his desk calendar and unfinished projects on his chair. "Dibs on first choice."

"Weasel," Sidney said. "Doesn't matter, anyway, because we don't eat the same things."

Giulia passed out two cups of coffee and one of peppermint tea.

"Jane, I don't know your caffeine preference, so I got sugar and creamers on the side."

"Wow. Thanks." Jane held the paper cup like she'd been transported direct to Christmas morning.

"Sidney, these are almond with raspberry cream and carrot with raw milk cream cheese." Giulia handed her two cupcakes on a Garden logo paper plate. "For the rest of us, I got an assortment: Two each of tiramisu, triple chocolate, strawberry shortcake, and snickerdoodle. The shortcakes are vegan too, if mini-Sidney is particularly ravenous this morning."

For several minutes silence reigned in the office. Giulia finished her second cupcake and tossed the paper in Zane's trash can.

"Tiramisu," she said.

"Triple chocolate," Zane said. "You can never beat three kinds of chocolate in one."

"If you people would ever try their vegan cupcakes," Sidney said, "you'd see that the almond-raspberry is unsurpassable."

Jane said in a hesitant voice, "Snickerdoodle?"

"See, the texture is all wrong for me," Giulia said. "My mouth agrees with the taste, but can't accept that it's not flat and chewy. Same with the shortcake, but the strawberry whipped cream filling makes up for it."

The phone rang.

"Interlude over," Zane said.

"Alas," Giulia said. She lowered her voice so Zane could hear the caller. "Go ahead with training, both of you. Zane and I will type our fingers raw for the rest of the day."

"Thanks for breakfast," Jane said.

"It's not a regular thing," Giulia said. "Driscoll Investigations went above and beyond yesterday."

Zane hung up the phone.

"New client." He wrote on a miniature legal pad. "Wants you to call him. Nothing urgent."

"That's good, because we don't have space for urgent today. I'll take the AtlanticEdge report because I wrote up Fitch's case in a lot more detail."

Giulia closed her door, opened the window and typed. Not twenty minutes later, the phone rang. Her buzzer sounded right after.

"Sorry, Ms. Driscoll, but it's Leonard Tulley. I thought you might want to take this one."

"You thought right. Thanks."

The transfer button turned red. She switched mental gears and pressed the button.

"This is Giulia Falcone-Driscoll, Mr. Tulley. How may I help you?"

"Remember when I told you about Roger and Colby's high school rivalry and then about his pregnant ex?" His voice was sharp without the lazy-guy camouflage.

How about "Good morning, Ms. F-D. Thanks for taking my call." All she said out loud was, "Yes."

"Did you tell Roger I told you about them?"

Giulia stiffened. "Certainly not. We are professionals."

"Didn't think so. Well, somebody told him, or he figured it out for himself, because he kept looking at me with his snake face yesterday."

"I'm sorry?"

"Jeez, don't you ever watch Animal Planet? When a snake's on the hunt it gets real still and its face sorta loses all expression. I know snakes don't have facial expressions. I'm not stupid. But it's like they get an aura or something."

"Mr. Tulley, I'm not sure what your point is. Is there anything I can help you with?"

"I dunno. You own a mongoose?"

Giulia laughed. "I'm sorry. I didn't mean to be rude, but that was a funny question. No, I don't own a mongoose. Are you worried that Mr. Fitch will try to retaliate for something he thinks you've done?"

"You're not the brightest bulb in the box, are you? I thought you had brains. Of course I'm worried. When Roger likes you, the world is perfect. If he changes his mind, watch your back. Free advice. Take it." He was silent for a moment. "It might have been my ex who talked to him. We got hammered a couple of times and I could've said something. Women. Can't trust 'em. Bye."

Giulia hung up the phone without slamming it. Tulley had more than an angry Roger Fitch to worry about. In a week or so, depending on how fast AtlanticEdge acted on the report she was writing, Tulley would be scrambling for bail money. What he'd stolen from them might not be enough to cover it.

She dismissed Tulley from her mind and typed for the next three hours. The traffic noises kept her alert, especially the occasional siren. The phone rang twice, but Zane didn't buzz her. She'd inserted the first screencap when Zane knocked on her door.

"Ms. Driscoll, I've got the summary typed up. Want me to bring it in?'

"I'll come out." She un-hunched and opened the door. "Oh, look. Four different walls."

Zane was alone in the office. "The other two went to lunch."

"Sure. Let's see what we've got." She walked around the office as she read, green pen in hand. "Good...good...no, I should've fleshed this part out more." She bent over Sidney's desk and added a few sentences. "Typo...Bah, that's not what I want it to say." She scratched out a paragraph and wrote several more sentences. "In conclusion...yes...not dramatic...logical. Good."

She handed it back to Zane. "It doesn't read too much like I wrote it at five o'clock this morning. Make those changes, please, and we'll send it to Petit along with all the documents he gave me. Which reminds me: I'd better put them back together."

Zane started retyping and Giulia took the rest of the Clue Collage apart. She carried them into her office and closed the window so they wouldn't blow around the room. Then she tipped everything out of the courier box and began to jog the removed pages back into their original places.

The phone rang.

"I'll get it." She picked up. "Driscoll Investigations."

"Ms. Falcone-Driscoll?" Colby Petit's voice. "Is that you?"

She closed her eyes and channeled her inner admin. "Yes, Mr. Petit. We're finishing up our final report right now."

"Oh, terrific. I knew you'd come through. But that's not why I'm calling. I'm neck-deep in last-minute preparations and I can't get hold of Roger."

"I'm sorry; is there something you think I can help you with?"

"Actually, yes. How close are you really to finishing the report for me?"

"I should have it to you by two o'clock."

"No, that's too late."

"I beg your pardon?"

"Oh. Sorry. I was thinking out loud." His voice added an extra layer of charm. "It's a huge favor, but would you be able to drive over to his apartment and drag him down to my office? He lost his temper last night and might have turned off his phone. I can't get hold of him and there's no one here I can ask to go over there. I don't rate my own errand-runner."

Giulia pounded her forehead on her desk. Did the man think no one besides himself had a desk full of work?

"Ms. Driscoll?"

Then again, the sooner she helped him, the sooner they'd both be off her back.

"I can squeeze it in, Mr. Petit."

"Wonderful. You're a life saver. I don't care if he's in his boxers and so hungover a whisper makes him cringe. All I ask is you throw him in your car and bring him to me."

"I would care if he's wearing nothing but boxers, but I get your point. Expect him in about an hour."

Zane was still typing when she took her jacket and purse off the coat rack.

"I'm going over to Fitch's apartment to drag his lazy butt out of bed. He turned off his phone and Petit needs him."

"Why'd he do that?"

"I called Petit last night with the highlights of what we found and he had the brilliant idea to tell Fitch."

Zane winced.

"For a lawyer he doesn't score high on the common sense scale."

"Olivier should get Petit into his office for a few sessions. Look at the way Petit is hanging onto a grudge from high school and trying to be the bigger person about it at the same time." She checked the time. "I'll be back in less than an hour if the traffic cooperates."

Zane made a move toward his leather jacket. "I should come with you. You know, as muscle."

"You were great on Saturday, but he won't be a problem this time." As soon as the words left her mouth, one of Frank's lectures began playing in her head: Don't underestimate any criminal suspect. Cornered animals attack.

"Are you sure?"

Giulia smiled at him. "You sound like Frank. Don't worry. He's either hung over or sleeping it off. I was a star pupil at my self-defense classes. I can take care of myself. Besides, I'm packing heat." She laughed at the expression on Zane's face. "I'm also going to take great pleasure in banging on Fitch's door as loud as possible."

Zane grinned. "Try to film it. We can upload it to YouTube under a throwaway account."

"Don't tempt me."

Forty

Lunch hour traffic plus the anticipation of a hungover Roger Fitch put Giulia in a miserable temper. By the time she pulled into the apartment's parking lot she briefly considered taking her Glock out of her locked glove compartment and placing it in her belt. The sight ought to give Fitch extra incentive to get dressed and out the door. After a moment of pleasant visualization she thought better of it and locked the Nunmobile as usual.

She buzzed his apartment a dozen times without result. Before she attempted to pick the lock, which might in turn trip a silent alarm, she remembered Geranium Asher. With a smile, she pressed the button for the old woman's apartment.

"Who is it?"

"It's Mrs. Driscoll."

"Hello! You come right on up."

The lock disengaged with another buzz and Giulia climbed the stairs to the second floor. Geranium was waiting in her doorway with a huge smile on her face.

"I never expected you to come back this soon. I made cookies again this morning. Chocolate-covered cherry. You come in and tell me what you think."

"I wish I could. Unfortunately I'm here to fetch your next-door neighbor. He's needed at his lawyer's and probably sleeping off an epic drinking bout."

Geranium wrinkled her nose. "You'll have to drag him out of

bed, most likely. I heard him late yesterday shouting into his phone and slamming doors. He always drinks when he gets mad." Her eyes got big. "I saw you on that nasty TV show with those young women throwing food and ripping each other's earrings out. This floor surely won't miss him when they throw him into jail." She tipped her head to one side. "That is, if you uncovered enough nastiness to send him to jail."

"Officially, I won't comment," Giulia said with a smile. "Unofficially, you all should be sleeping a lot better soon."

Geranium nodded. "I didn't hear you say a thing. Well, you have a job to do. For my part, I think it's time to rearrange a chair over by a certain wall. I'm trying out that *feng shui* I've heard so much about." She winked and closed her door.

Still smiling, Giulia rang Fitch's doorbell. She hoped he'd do Geranium a favor and shout. Maybe even throw something. That would give her an entertaining morning. A minute later, she rang again, this time leaning on it for a good thirty seconds. Still no sound from the other side. She pounded on it with the side of her fist.

"Roger Fitch! Wake up!" She pounded again. "Ro-ger Fitch!"

Her hand started to hurt, so she took off one red shoe and banged on the door with the heel.

"Roger Fitch! Wake up! Let me in! Roger Fitch!"

She leaned in closer to the door. Another groan and a thud.

She put her shoe back on and reached into one of the zippered compartments in her purse for a large paper clip. With a sharp twist she snapped it in half and crouched so the lock was at her eye level.

"From the convent to breaking and entering. Sister Bart would be thrilled to watch this." Her hands worked as she muttered to herself. "Insert the hook end into the lock below the pins so the L shape points up. I should've practiced this more often. Push it down...do it right so it doesn't pop out...turn the L away and stick the other half right up underneath the pins. There. Felt it. Hands, find some muscle memory." She wiggled the top half and applied clockwise force to the bottom half. "I felt that. A little more until it...pops."

The lock disengaged.

"That should've been harder. Either it's a cheapo lock or I'm getting better at criminal activities." Giulia dropped the paper clip halves back into her purse. "Rise and shine, Mr. Fitch. Your attorney awaits."

She opened the door. The hall was way too dark for just past noon and the air stank of nachos and old pizza. She thought she remembered a light switch...there it was, beneath a framed photo of a microbrew tasting at Long Neck.

With a muted click, ceiling fixtures illuminated the hall. She walked into the open space between the kitchen and living room and called, "Mr. Fitch? It's Giulia Falcone-Driscoll."

She walked all the way into the kitchen. Nothing. She turned toward the living room and saw a sneakered foot next to the chrome and glass coffee table. A step further and she saw a denim-clad leg and two empty bottles of vodka. A third bottle rolled back and forth on the edge of the table, spilling clear liquid with every swing. Empty beer cans lay in an open pizza box.

Another step and she got a full view of her client. He lay passed out on the rug, vodka splashes on his arms and two empty pill bottles mixed in among the beer cans.

Giulia leapt the rest of the distance and snatched up one of the pill bottles.

"Hydrocodone, ten milligrams. Fitch, you idiot."

Giulia dropped her purse, picked up Fitch's arm with one hand, and pushed up his damp sleeve with the other. He still had a pulse.

She yanked open her purse and found her phone. Her fingers hit the password on the first try and she started to dial 9-1-1. Fitch grabbed the phone out of her hands before she could hit the last digit.

"Sorry, darlin'. That's not part of the plan."

Giulia stared at the Smith & Wesson in his right hand. Fitch's eyes were clear and his voice was crisp and pleased. "You really are a useless bleeding heart." He pocketed her phone and got to his feet. "Colby sent you, didn't he? I figured he would when I didn't answer his calls all morning. Knew his famous charm would get you to do what he asked."

Giulia was flogging herself harder than Fitch was sneering. She should've been more careful. She knew he couldn't be trusted.

Fitch kept the gun aimed at Giulia's stomach.

She had never wanted to curse more than at this moment. If he shot her at that distance, it would disable her enough for him to get away. He was the type to use more than one bullet to make sure of the kill, too. Her scattered thoughts scrambled for a way out.

Then her brain rebooted. Fitch had called her "bleeding-heart" and "soft" more than once. He thought she was gullible—well, he was right about that. Why else was she standing here with a Smith & Wesson aimed at her gut? He thought she was still the timid church mouse who'd joined the community theater orchestra four years ago. He'd given her the perfect camouflage. He also had no idea that she could cry on cue.

"Move, Driscoll." Fitch gestured with the gun.

"I—but—where do you want me to go?" She made her eyes big and round.

"You're my driver, woman. It's time for me to get out of Dodge."

Giulia planted her feet but made sure her hands trembled. "I'm not letting you take my car."

He laughed. "What would I want with that used toy car you drive? We're taking my car, now that it's fixed up. A nice, anonymous dark blue Buick."

"Mr. Fitch, you don't have to go anywhere. We believe our investigation proves that you didn't kill Loriela Gil."

She pulled up her mental map of the apartment. The balcony was too far from the living room. The window above the sink was too small to squeeze through. The front door was the only option.

"No shit, Sherlock. I've been telling everyone I didn't kill Lori for a year. Come on. We're heading out." He prodded the small of her back with the gun.

She deliberately stumbled. He grabbed her arm and wrenched her upright.

She held her breath for a moment and tears grew in the corners of her eyes. She turned her face to give Fitch the full effect.

"You're crying? Good God, how do you function in normal society?" The gun jabbed her ribs. "Let's go, little girl. It's time to drive daddy to freedom."

At that moment she remembered Geranium was listening. How could I forget? Have to make noise.

"No! Please, Mr. Fitch, put down the gun!" Giulia snatched one of the empty vodka bottles and skidded around the coffee table.

"Get back here, bitch!"

"Help!" Giulia threw the bottle so it bounced off the coffee table.

Fitch made a grab for it but missed. The bottle hit the TV stand and shattered with a lovely loud smash. Giulia ran for the door but Fitch moved much faster than she expected. He caught her by the hair and yanked. The false tears in her eyes became real ones.

He jerked her head back so she looked up into his face. "None of that escape crap. We're going out the back stairs now. You and me." He dug the gun into her spine at every other word. "You will not. Say. One. Word. You don't want to end up like Lori. You want to get back home to your big, strong cop husband."

Giulia nodded, making sure she trembled enough for Fitch to notice.

He snickered. She was satisfied. He opened the door and they went through. Giulia tried to see Geranium's door out of the corners of her eyes. It looked closed. She tried to send her thoughts to Geranium through the door: Please be listening. Please call the police.

He marched her to the stairs at the end of the hall, keeping close to her side.

Giulia pushed open the door to the back stairs and they walked down each tread together. The awkward descent took twice as long as Giulia did walking it alone and she hoped the delay would give the police more time to arrive. Fitch cracked open the door to the back parking lot. "Stick your curly head out and check for innocent bystanders."

Giulia complied. "No one."

"Good. We're walking straight to my car, which is conveniently parked against those nice bushy pine trees." He gave her a calculating look. "While we walk, let's have a conversation. If any nosy old ladies are looking out their windows, they'll see two people having a casual conversation. Who do you think killed Lori?"

Giulia pushed open the door and they walked into a smaller parking lot surrounded on three sides by other buildings and on the fourth by stunted pine trees. Four cars and two pickups were scattered among the twenty lined spaces.

Fitch aimed them at a dark blue Buick with its back against the trees.

"Well? Who'd you pin her murder on?"

"Leonard Tulley." She glanced around the parking lot. The street wasn't visible from there, leaving no way to signal anyone.

"Ding ding ding! The kids playing detective get one right." He laughed. It was an ugly sound. "Twenty more steps. Don't get stupid, or no happy reunion with coppy."

"I understand, Mr. Fitch." The one time she should've brought her gun in with her...

He whispered into her ear, "I bet you don't know why he killed her."

His breath steamed up her skin. She repressed a shudder and remembered to play dumb. "We didn't get a handle on that. When Mr. Petit called to say the trial had been moved up, we spent the time writing up all we found so he could use it in his arguments to the jury."

"And people say no one is willing to work hard for their paycheck these days." He pulled a key ring from his pants pocket and pressed a button. The door locks released.

"You're going to sit in the driver's seat, and you're not going to do anything stupid while I get into the passenger seat."

Giulia climbed into the seat without replying. Fitch crossed in front of the car and opened the passenger door, keeping the gun visible to Giulia with every step.

"Buckle up, Driscoll. First rule of criminal activity: don't draw unnecessary attention to yourself." He waited so they buckled together. "Here's the plan. We're heading west on 376 'til we get to the Ridge Road exit."

"And then?"

"Nope. That's all you need to know for now. Start the car."

Giulia couldn't come up with an escape route that didn't involve Fitch shooting her at point-blank range. Yet. She started the car.

"Don't speed," Fitch said. "Don't drive too slow. Keep to the exact speed limit. Let's go."

She put the car in gear and drove around the side of the apartment building to the street. Fitch kept the gun in her ribs, out of sight of anyone driving in the lane next to them. She merged into the street and got up to speed without gunning the engine.

"It's hard to concentrate with a gun pointed at me."

"Too bad. Keep your goal in mind: getting home alive. I always keep my goals right in front of me. That's why I'm leaving town with a hundred thousand in the bank and another hundred in the trunk."

Play dumb. "Did you steal that money?" She stopped as the corner light turned yellow.

A long, braying laugh. "I didn't get it panhandling on the streets."

A minivan pulled up next to her, two small girls in the backseat beating each other with sock monkey dolls. Giulia kept her eyes on the light. The mother driving yelled without effect at the girls.

The light changed. The minivan pulled into the intersection. Giulia followed suit.

"Very good."

Giulia thought with satisfaction about breaking his jaw. No, his nose because they were in tight quarters.

Fitch settled his shoulders into the bucket seat and braced the gun with both hands. "We have time. Let me tell you a story about a lovely woman, a handsome man, and their clueless flunky."

Forty-One

Giulia reduced her speed to forty as she attempted to merge onto the interstate. An eighteen-wheeler changed to the right-hand lane directly in front of her, cutting her off. She took her foot off the gas, but Fitch dug the gun in deeper. "Speed up. Merge directly into the middle lane. Now."

"I have no desire to die under the wheels of a semi."

"Me neither. I could've managed that merge without instructions, though. Didn't they teach you to drive in the nunnery?"

She didn't bother to answer.

Giulia drove in the right-hand lane, letting everyone pass her. She hadn't realized how few cars actually drove the speed limit. Funny.

Amazing what her brain came up with when she was in mortal danger. Because she was. Fitch wasn't about to let her go. If she wanted to survive, she had to take his gun away.

"To continue the story of our three-way strategy game. There we were, Lori and I, working for The Man. It wasn't enough." He watched the traffic for a few seconds. "Look out for that moron changing lanes without signaling."

Giulia bit her lip so she wouldn't talk back to the guy holding a gun on her. "But Loriela became head of accounting in less than a year and you're head of sales. Those positions must come with impressive salaries."

A set of three minivans whirred past them on Fitch's side. A moving van rumbled by Giulia.

"Impressive by some standards, maybe. The trouble was, Lori and I were tired of waiting, doing it the slow way. That's for grunts and women on the Mommy Track." He glanced out the windshield again. "Cop on your left. Be a good girl now."

Giulia amended her earlier promise to herself. She was going to break more than his nose.

The police car hit its siren. A silver mustang accepted defeat and signaled its trip to the right shoulder and a speeding ticket.

"Back to the plan. What's a great set up without some eager fanboy to do the real work? Tulley had it bad for Lori. He practically drooled when she wore shirts that showed cleavage, and Lori knew how to use people." He leaned closer to Giulia. "Right at the speed limit. You obey orders so well it's a wonder how you haven't run your husband's agency into the ground."

Her fingers tightened on the steering wheel, but she loosened them a moment later. Body language could give her away.

"I know what you're thinking. Lori used me. Yep, she did, and I used her. We both knew it. Then Len got the idea that Lori would be better off with him." The ugly laugh reappeared. "Lori and I used to laugh our asses off about Len. I kept laughing even when Lori started to turn into her shrew of a mother. That's when I went to work on Len. Took that lump of fat an entire year to figure out I played him."

Traffic thinned. Giulia kept checking for the marked or unmarked police car that should be following her. If Geranium had been listening. If Geranium made that call.

Fitch pointed to the upcoming exit sign. "Ridge Road. Don't get any ideas."

Giulia changed lanes.

"Can't leave this story without a punch line. When I found out the other day somebody tried to pin Lori's murder on me because of that old abortion story, I didn't have to look far. Only Lori and Colby and Len knew that story." His foot beat a pattern on the floor mat. "Nobody plays Roger Fitch. So I changed plans fast. Withdrew everything from our shared bank accounts except a hundred bucks. Who's he going to complain to? Not the cops. Not the bank. Now he's dumb and broke and screwed. I'm free and rich and about to drive off into the sunset. Starting tomorrow, there will be no Roger Fitch to track down."

Giulia went with the obvious TV show dialogue. "Mr. Fitch, there's no way you can escape the police. They know your car because you reported the theft."

Another laugh. "Planning, Driscoll. Planning is everything. I've got a spare set of plates stashed in one of the cabins. Rented it last week under a fake name and paid cash. There's the off-ramp. Exit now."

She left the expressway and circled onto Ridge Road. This wasn't good. If Geranium had made that phone call, surely the police would've caught up to them on 376. And if she did call and the police were searching, how were they going to find the car now that they were off the main road?

"Speed limit change. Slow down."

Shut up, Fitch.

"Turn right on Bayer. See it? About a hundred yards ahead."

Giulia couldn't think of a reason to stop the car while they were still on a somewhat busy road. She stopped it anyway.

"What the hell? Drive!"

Timid Giulia said, "I can't do this. It's wrong. I work for the good guys—"

He clipped her across the face with the barrel of the gun. Her lip split.

"Move!"

She shook her head, making it a tight, scared movement.

A siren reached her ears at last. Loud and getting louder with every revolution.

Fitch cursed. "Drive the car."

Giulia gripped the wheel and kept her foot on the brake. A green hatchback drove past them on the other side of the divided road. In her rearview mirror a school bus appeared from the same exit ramp. She looked right and left.

The shoulders on both sides of the road dipped and rose before they met the treeline.

He hit her cheek twice, harder than the blow to her mouth. "Drive the car or I'll beat you blind on one side and shove your foot onto the gas pedal myself."

Her ears rang, but she still heard the siren—sirens, plural—closing the gap between them. Fitch clubbed her knee with the butt of the gun. The sharp pain knocked her foot partially off the brake. The car jerked forward. Giulia caught a flashing red and blue light angling toward them from the exit ramp.

She floored it. Fitch fell back into his seat. She swung onto Bayer and increased speed. Fitch spewed threats and curses at her. The sirens grew loud enough to force him to shout over them. A VW bus chugged along in front of her. She swung around it much too fast and grazed its side mirror when she cut back in front of it.

The VW driver leaned on the horn. Fitch grabbed the wheel with his left hand and tried to spin it out of her grip. The car swerved across both lanes. The sirens got louder. The VW braked and faded from the rearview mirror.

Fitch shouted until Giulia thought she'd go deaf from his voice on top of the sirens. "Slow down! You're gonna wreck us! Slow down!" They fought for control of the steering wheel. The speedometer inched past seventy. The Buick caught the rear bumper of a Mini Cooper. The Cooper spun and landed with its back wheels in the ditch by the opposite side of the road.

Giulia saw flashing lights in the rearview mirror.

Now.

She wrenched the steering wheel to the left. The front wheels hit the grass. The tires skidded for a heartbeat. The car flipped over on its side and kept rolling. The roof straddled the ditch and the car tilted one last time.

It stopped when its roof smashed against three pine trees, lower branches crunching against the windshield and the passenger windows. The Buick's wheels still spun, the engine notching down step by step from racing speed.

Fitch sprawled against the door, his seat belt pressing down on his ear. Giulia hung sideways in hers, the edge cutting into her waist. Her ears rang. Her heart pounded. Her face throbbed from Fitch's blows. Her knee twinged when she tried to move it. She shook her head to get it clear.

She peeled her fingers off the steering wheel. Fitch's knuckles were white from his grip on the gun and he muttered as he tried to free his trapped elbows.

"You can't do this to me." Blood dripped down the side of his face. "I'll shove your dead body out that door in front of your cop husband."

He aimed the gun at last. Giulia grabbed his hands. His finger groped for the trigger. She pushed his hands toward the dashboard, away from her. He jerked. She lost her grip for an instant, got it back, and wrenched Fitch's wrists a hundred and eighty degrees. His bones snapped like the paperclip she used to pick his lock.

He yelled louder than the approaching sirens. Giulia got one hand on the gun barrel. Fitch's left hand flopped away but his right hand clutched it tighter. His spit struck her face as he screamed at her.

Giulia's other hand closed around his right wrist. She used that leverage to clamp his elbow to his side. She pushed his wrist into his chest and wrenched it toward the dashboard. *Crack.*

The gun fell into her hand.

His swollen, red eyes stared at her. "You broke my wrists."

If Giulia had been the sheltered convent refugee Fitch had assumed all along, she would've been appalled. As it was, she only wanted him to shut up.

"How the hell did you do that, you spineless bitch?"

Giulia trained the gun on him as the sirens reached deafening levels and then cut off.

"Jackie Chan movies."

His stupefied look was a satisfactory reward.

Forty-Two

The door above Giulia opened. She kept her eyes and the gun on Fitch.

"Honey, isn't this a little over the top?" Frank's voice said.

"You're just jealous of my driving skills." Giulia was ridiculously pleased at how steady her voice was.

Fitch started up again. "Your wife broke my wrists! I'll sue her for assault! I'll take you for every penny you've got! She's a lying, treacherous bitch! She's—"

"Shut it, Fitch." Frank's hand reached over Giulia's shoulder and covered the gun. "Why did we bother to get you your own gun if you're not going to use it? I'll take this."

Fitch stopped whining long enough to hear Frank's last sentence. The look of shock on his face was so priceless both Giulia and Frank laughed.

As soon as her hands were free she turned off the ignition. She turned her head and managed a shaky grin.

A uniformed police officer's head appeared next to Frank's. "Detective, the Fire Department wants to check them out to see if they can put the car back on its wheels."

"Sure." Then with extreme politeness: "Fitch, if you'll look to your right, you'll see two well-trained police officers with guns. They are prepared to shoot you if you breathe the wrong way. I'd advise you to sit still."

Frank squeezed Giulia's shoulder and stepped away. Several

firefighters came up to the car and inspected it without obstructing the police officers' line of sight. Giulia caught only bits and pieces of what they were doing, because she refused to take her attention away from Fitch.

After some discussion, measuring, and more discussion, one of them tapped Giulia on the shoulder. She turned her head enough to see a Fabio-clone looking earnest and businesslike.

"Ma'am, we're not going to try to turn the car upright with you in it. Here's the plan. I'm going to support you and Ibanez here is going to cut the seat belt. Then we'll both lift you out. Can you handle that?"

"No problem. Watch out for him, though." She indicated Fitch with her head.

Firefighter Fabio said, "He'd be pretty stupid to try anything in front of all these witnesses."

Fitch ordered them to perform a physically impossible act. The firefighters laughed.

"Okay, ma'am, here we go."

Fabio took hold of Giulia's arms. Ibanez leaned into the car and sliced through the seat belt across her hips first. She braced her legs against the center panel, swallowing the stab of pain in her knee.

Ibanez cut apart the shoulder harness and Fabio's grip was all that stopped Giulia from crashing onto Fitch. Ibanez wrapped his arms around her legs and the two men hauled her out into the open.

"Of course. A ladder." Giulia made a wry face. "I should've wondered how you could reach me so easily."

They carried her several feet north of the car.

"You should get those bruises looked at, ma'am," Fabio said. "I'll send the EMTs over."

When they set her on the ground her knee buckled, but she recovered right away. Not before Frank saw it.

He cut off his conversation with his partner and ran over. "What's wrong with your knee—dammit." He touched her cheekbone and she flinched away. "What did that bastard do to you?"

"I wouldn't obey his orders. He didn't like it." She got a death grip on his arm. "Frank, don't. He can't fight back, remember? I broke his wrists."

He stopped trying to break away. "You did? Really? He wasn't exaggerating?"

Giulia shook her head and sighed with feeling. "O ye of little faith."

Nash VanHorne, Frank's partner, came up in time to hear Giulia's reply. "Giulia, you've got to teach me some of those Bible comebacks to use on my kid sisters."

An EMT came over and made Giulia sit on the grass. She worked her hands into disposable gloves and palpated Giulia's cheek and lip.

"Not too bad. He missed your eye, so you won't look like a raccoon for a week." She snapped open an instant cold pack and placed it on Giulia's cheek. "Hold that while I fix your mouth. This is going to feel cold."

She dabbed a swab soaked in something medicinal on Giulia's split lip.

Giulia inhaled sharply. "That stings like a dozen bees."

"Yeah. I lied." The EMT smiled. "You took it like a fighter. Keep that ice on at least twenty minutes every hour, then swap it out for heat tomorrow. Got any arnica gel?"

"No, but my admin will. She'll be thrilled to preach the gospel of nature to me again."

"I'm with her. Use the arnica on your face. The bruise will heal quicker."

Behind them, Fitch started yelling at everyone in sight.

The EMT rolled her eyes. "He's going to be so much fun. You hurt your knee, too?"

"That one over there hit it with his gun."

"What a charmer. I've either got to ruin your jeans to treat it or all these guys get to see your underwear."

"Sacrifice the jeans, please."

"I thought you'd say that." She cut open the jeans on Giulia's right leg with scissors. "Hmm." She palpated the kneecap and both sides, then activated another cold pack. "I've got pink tape and green tape today."

"Green. I'm not feeling particularly feminine at the moment."

The EMT chuckled and strapped the tape around the ice pack and Giulia's knee.

"Get an x-ray this afternoon," she said, packing up. "I don't think it's more than another bruise, but never mess with your knees."

"I will," Giulia said. "Thanks."

"No problem. You were easy. Now I earn my pay."

Screeching tires drowned out Fitch's voice. Giulia and the EMT turned toward it in unison.

"Oh, no."

"What?" the EMT said. "Oh. The ambulance chasers had their police scanner on."

The Scoop's white van skidded off the road and stopped on the grass. Both doors opened at the same time. The camera's spotlight swung wildly across the faces of the group around the fire truck as the cameraman ran down the culvert and up the other side. Kanning waited 'til he got onto flatter ground before bringing up his microphone.

"Ken Kanning here for *The Scoop*." His voice bounced as he ran. "We're center stage at the Silk Tie Killer's latest crime."

For an instant the smorgasbord of potential interviewees appeared to paralyze him. Then he spotted Giulia.

"Mrs. Falcone-Driscoll." He vaulted over to her. "We rushed here to get your story as it happens."

Giulia turned her face away from the camera. *God, if you'll show me what sin I committed to rate this ongoing punishment, I promise never to repeat it.*

"Back off, Kanning," the EMT said. "I've got injured people to treat."

Kanning barreled on as though the EMT hadn't spoken. "Scoopers, brave Giulia Falcone-Driscoll sustained terrible injuries in her successful battle with the Silk Tie Killer. Look at this courageous woman."

The camera moved in for a close-up.

"Look at the beating she endured. See the bruises, the blood! This is the face of a woman who risked her life in the cause of justice." Kanning photobombed the shot. "Remember our promise, Scoopers: If we're ever wrong, we're ready to admit it. This is one of those rare times."

He switched the mike to his left hand and held out his right. "Congratulations. You sure had us convinced you were trying to pervert justice instead of uphold it."

Giulia didn't shake his hand.

"Mrs. Falcone-Driscoll, everyone's waiting to hear your harrowing story. The Scoopers are on the edges of their seats." He stuck the mike in her face.

From the treeline, Roger Fitch yelled, "I'll sue you for police brutality!"

Kanning's head snapped around. He jerked it toward the Fitch tableau and *The Scoop* deserted Giulia for bigger prey.

The police couldn't restrain Fitch's broken wrists, so they had cuffed his ankles. Only the assistance of two police officers kept him still long enough for the other EMT to apply splints. When the EMT finished, he hefted the strapping tape and glared at Fitch's flapping mouth. That shut him up for half a minute.

Giulia's EMT packed up her supplies. "What a douchenozzle."

"Kanning or Fitch?"

"Do I have to decide?"

Giulia laughed and a moment later pressed a hand to her face. "Ow."

While Kanning grilled Fitch, the police photographer finished taking pictures of the car, the chewed-up grass, and the skid marks on the road. Now he stepped back. With creaks and groans and metal scraping against metal, the firefighters tipped the Buick back onto its wheels. It bounced a few times then settled, listing to one side where the crash had blown out a tire.

More photos. The smell of gasoline filled the air and Fitch struggled to get up. Two sets of hands on his shoulders held him down.

"Spray it down! Don't let the trunk catch on fire! Let me up, you—"

Frank and VanHorne looked at each other. The firefighters coated the entire car with chemical spray, waited, sprayed it again, and waited some more. The chief got flat on the foam-covered grass and inspected the undercarriage, then walked all around it.

"Go ahead," he said to Frank and VanHorne. "It wasn't going to go up, but we like to make sure."

VanHorne reached inside the car for the switch and popped open the trunk.

Frank raised it all the way. "Well, well, well. Close out a few bank accounts today, Fitch?"

"You'll never see that much in your lifetime, cop! I busted my hump for that cash. You can impound it, but I'll beat this murder charge and it'll be mine again."

The police photographer snapped more pictures. Kanning's cameraman squeezed in next to him until Frank ordered him away. Kanning's commentary ran nonstop.

Giulia limped over to the Fitch grouping. "You said all three of you stole that money—you, Loriela Gil, and Leonard Tulley."

Fitch waved a splint at her. She repressed a laugh at the failure of his grandiose dismissive gesture.

"Do you really think I'm going to fall for that? I'm not saying another word 'til Colby Petit gets here."

"Thank God for small favors," the uniformed police officer said.

Forty-Three

Colby Petit arrived breathless at the precinct as Giulia was reading over her statement, leg propped on a spare chair.

"Ms. Driscoll? Where's Roger? What happened?"

Giulia tried hard to keep her voice professional. "Here's the short version: Your client kidnapped me at gunpoint, forced me to drive him to Settlers Cabin Park, took a stab at pistol-whipping me, and is now in a holding cell. If you listen, you can hear him screaming for you amidst the other voices back there."

He stared at her without moving until Fitch's voice rose above the holding cell chaos: "Let my lawyer in here, you bastards!"

Petit startled into action. "I—that is—I'll go talk to him. May I ask you some questions when I come out?"

Giulia shook her head. "I don't think so. You'll have to hear about it when I get on the witness stand."

Petit turned greenish. Then he ran to the door to the holding area. A cacophony of angry voices flooded the room. Fitch still managed to be the loudest.

Giulia signed the statement and gave it back to VanHorne. "Looks good. I think it's time I got this knee x-rayed."

Frank came through the door from the interrogation rooms. "You'll never guess who I've been talking to."

"Too tired for guessing games. I want ibuprofen and more ice."

Frank came around behind her and massaged her shoulders. "Leonard Tulley."

Giulia paused in the midst of melting against his chest. "You're kidding. Why? How?"

"Relax. Don't undo this shoulder rub. He came in about an hour ago, Jimmy says, looking like David Beckham on a breakaway with the entire New York Red Bulls team after him. Says his half of the money he and Fitch stole from two different workplaces vanished from their checking accounts. He called your office and heard you were headed to Fitch's."

"That shouldn't have meant anything to him."

"You forget about guilt. Apparently Tulley isn't cut out for a criminal career. He came with a lawyer in tow and wants to deal. One of the state lawyers is in with them now."

Giulia's eyes closed and she said in a slow voice, "He's going to expose everything he and Loriela and Fitch did in exchange for no death penalty option at his trial."

Frank's hands stopped. "Death penalty?"

"Your hands are not on break, please. Thank you. Did you forget my brilliant deduction last night? I said that Fitch got Tulley to kill Loriela. During our car trip today, Fitch practically confessed to it."

"Who is he? Svengali?" VanHorne said.

Giulia said, "Perhaps. Tulley is singing in the other room, in one sense."

VanHorne groaned.

"Sorry. Blame the stress reaction." She opened her eyes to see Frank looking from VanHorne to her, puzzled. "Classic book and movie. Svengali hypnotizes Trilby, who can't carry a tune in a bucket, and makes her a great singer. It all goes wrong, of course, in the same way Fitch's ascendance over Tulley has bit Fitch in the butt." She patted Frank's hands and lifted them off her shoulders. "We need a movie night. Your education has been neglected."

"Good. You find that and I'll look for an explosions-and-boobs action film you haven't seen."

Giulia concealed her sigh. "Deal. I require a trip to the emergency room for an x-ray now, please."

"At your service." Frank helped her out of her chair. She hobbled on his arm out to the front entrance.

"Frank. Wait." Captain Jimmy Reilly ran up to them. "The lawyers finished bargaining. Get this—Tulley confessed to the murder of Loriela Gil, but claims Fitch masterminded the whole thing. Says Fitch showed him the easiest way up their balcony, promised to get her drunk and set up the neckties, bought the glass cutter, everything. Says Gil led him on and Fitch worked on him 'til he wasn't thinking straight."

Giulia batted her eyes at Frank.

"Jimmy, you're killing me," Frank said. "Giulia figured that out last night. I'm losing my status as superior thinker in this marriage."

Jimmy laughed. "I'm on Giulia's side. You know that. Let me open the door for you."

Giulia clutched the iron railing. "I can make it," she said to Frank.

"I'm going to prepare a statement for the legitimate news," Jimmy said. "I'm already getting phone calls."

The glare of a spotlight made Giulia throw her free hand in front of her eyes.

"Ken Kanning here for *The Scoop*! You got away from us at the scene, but our viewers are still waiting for the blow-by-blow account of your capture of the Silk Tie Killer." He pushed the microphone into Giulia's chin.

Frank loomed over Kanning. "Remove that microphone."

Kanning attempted a charming smile. "Come on, Detective. Everyone loves a gutsy heroine. Especially a pretty one like Mrs. Driscoll."

Jimmy came down the stairs. "Kanning, get off police property."

"Captain, the press has universal access to—"

"Get off police property and stop harassing Mrs. Driscoll."

"Or what?"

Jimmy held out a hand to Frank, palm up. Frank slapped his

phone into it. Jimmy pressed a button and began dictating. "Kanning, Kenneth. Trespassing. Harassment. Violation of privacy. We confiscated one video camera and all recordings."

Kanning's bravado evaporated. He retreated two steps and bumped into his cameraman. "Shut it down, Larry."

"What?" the cameraman said. "We're gonna cave?"

"Shut it down and let's go." Kanning's voice lost its sleekness when he spoke through gritted teeth.

The cameraman muttered something insulting, whether at Kanning or at Jimmy, Giulia couldn't tell. *The Scoop* covered the distance to their creeper van in a remarkably short time.

Jimmy handed Frank back his phone, its screen black. "Good thing they couldn't tell I don't know your password."

Forty-Four

After two hours at the ER, Giulia's knee x-ray showed a deep bone bruise but no break. She picked up the Nunmobile at the police station and drove it back to the office. Frank followed her in his Camry and promised to throw her in the trunk if she attempted the stairs.

She called Sidney and all three of them came running down.

"You didn't say anything about your face," Sidney said. "Did you get that when you crashed the car?"

"Nope. Fitch didn't like it when I wasn't an obedient little hostage." She smiled at Jane. "Please come back tomorrow. It's a wacky job sometimes, but it's nowhere near this violent. Most of the time."

"Um, yeah. Of course I'll come back. I like eating and paying my rent. Are you okay?"

"I've been worse. Oh, wait. I shouldn't have said that."

Zane coughed. "It's the reaction. Want some good news?"

"More than anything except ibuprofen."

"The Diocese called and wants to talk about putting us on retainer. Great minds think alike?"

Giulia laughed. "Our bank account will be fat and happy soon. AtlanticEdge always pays on time. It might take longer for the State to release the money Fitch owes us, but now that the Diocese brought up the retainer, we have the upper hand." She put pressure on her injured knee and winced.

Sidney said, "Frank, she should be home with you attending to her every need."

"I'm trying to get her there."

"Oh, Sidney, that's right. The EMT said I should use arnica on my bruises. Do you have any?"

"What a silly question. Of course. I'll bring it over tonight. Olivier's taking me out to dinner at the new—" She grimaced and clutched her belly. "That's the third one this afternoon."

"No, no, no, mini-Sidney." Giulia shook her finger at Sidney's midsection. "No greeting the world until Mama trains Jane."

"I'll do my best—ow." She breathed through the contraction. "It's probably false labor."

Giulia dropped her head into her hands. "Frank, let's go home. This might be my last calm evening for the foreseeable future."

Alice Loweecey

Baker of brownies and tormenter of characters, Alice Loweecey recently celebrated her thirtieth year outside the convent. She grew up watching Hammer horror films and Scooby-Doo mysteries, which explains a whole lot. When she's not creating trouble for Giulia Falcone-Driscoll, she can be found growing her own vegetables (in summer) and cooking with them (the rest of the year).

Henery Press Mystery Books

And finally, before you go...
Here are a few other mysteries
you might enjoy:

DINERS, DIVES & DEAD ENDS

Terri L. Austin

A Rose Strickland Mystery (#1)

As a struggling waitress and part-time college student, Rose Strickland's life is stalled in the slow lane. But when her close friend, Axton, disappears, Rose suddenly finds herself serving up more than hot coffee and flapjacks. Now she's hashing it out with sexy bad guys and scrambling to find clues in a race to save Axton before his time runs out.

With her anime-loving bestie, her septuagenarian boss, and a pair of IT wise men along for the ride, Rose discovers political corruption, illegal gambling, and shady corporations. She's gone from zero to sixty and quickly learns when you're speeding down the fast lane, it's easy to crash and burn.

Available at booksellers nationwide and online

Visit www.henerypress.com for details

PORTRAIT OF A DEAD GUY

Larissa Reinhart

A Cherry Tucker Mystery (#1)

In Halo, Georgia, folks know Cherry Tucker as big in mouth, small in stature, and able to sketch a portrait faster than buck-shot rips from a ten gauge -- but commissions are scarce. So when the well-heeled Branson family wants to memorialize their murdered son in a coffin portrait, Cherry scrambles to win their patronage from her small town rival.

As the clock ticks toward the deadline, Cherry faces more trouble than just a controversial subject. Between ex-boyfriends, her flaky family, an illegal gambling ring, and outwitting a killer on a spree, Cherry finds herself painted into a corner she'll be lucky to survive.

Available at booksellers nationwide and online

Visit www.henerypress.com for details

FIT TO BE DEAD

Nancy G. West

An Aggie Mundeen Mystery (#1)

Aggie Mundeen, single and pushing forty, fears nothing but middle age. When she moves from Chicago to San Antonio, she decides she better shape up before anybody discovers she writes the column, "Stay Young with Aggie." She takes Aspects of Aging at University of the Holy Trinity and plunges into exercise at Fit and Firm.

Rusty at flirting and mechanically inept, she irritates a slew of male exercisers, then stumbles into murder. She'd like to impress the attractive detective with her sleuthing skills. But when the killer comes after her, the health club evacuates semi-clad patrons, and the detective has to stall his investigation to save Aggie's derriere.

Available at booksellers nationwide and online

Visit www.henerypress.com for details

THE AMBITIOUS CARD

John Gaspard

An Eli Marks Mystery (#1)

The life of a magician isn't all kiddie shows and card tricks. Sometimes it's murder. Especially when magician Eli Marks very publicly debunks a famed psychic, and said psychic ends up dead. The evidence, including a bloody King of Diamonds playing card (one from Eli's own Ambitious Card routine), directs the police right to Eli.

As more psychics are slain, and more King cards rise to the top, Eli can't escape suspicion. Things get really complicated when romance blooms with a beautiful psychic, and Eli discovers she's the next target for murder, and he's scheduled to die with her. Now Eli must use every trick he knows to keep them both alive and reveal the true killer.

Available at booksellers nationwide and online

Visit www.henerypress.com for details

MACDEATH

Cindy Brown

An Ivy Meadows Mystery (#1)

Like every actor, Ivy Meadows knows that *Macbeth* is cursed. But she's finally scored her big break, cast as an acrobatic witch in a circus-themed production of *Macbeth* in Phoenix, Arizona. And though it may not be Broadway, nothing can dampen her enthusiasm—not her flying caldron, too-tight leotard, or carrot-wielding dictator of a director.

But when one of the cast dies on opening night, Ivy is sure the seeming accident is "murder most foul" and that she's the perfect person to solve the crime (after all, she does work part-time in her uncle's detective agency). Undeterred by a poisoned Big Gulp, the threat of being blackballed, and the suddenly too-real curse, Ivy pursues the truth at the risk of her hard-won career—and her life.

Available at booksellers nationwide and online

Visit www.henerypress.com for details

CROPPED TO DEATH

Christina Freeburn

A Faith Hunter Scrap This Mystery (#1)

Former US Army JAG specialist, Faith Hunter, returns to her West Virginia home to work in her grandmothers' scrapbooking store determined to lead an unassuming life after her adventure abroad turned disaster. But her quiet life unravels when her friend is charged with murder – and Faith inadvertently supplied the evidence. So Faith decides to cut through the scrap and piece together what really happened.

With a sexy prosecutor, a determined homicide detective, a handful of sticky suspects and a crop contest gone bad, Faith quickly realizes if she's not careful, she'll be the next one cropped.

Available at booksellers nationwide and online

Visit www.henerypress.com for details

CPSIA information can be obtained at www.ICGtesting.com
Printed in the USA
LVOW10s1755160115

423151LV00017B/629/P